ALSO BY ANDREW VACHSS

Flood

Strega

Blue Belle

Hard Candy

Blossom

Sacrifice

Shella

Down in the Zero

Born Bad

Batman: The Ultimate Evil

Another Chance to Get It Right:
A Children's Book for Adults

FOOTSTEPS OF THE HAWK

FOOTSTEPS OF THE HAWK

ANDREW VACHSS

ALFRED A. KNOPF   New York   1995

THIS IS A BORZOI BOOK
PUBLISHED BY ALFRED A. KNOPF, INC.

Copyright © 1995 by Andrew Vachss

Library of Congress Cataloging-in-Publication Data

Vachss, Andrew H.
Footsteps of the hawk / by Andrew Vachss. — 1st ed.
p.   cm.
ISBN 0-679-44500-5
1. Burke (Fictitious character)—Fiction.   2. Private
investigators—New York (N.Y.)—Fiction.   I. Title.
PS3572.A33F66   1995
813'.54—dc20   95-17596
CIP

This book is a work of fiction. Names, characters, places,
and incidents either are the products of the author's
imagination or are used fictitiously, and any resemblance
to actual persons, living or dead, events, or locales is
entirely coincidental.

Manufactured in the United States of America

FIRST EDITION

for Baby Boy E . . .

> You took Death all the way through the last round.
> And got jobbed by the judges.
> Again.
>
> No more fixed fights for you, little warrior.
> Now it's—finally—time to play.

ACKNOWLEDGMENT

To Alan Grant
a volunteer in a war not his own
to free all the Children of the Secret

FOOTSTEPS OF THE HAWK

In my business, if you're the last one to a meet you could end up being left there when it's over.

I watched the refrigerator-white Range Rover work its way around the broken chunks of concrete dotting the asphalt that used to be a parking lot. Those luxo four-bys cost big bucks—I guessed Saunders had come into some serious money since the last time we did business. The big rig nosed forward, came to a halt at the start of the pier, then reversed so its rear end was backed against the abandoned building.

I trained the binoculars on the driver's door, watching the man get out. It was Saunders all right, dressed in a suburban safari outfit, right down to a pair of gleaming black boots. The passenger door opened. Another man. Medium height, with a face too chubby for his build, wearing a camo jacket and combat boots, eyes covered with mirror-lensed aviator sunglasses. I climbed down from my perch atop a heavy crossbeam using a rope ladder dyed black. As I moved closer to the door, the ladder merged into the shadows.

The mid-afternoon light was strong, fractured by the wreckage inside the abandoned warehouse—I could see all the way across the grimy Hudson to the Jersey waterfront. The door swung open and they stepped inside.

"Burke," Saunders said, offering his hand. "Long time no see."

"You said business," I told him.

"Same old Burke," he chuckled, dropping his hand . . . but keeping it in view. "This is the guy I told you about. Roger Cline."

"That's Cline like Patsy, not Klein like Jew," the guy said, smiling with his mouth, his eyes invisible behind the mirror lenses. "Saunders here tell you what we need?"

"Yeah," I told the man. "Ordnance."

"*Heavy* ordnance, my friend," he said. "Can you do it?"

"Sure," I told him. It was the truth—with all the military base closings, it's easy enough these days.

"What we need is—"

"You ever do time?" I interrupted.

"Huh?"

"You ever do time?" I repeated, watching my reflection in the mirror lenses.

The man turned his head slightly to his right, looking for an ally, but Saunders only shrugged, shifting his weight slightly to his outside foot, letting his body language tell the story.

The man turned back to me. "Yeah, I pulled some time," he said, a hostile undercurrent to his reedy voice. "So what?" He pulled off the sunglasses and glared at me all in the same motion—I guess it had worked better when he'd practiced it at home.

"Not *so* what," I told him. "*For* what?"

"What's it to you?" he asked.

"I like to know who I'm dealing with," I told him in a reasonable voice.

"Hey, I ain't asking your daughter for a date, man."

"Suit yourself," I said.

He was quiet for about fifteen seconds, still trying to stare me down—good fucking luck. Then he ran a palm over his close-cropped brown hair, bit into his lower lip for a split-second, said, "Armed robbery."

I nodded as if I was absorbing the information. "You go down alone?" I asked him.

"Huh?"

"When you went to the joint, your partners go with you?"

"No. I mean, I didn't have no partners."

I nodded like that made sense too. "All right," I told the man. "I'll see what's available. Take about three, four weeks. No guarantees, though."

"I thought you could—"

"What? Go over the wall and *steal* the stuff? Get real, pal. I got an inside man—that's the only way to pull off this particular thing. What's for sale is what he can get, that's the story. Whichever way it comes up, that's the way it is, that's the way it *stays*, understand?"

"Yeah. But . . ." He let it trail off, looking over at Saunders.

"Let me talk to you for a minute," Saunders said. "Just a little one-on-one, okay? For old times' sake?"

I nodded.

"Wait for me outside," Saunders told the other man. "Here's the keys."

Cline-like-Patsy started to say something, changed his mind. He took the keys from Saunders, walked out through the sagging doorway.

"What was that all about, Burke?" Saunders asked me.

"He's counterfeit," I told him. "A three-dollar bill."

"How do you know?"

"Nobody says they went inside for *armed* robbery—that's social-work talk. You say you went down for stealing, or you say you're a thief. You gonna rob, you're armed—how else would it be? And you see his face when I asked him about partners? He never *had* partners—not for what he was doing."

"So what do you care about his pedigree?"

"Look, this guy may be one of those lame Nazis or whatever they call themselves this week, but he's no white-tribe warrior—he's a fucking tree-jumper. And he ratted out a bunch of people when he went in."

"So?"

"So he's not reliable. You know it, and I know it."

"His money spends just as good."

"And you already got some," I said.

"Look, I—"

"Drop it," I told him. "You had an order for hardware, you would have come to me yourself—we did business before. Then you would have marked it up, sold it right over to the chump without me ever knowing."

"I—"

"But you wanted to stay out of the middle on this one, right? So it's one of two things: either you don't think this guy's good for the money or he's got you spooked."

"I don't spook," Saunders said, a hurt tone in his calm hustler's voice.

"How much did he pay you to set up the meet?"

"Five."

"Half's mine."

"How do you figure?"

"I'm not doing business with him, and neither are you. You stung him for five to make the meet. Later you'll tell him I couldn't pull it off. He won't be mad at me—I didn't take any of his cash. So you figure it's harmless . . . a nice score for a few hours' work."

"If it was a score, it's *my* score," he said.

"You think I'm a fucking 800 number? Toll-free?"

"I was up front with you, Burke. Come on, no hard feelings. How does a grand strike you?"

"You told me five, he probably duked ten on you. Cut me a deuce we stay okay, you and me."

"And if I don't?"

"You never know," I said quietly.

Saunders reached into the side pocket of his safari jacket. Slowly, with two fingers. Pulled out a pack of cigarettes. Held it forward, offering me one.

"No thanks," I told him. "I don't smoke."

"The last time I saw you, you did."

"The last time you saw me, we were doing some real business."

"Ah . . ." he mused, firing up his smoke. "Tell you what. I don't want hard feelings, all right? How about if I give you the deuce, but I throw in some information? Valuable information. You pay whatever it's worth, okay?"

"I'm listening."

He stepped closer to me, dropping his voice. "I've been working out of the city. Understand you were doing some work up there too. In Connecticut?"

I kept my face calm, waiting.

"A cop's on your trail, Burke. A lady cop. She was up there, asking around."

"That's what cops do."

"It doesn't concern you?"

"No. I never do anything to bother the locals."

"Okay. Whatever you say. Just trying to do an old friend a favor."

"I'll remember," I said, holding out an open hand. For the money.

The creep with the sunglasses hadn't gone to prison alone. I had—more than once. But I never come that way to a meet. Max the Silent dropped out of the shadows, disdaining the rope ladder, landing as softly as moonlight on dark water.

Max is my partner. If I'd lit a cigarette while talking to Saunders, Max would have dropped on him like an anvil on an egg.

I pocketed seven fifty off the roll Saunders had finally handed over, gave the same amount to Max. The extra five would go into our bank.

Max nodded his acceptance. I heard the Range Rover pull away. Max was in motion before I was—he can't hear, but the vibrations of that big rig on the rotting boards of the old pier were so strong even I could feel them. Max glided to the warehouse door, looked outside.

When he nodded again, I followed him out the door.

My old Plymouth was parked on the other side of West Street, looking the way it always does—abandoned. I unlocked it and we both climbed inside.

I keyed the motor and we took off, heading for the bank.

We cruised by the front first. The white-dragon tapestry was in the window—All Clear. I stopped in the alley behind the restaurant. The seamlessness of the dirty gray wall was broken by a pristine square of white paint. Max's chop was inside the square, standing out in meticulous black calligraphy. You didn't have to read Chinese to understand it: No Parking. Ever.

The steel door to the back of the restaurant opened as we approached. A pudgy Chinese man stood in the opening, wearing a white chef's apron, a butcher axe in one hand. When he saw who it was, he stepped aside. I heard the door snap closed behind us.

We walked through the kitchen, past the bank of pay phones. Took my booth in the back, sat down.

Mama left her post at the cash register and came over to our table, snapping out some instructions in Cantonese. The waiter was way ahead of her—he vanished, then reappeared with a large tureen of hot-and-sour soup.

Mama served me and Max first, while she was still standing. Then she sat next to Max and used the ladle to fill her own bowl. Max and I each took the obligatory sip, made the required gestures of appreciation.

"We got—" I started to say.

"Finish soup first," Mama replied.

Okay. We drained our bowls, sat for a second helping. Worked that one more slowly, mixing in some dry fried noodles. The waiter came and exchanged our bowls for a blue glass ashtray.

"So?" Mama asked.

I handed her the five hundred. "For the bank," I told her.

"From both?" she wanted to know.

I nodded. Mama made the cash disappear. Max and I would each get two hundred dollars' credit in Mama's bank—the remaining 20 percent was her fee. The score was really too small to go through all that—we turned it over as a gesture of respect.

"That girl call again," she told me.

I knew who she meant. The same lady cop Saunders told me about. Belinda Roberts. That was the name she'd told me one day in Central Park. I was tracking, setting up a job, had Pansy along with me for cover. Belinda was jogging along, a fine-looking woman with a careless mass of reddish-brown hair topping a curvy, muscular body. She said she liked my dog. Said she liked me too. Gave me a number, asked me to call.

I never did. When I saw her again, she was in the same place. It was Clarence who made her for a cop. She was in the park, working. Maybe undercover to catch a rapist, maybe on observation for a drug deal. Maybe working me. No way to tell.

No way . . . until she called the restaurant, asking for me. Asking for Burke. I'd never given her my right name, never gave her the number.

Lying Belinda. Persistent bitch. Whatever she wanted, she'd get tired before I would—I'm a sensei of patience, a Zen master at waiting.

Max coiled his fists, cocked his head—a boxer assuming his stance. Looked a question over at me.

I shook my head, tapped my watch. Too early.

"Good investment, Burke?" Mama asked.

I guessed Max had told her about the Prof's latest get-rich-legit scheme. Some fighter he was training in a converted warehouse in the South Bronx. I had wanted us to all pool our cash and get a racehorse—I've always coveted a trotter of my own. But convicted felons can't own racehorses—the authorities don't want the wrong kind of people in that game. They run an extensive background check, photo, prints, checkable references, all that kind of thing. That's for owning a racehorse—you want to open a nursery school, they don't care about any of that background crap.

"I don't know, Mama," I told her honestly. "I never saw this kid work."

"Prof says maybe big money," she said, her dark eyes alive with the flame of cash. "You invest?"

"Yeah. He took me for five large."

"Max too?"

"Sure."

"Why no ask me?"

"It's *gambling*, Mama," I said, keeping even the slightest tinge of sarcasm from my voice.

"Not gamble, Burke. Invest, right?"

"If you say so."

"So! How big piece you get for five thousand?"

"I guess I never asked."

Mama made a clucking sound with her tongue. Then she turned and said something over her shoulder to one of the waiters. He bowed, disappeared. When he came back, he was holding a battered gray metal box. Mama opened the lid, reached inside without looking. Handed me a stack of hundreds.

"Five thousand," she said. "I get same piece as you and Max, okay?"

I nodded, awestruck as always with her ability to count money by feel.

M ax and I played a few dozen more hands in our life-sentence gin game. Mama was more animated than usual, shouting advice at Max, once smacking him on the back of his head when he made a spectacularly boneheaded play. Max ignored the slap, but kept following her advice. As a result, I was up another three hundred bucks by noon. I made a steering gesture with my hands. Max flashed a smile—time to ride.

We took the FDR to the Triborough, exited at Bruckner Boulevard and motored peacefully until I found the block. It was dotted with Bronx burn-outs, abandoned buildings with that charred look they get after a while. The warehouse was set back from the street, past a concrete apron once used to load trucks. I pulled onto the apron, climbed out and activated the security systems. The Plymouth didn't look worth stealing and it came prevandalized—but even all that won't protect a car once you're into the Badlands.

Clarence was just inside the door, comfortable in an old easy chair, resplendent in a goldenrod silk jacket over a black shirt. He's always dressed to the nines—as in millimeter. The young gunman got to his feet, said "Burke" to me, bowed to Max.

"He's here?" I asked.

"Oh yes, mahn. My father is in the back, working with our gladiator."

Clarence led the way through a maze of young men. Some were skipping rope, others working heavy bags or speed bags. A makeshift ring was set up in the far corner. Most of the fighters were black, with a mixture of Latins and a pair of Irish kids who looked like brothers.

"Put that iron down, fool. You training for a fight, not a goddamn pose-off." It was the Prof, drawn up to his full height, which put him right around this kid's chest. The kid was holding a barbell in both hands, waist-high, listening intently. A big kid, maybe six two and a piece, looked like he went right around two hundred pounds. He had Rome stamped all over his features, especially his nose, but his skin was fair and he had blue eyes under black hair combed straight back from his forehead.

"Sammy said—" the kid started to say, but the Prof was on him quicker than you could bribe a politician.

"Sammy? That chump's game is lame. You listen to that big stiff, you be seeing your name in the obituaries, not on the sports page."

"Okay, Prof," the kid said.

But the Prof wasn't done. "*This* is what wins fights, boy," the little man said, pounding his chest with a clenched fist.

"I know," the kid said. "Heart—"

"I ain't talking about heart, kid—you didn't have heart, you wouldn't get in the ring in the first place. I'm talking conditioning, see? Pure conditioning. A good heart is a nice start, but a bad lung will get you hung. Got it?"

"Yes," the kid said. Serious, not sulky.

"Righteous. Now drop that bar and shake hands with my man. Burke, this is Frankie Eye, do or die."

"That's what he calls me," the big kid said, smiling. "It's short for Ianello."

He had a powerful grip, but he wasn't trying to impress anybody with it. His eyes were clear and direct, his stance respectful.

"And this here is Max the Silent. The life-taking, widow-making wind of destruction," the Prof told the kid, indicating Max. The Mongol warrior bowed. The kid had one hand stuck out but he quickly pulled it back, imitating Max's ceremony with a bow of his own. I didn't know if he could fight yet, but he was no dummy.

"Heavy bag's free," the Prof said to the kid. "Come on."

The kid followed the Prof over to the now-vacant bag, slipping on a pair of training gloves as he walked. He stepped up to the bag like a man going to work, started pounding it with alternating hands, left-right-left, a steady stream of hooks, breathing through his nose, well within himself. He had a perfect boxer's body—you couldn't see any muscle development until he moved.

The Prof stood to the side, watching the kid like an air-traffic controller with too many planes on the radar screen. The kid kept working the bag, steady as a metronome. When the Prof finally called a halt, the kid didn't look winded.

"We need a hundred punches a round. *Hard* punches. *Every* round," the Prof told the kid, tossing an old terry-cloth robe over his fighter's shoulder. "This whole game is about conditioning, remember what I said? You get tired, you get weak. You get weak, you go down." The kid nodded—he'd obviously heard all this before.

"What you think of our boy?" the Prof asked me.

"Don't know yet," I told him. The Prof knew what I meant. The world's full of good gym fighters—it's when they get hit that you find out the truth.

Max stepped forward, shaking his head in a "No!" gesture, pointing at the kid. He bowed to the Prof, pointed at the kid, then at himself.

"Forget that!" the Prof snapped at him. "Ain't no way in the world you gonna spar with my boy."

Max ignored the Prof, stepped close to the kid, guided him back toward the heavy bag. I pulled the robe off the kid's shoulders as Max turned him so he was facing the bag again. Max stepped behind the kid, put one hand on each side of the kid's waist, fingers splayed around to just below the kid's abdomen. When he nodded, the kid started to throw punches, slowly at first, then harder and harder. Max stepped away, bowed again, and changed places with the kid.

"Put your hands where Max had them," I told the kid. He tentatively put his gloved hands on either side of the Mongol, confused but going along.

Max ripped a left hook, a jet-stream pile driver that actually rocked the bag.

"Look at your hands," I told the kid. The kid's left hand was dangling in the air, his right still on Max's waist. He put his hand back, bent his shoulders forward so he was closer to Max. The warrior fired several shots with each fist. The kid lost his grip again. Max stepped away, pointed to the kid's hips, made a maître d's gesture, inviting the kid back to the bag.

Frankie got it then. He took his stance, started slowly, driving each punch by torquing his hips, increasing the tempo as he felt it working. The heavy bag danced, the blows much heavier than when the kid first worked it. When he stopped, he was smiling.

"I never realized . . ." he said, turning to Max, bowing his thanks.

"Yeah, yeah—the mope can smoke," the Prof said, reluctantly acknowledging Max's expertise, guarding his own territory. "But fighting's a mind game. It's all in the head, Fred."

"When's he gonna go?" I asked.

"Friday night," the Prof said. "We got this showcase gig. Over in Queens. Exposure's good, and the purse could be worse."

"How much?"

"One large."

"That's not a whole lot to get beat on," I said, dubious.

"Look here, schoolboy. It ain't about bucks, not at first. Way I hear it, one of the cable scouts'll be there—it's their show. National, get it? There's a big-time shortage of heavyweights. And *white* heavies . . . hell, you can write your own ticket. They so desperate for white, they settling for some of those Afro-mocha, too-much-cream-in-the-coffee brothers. The heavyweights? I tell you, there ain't no bop in that crop. The ones they got, they just nursing them along. You see these clowns, records like thirty-two and oh. But they never fight each *other*, see? They got to have that undefeated record to get a shot. Then they score, but there ain't no more. One fight, that's right. And then it's over, Rover. We not going that route. Frankie's gonna fight anybody wants to play, all the way. So when he gets his shot, he drops the hammer."

"But for a first fight . . . ?"

"Look, Burke. Frankie got a whole *bunch* of fights before this. Amateur, sure, but plenty of fights."

"How'd he do?"

"Ah, he was jobbed most of the time. He fights pro-style. Body punches, chopping down the tree, see? But the amateurs, it's all about pitty-pat. Slap each other like bitches in a pillow fight. That wasn't Frankie."

"That's where you found him? In the amateurs?"

"Nah. He was in this club over to Jersey. Fighting smokers. In the basement, you know how it works. You get paid to cook, but it's off the books. Don't go on your record, neither."

I looked over to where the kid was skipping rope under Clarence's watchful eye. "Speaking of records . . ." I let it trail away.

"Down twice," the Prof came back. "One in the kiddie camps, once upstate. Assault, both times. Kid's got a real nasty temper."

"Who's he been . . . ?"

"Anybody, babe. He was a brawler. Half-ass burglar too. Booze was his beast. But now that's all done, son. My man don't touch a drop, and that's a Medeco lock."

I watched the kid spar for a while. Nothing spectacular—steady and dedicated, learning the fundamentals. I slipped the Prof the five grand from Mama, told him she was in. Then I signaled Max it was time to split. He would have happily stayed there all goddamn day, but I had work to do.

I pulled the Plymouth into the garage of the warehouse where Max lives. He pointed up, making a "come on" gesture, inviting me to say hello to Immaculata and the baby, Flower. I tapped my watch, held my thumb and forefinger close together, showing him I didn't have time.

I stood on the sidewalk, watched the Plymouth disappear behind the descending garage door. As soon as it disappeared, I walked over to the subway on Chrystie Street and dropped into the underground, heading uptown.

A small group of people clustered near the middle of the platform. Timid rabbits—knowing one of the herd would be taken, praying it wouldn't be them, never thinking that together they could have a fox for breakfast. I walked away from them, toward the rear. The end of the platform was deserted. I stood there quietly, settling into myself. A bird flew past my face, almost too quick to see. I was used to rats in the subway, but I'd never seen a bird before. I trained my eyes on where the bird had vanished. Nothing. Then I heard a chirping noise and refocused. A nest was neatly tucked into the hollow part of a crossbeam. The mother bird hopped about anxiously, trying to quiet them down. I walked a few feet back toward the center of the platform, turning my back. In a minute, the mother bird swooped by again. A sparrow, she looked like. Down here, the squatters aren't all humans.

The train finally rolled in. It wasn't crowded at that hour. I found a two-person seat at the end of the car. Two stops later, a pair of black teenagers got on, doing the gangstah strut. One of them sat next to me, bumping my shoulder slightly. I stiffened my left arm, ready for a move, but the kid said, "Excuse me, sir," in a polite voice. His pal took the seat facing us, and the two started a rapid-fire conversation.

"Ain't no way the bitch gets away from me," the kid next to me said. "My game is too strong."

"Why you gotta be referring to sisters like that?" the guy across from us said.

"What you mean?"

"I mean, man, what is all this *bitch* thing with you? You not showing no respect. Why you call your own woman a bitch?"

The kid next to me considered the question for a minute, then he leaned forward, said, "Well, what *else* I gonna call the ho'?"

His pal gave me a "What can you do?" look. I nodded to show I understood his dilemma. When the train rolled up to my stop, they were still going at it.

The private clinic was housed in a discreet brownstone on a quiet East Side block. I rang the bell, standing so the video eye could pick up my image easily. In a minute, the door was opened by a young woman in jeans and a white T-shirt. "You're Mr. Burke?" she asked. I nodded to tell her she had the right man but she had already turned her back to me and was walking away. I followed her into a small room just past a receptionist's desk, took the seat she indicated. She walked out without another word.

Doc showed in a couple more minutes. Medium height with a husky wrestler's chest, his eyes unreadable behind the glasses he always wears.

"Thanks for coming, hoss," he said.

"I owe you one," I told him. It was the truth. Hell, more than one, maybe. "Besides, I wanted to see how your new setup was working out."

"So far so good," he said.

"It's a long way from Upstate," I told him. Upstate—the prison—where we first met. I was a convict, Doc was the institutional psychiatrist. Later, they put him in charge of all the institutions for the criminally insane. I'd heard he packed it in. Quit cold. Moved down here to the city to open up this clinic for damaged teenagers.

"I'm still the same," Doc said, just a faint trace of Kentucky in his voice.

"Me too," I assured him.

Something shifted behind the lenses of his glasses. A microscope, focusing. "Heard you might have bought yourself a bit of trouble a while back."

"That wasn't me," I said.

Doc just nodded. I lit a cigarette. "I used to—" he started.

"I heard this before," I interrupted. It was self-preservation.

Doc's a great storyteller, has a real narrator's gift. But it doesn't work so well from a soapbox—I'd heard about his heroic triumph over evil cigarettes too many times already.

"Okay, hoss. Whatever you say. Here's the deal: we have a client who's expecting—"

He stopped talking when a teenage girl burst into the room. A brunette with long, thin hair flowing all the way down past her shoulders. Her face was a skeleton, her body too scrawny to cast a shadow. Her skin was that dull-orange color starvation freaks get from a heavy carrot diet—there's some bullshit going around about how carrots fill you up but have no calories—every teenage girl in the world seems to believe it.

"I'm not going to—" she started.

"Susan, I'm with somebody," Doc said mildly.

"I don't care! They can't make me—"

"Nobody is going to *make* you do anything, Susan. But if you don't—"

"I *won't*. I know what I'm doing. I . . ."

Doc held up a hand, palm out like a traffic cop, but it was no good. The girl just charged ahead. "Just let me *explain*, all right? Let me tell you *why*. Please?"

"As soon as I'm finished with—"

"No! *Now!* I don't care if another shrink hears—"

"Burke isn't . . ." Doc started to say. He caught my eye. I nodded. He went with it, settling back in his chair, spreading his arms, palms out and open. "Tell me," he said.

"There's a *reason* for it," the girl said, standing with her hands on what should have been her hips. "I don't have anorexia. I mean, it's not an addiction or anything. I'm not like Aurora."

"Tell me the reason," Doc said, gently.

The girl's face contorted. She shook off the spasm, wrapped her arms around herself, whispered: "I don't want to look sexy."

"Susan . . ." Doc tried.

"I *won't!*" the girl lashed out. "You can't make me."

"How old were you when it happened?" I asked.

Her face whirled around toward me. Only her head swiveled—her body was still facing Doc. "What?"

"How old were you when . . . ?" I repeated, holding her close with my voice, cutting off the exit roads.

Her eyes screamed at me, but her voice was low-pitched. "Nine," she said.

"You have a lot of curves then?"

"What?"

"Did you look sexy then, Susan? Like a woman?"

"No . . ."

"You keep starving yourself, you end up looking like a child again. No curves, no shape. All flat lines, right? Like a skinny little girl again."

"I . . ."

"They don't want grown women," I told her, sharing the truth— we both knew who "they" were. "They want *little* girls," I said quietly. "You're not keeping them away, Susan—you're playing your old tapes."

"I *hate* you!" she shrieked at me. Then she started to cry. Deep, racking sobs. Her bird's-wing ribs looked like they were going to snap from the pressure and Doc was on his feet in a split-second, arms around the girl, crooning something soft in her ear, patting her back until she stopped holding herself so rigid, walking her out the door.

I finished my cigarette, looking around the office, someplace else in my head. But I wasn't that far gone—I used the time to slip a couple of Doc's ℞ pads into my pocket.

Doc was back in a few minutes. If he noticed the missing pads, he didn't say anything. "You should have been a therapist, hoss. We've been discussing how we could confront Susan with her real agenda for weeks now."

"I'm sorry. I—"

"Don't be sorry. I wasn't kidding you—that was what she needed. I guess it was better hearing it from a stranger. She was sent to us for anorexia, but we weren't getting anywhere. Another week and she'd have had to go on IV."

"Who sent her?"

"Her dad."

"The same one who . . . ?"

"No. It was her grandfather. Happened maybe ten, twelve years ago. They never did anything about it. Oh sure, they kept her away from him, but that was it. They thought everything was fine until she just stopped eating."

"The weight she's trying to lose, it's got nothing to do with calories, huh?"

"Right on the money, hoss. But now we got ourselves jump-started. And Susan got herself a chance." Then he leaned back in his chair and told me what he wanted.

I told Doc I couldn't handle a 24-7, but he promised that his client's daughter would be on the midnight bus out of Cincinnati. That was the job—a runaway. At least that's what *she* thought. The kid's parents made the arrangements with Doc. She'd go right into his clinic. And she wouldn't have to go home if she didn't want to. If you wanted Doc to treat your kid, you had to sign that last part. Notarized.

I didn't ask Doc anything else. I got up to leave but he stopped me, using the same traffic-cop gesture he'd used on the girl with the carrot skin.

"You know, Burke . . . the way you handled that thing with Susan . . . I don't understand why you live the way you do."

"You don't know how I live," I told him, trying to shut this off.

"I've got an idea," Doc replied. "Look, I know *you*—I know you a long time. Even back . . . inside . . . you were always studying something. Reading, asking questions. You've got an amazing vocabulary—it's almost like you're bilingual—sometimes you sound like a mobster, sometimes you sound like a lawyer, sometimes you—"

"I do have a great vocabulary," I interrupted. "It's so fucking big, I even know what the word 'patronizing' means."

Doc nodded—like he'd tried his best, but the case was hopeless.

When I walked in the Eighth Avenue entrance everyone was in their places. The Prof was sitting on his shoeshine box, industriously working over a pair of alligator loafers. Clarence was in the loafers, eyes sweeping the terminal. Max was slumped on a bench, his body disguised under a filthy old raincoat, a battered felt hat shielding his eyes.

I was wearing one of the suits Michelle had made me buy. Gray silk, fall weave. Carrying a black anodized-aluminum attaché case in my left hand.

I strolled past a bank of pay phones, listening to a United Nations babble—all kinds of people, calling home. Calling home is a big business in this city. You can find special setups in any heavy ethnic neighborhood—phone centers, they're called. They set them up almost like tiny apartments—nice comfortable chair to sit in, couple of spares in case you want to crowd the whole family in too. Some of them have desks, shelf space, writing paper. And their rates are cheaper than you could get on your own phone, because the guys who run it buy blocks of trunk time to specific locations. In Flushing, it's Korea, India, Southeast Asia: two seventy-nine for the first minute, then seventy-five cents for each additional minute. In Jackson Heights, it's Colombia: a buck twenty-six for the first, forty-nine cents after. People who use the centers, they're not thinking of a quickie call—some of them stay for hours.

Down in the Port Authority, they have the low-rent version—you make your call with someone else's credit card. Thieves rent the credit-card numbers—all you can use for twenty-four hours, one flat fee. The Port Authority is the best place to use them—plenty of pay phones always available, impossible to stake out, anonymous.

My watch said it was eleven-forty. Plenty of time even if the bus was on schedule. The Port Authority cops were all around, watching for runaways. No shortage of pimps either, trolling for the same fish, using different bait.

It went so smooth I almost didn't trust it. While the predators hovered, I walked straight on through. I met the bus, told the girl I was with Project Pride, a safe house for runaways. Promised her a nice private room, free food, and counselors to help her find a job. She told me she was going to be an actress. I told her lies of equal weight. She got into my Plymouth. I drove her to the clinic, half-listening to her stream of chatter, hating how easy anyone could have gotten this little girl to come along with them.

I found a place to park, rang the bell. The door opened. I left the kid there.

The next morning, I went back to work. Ever since I got back from Connecticut, I've been bottom-feeding, picking at carrion. I run my scams in the Personals—promising whatever, delivering never. I also use my P.O. boxes—offering losers a real pipeline to "mercenary opportunities." The only mercenary they'll ever meet that way is me. Kiddie-porn stings don't have much bite to them today—the freaks all want to sample the merchandise over a computer modem before they buy. Or they want you to fax a teaser. And even the pedophiles who want hard copy insist you use FedEx so the *federales* can't bust you for trafficking through the U.S. mail. But that's okay—there's never a shortage of targets who can't go crying to the cops when they get fleeced.

I deal with citizens too. Every time the government adds a new tax to cigarettes, the market for bootleg butts goes bullish. And brand-name counterfeiting is always a sure thing: Mont Blanc pens, Rolex watches, Gucci bags—they're all best-sellers for street merchants. Most of it's made in Southeast Asia, where child labor is real cheap. In Thailand, the Promised Land for baby-rapers, it's so cheap that the freaks organize tours: for one flat rate you get round-trip to Bangkok, a nice hotel . . . and babies to fuck. The planes are always filled to capacity.

But even if hustling, scamming, and grafting all dried up, I could always sell firearms—hate never goes out of style. I only deal in bulk, like a case of handguns. And I won't touch the exotics—titanium crossbows that cost three grand, mail-order SAMs—that kind of stuff's for the borderlands, the far-out frontier where psychosis and technology overlap.

I sell to the usual suspects, mostly far-right dim-bulbs who sit in their basements stroking the gun barrels . . . the firearms equivalent of the inflatable women they sell in the freak-sex catalogs. Most of my customers are pretty easy to scope out, but when an unsmiling young woman in overalls and a flannel shirt wanted to buy enough *plastique* to level a high-rise, I raised my eyebrows in a question. She told me she was an animal lover, like that explained it all.

I passed on that one. I don't play much—and when I do, it's with my deck.

My bottom-feeding wasn't limited to business. I've known Vyra forever, met her when she was engaged to marry an architect. She didn't go through with that one. After working her way through another half-dozen guys, she eventually settled on an accountant. All throughout that, we'd get together once in a while. We never had that much to say to each other—came together as smooth as chambering a round, parted as easy as firing it.

Vyra was a slim girl, not very curvy, with breasts way too big for her frame. The only bras she could wear had industrial-strength underwires—when she took them off you could see the violent red marks where they had cut into her. They made her back ache too, she said. And sometimes her neck hurt so badly she had to have it braced.

"Why don't you get them fixed?" I asked once, lying next to her on a hotel bed.

"You mean like the rest of me?" she asked, not sure whether to try sarcasm or tears—she always had both on tap. I'd known Vyra before she started on the plastic surgery—hell, I knew her when she was still Myra—but I'd never tried to talk her out of it. She finally got her nose reduced, earlobes cut down, and an implant at the tip of her chin. All in one visit—I didn't see her for about three months. When I did, she was the same sweet bitch-on-wheels she'd always been, only with more confidence.

"Why not?" I replied. "You could get the best—"

"Men *love* them," she said. "I mean, they *worship* them. You have no idea. . . ."

"But if it's going to keep you in pain all the—"

"Don't worry." She smiled, her perfectly capped teeth white in the afternoon dimness. "I make them pay for it."

When I first saw Vyra, she was a hat-check girl in a nightclub, wearing one of those imitation bunny outfits—a one-piece bodysuit cut high on the thighs with a deep V at the chest. A customer gave her ten bucks to reclaim his hat, watched hungrily as she stuffed the bill deep into her cleavage.

"I'll bet you could stuff a hundred bucks down there," the guy said. "All in singles."

"I don't play with singles," Vyra shot back, telling him the score.

She married a guy she met in the club. Or a guy she met in the club introduced her to the guy she married. Or the guy was married when she met him and divorced his wife over her. Or something like that . . . When Vyra tells her stories, I don't listen too hard.

Next time I ran into her, it was an accident. I was working a tracking job over in Jersey—she was sitting out in front of a café, at one of those little round tables with big Euro ashtrays, sipping something from a tall narrow glass. I sat down across from her, grateful for the vantage point and the cover.

Vyra told me about her life, flashing a diamond ring that must have cost five figures wholesale. She gave me her phone number, but the calling instructions were so complicated—only on Tuesday and Thursday, between two and four in the afternoon, but not if it falls on the first day of the month . . . crap like that—I never got around to it.

But when she called me, she caught me just right. I was in Mama's, not doing anything, and she was in the Vista Hotel, right across from Battery Park. It only took me a few minutes to get there. About the same time it took both of us to get done with the only thing there ever was between us.

She was good at it—a lifetime of faking passion blurred the line so much that, sometimes, she actually thought she was letting go.

"You're the only one who ever made me come," she told me. It was a good line, as such things go. "You were the first" would have been deeper sarcasm than "I love you," but making a woman come for the first time in her life—hell, most men's egos would slip-slide around that credibility gap with ease.

Vyra's good at sex. Practiced, athletic, responsive . . . controlling enough so she does most of the work, but not so much so that you *feel* controlled. On a good day, she can bite a pillow hard enough to make you think you were driving steel like John Henry never dreamed, the Boss Rooster with his pick of the chicks. Vyra must have learned the truth early on in her life—faking love is a snap, but faking lust is a bitch.

Vyra's great at girl-gestures—whipping off an earring to make a phone call, tossing her hair off her face with a quick movement of her neck, walking with one hand on her purse, the other swinging in time with her hips, like a conductor directing musicians—not an original move in the lot, but all of them sweet, smooth and sexy.

Vyra's a good person too—just tell her about an abandoned baby or a wounded animal, her checkbook opens faster than a bagman's hand. She's one of those girls . . . I really can't explain them. It's like they're running parallel to you all the time. The lines never cross, but, sometimes, they get close enough to almost touch.

It was always hotel sex, except for one time in her car. She never asked to come to my place—never asked me much of anything. Sometimes we made a date on the phone, sometimes she'd just call when she was around . . . and if I was too, we'd get together.

It's as though our lives are checkerboarded—when our pieces land on the same square, we get together, take care of business, and move on.

Vyra wants something she can't call by name. I know what to call it, but I don't want it.

She offered me some money once. Real money, so I could go into a business or something. It was a sweet thing she was trying to do, maybe the only way she knows how. I didn't take it—told myself it was better to leave that kind of offer in the bank, for when I might really need it.

I didn't need Vyra, either. But when I called in, and Mama said there was a message from her, I aimed the Plymouth at the Vista without thinking much about it.

Vyra had a new pair of shoes. Blue spikes, with little red bows at the back. She liked them so much, she kept them on.

Afterwards, she wanted to tell me all about what she'd been doing—she was a volunteer counselor in some "therapeutic community" on the other side of the Hudson. I lay on my back, blew smoke rings toward the ceiling. She propped herself on one elbow, sprouting prepackaged wisdom—"there's no such thing as a free lunch" seemed to be her favorite. I closed my eyes, letting her voice wash over me.

"Are you *listening* to me?" she finally said.

"Sure."

"Listen, Burke, you're not the only one with problems. Everybody has to carry their own baggage through life."

"But everybody doesn't have to go through Customs, do they, little bitch?" I asked, my voice gentle.

I don't know why that started her crying, but I held her against my chest until she was done.

I pulled my car out of the hotel's underground garage, thinking about how Vyra had offered me money again—she was one of those goodhearted women who could offer to lend you money without wanting your balls for a down payment. And my ego wasn't stupid enough to tell her I still had a big piece of my last score stashed away.

I don't want to live large—it just makes you a bigger target. I live a small, low-maintenance life. I'm just trying to get through it.

I was just trying to get through the intersection at West Broadway and Chambers, heading for the West Side Highway, when it happened. I was coming through at the same time as a bright lipstick-red low-slung sports coupe—a Dodge Stealth, it looked like. My Plymouth has so many dents in its primer-coated body that I usually carry major bargaining power over any contested space in city traffic, but the driver of the red car wasn't having any, bulling his way through, oblivious to the blaring horns and screech of brakes. I let him through, tucked in behind, followed him to the Highway.

He made the right turn ahead of me. I cranked the wheel hard into the service road and pulled ahead. I took a quick glance at the red Stealth—it sported blackout windows and I couldn't see inside.

I felt it somewhere to my left but, after a while, I couldn't even pick it up in my left-side mirror.

The Highway forked just before the Meat Market. I stayed right, heading for the whore stroll on Tenth Avenue. A working girl was having trouble leaving her pimp—and she'd gotten word out to me. I promised the broker who gave me the word that I'd listen to the offer, make my decision after I'd heard the pitch.

I was motoring sedately along Tenth Avenue when the idiot in the red Stealth shot across my bow at Eighteenth Street, sliding so I'd have to hit him or stop. I floored the brakes—crazy bastard. I was checking the rearview mirror to see if there was room to back away when I heard a car door slam. A man with the build of a fire hydrant was walking toward my car. Walking fast. I recognized him. Morales, the no-neck thug who partnered with McGowan for NYPD.

Damn.

I climbed out of the Plymouth, put on a "What the hell's this all about?" expression. Morales stepped right into my face, showing teeth. It wasn't a smile.

"I fucking *thought* that was you," he snarled.

"What's the beef?" I asked him.

"Oh, let me see. Burke, right? What *could* the beef be? Parking tickets? Drunk driving? No . . . how about fucking homicide, that more up your alley?"

"We already did this once," I reminded him, keeping my voice soft. It's a tightrope dance with Morales. He's a pit bull in human form—you show him fear and you're done. But if you challenge him, that just lights his fuse. With Morales, the only safe place is *away.*

Traffic flowed past. The drivers didn't rubberneck us—it takes more than a couple of men talking in the street to get attention around here.

"I never mind going another round," Morales said. "You wouldn't happen to know anything about this house up in the Bronx, would you? A house with all kinds of dead bodies in it. Kid's body too. A little kid. You know anything about that, Burke?"

"No. Was it in the papers?"

"Yeah, motherfucker, it was in the papers. All *over* the papers, a couple a years back. Remember now?"

"It doesn't ring a bell," I told him, keeping my eyes away from his. Morales wouldn't take that as a sign of guilt: his eyes are little black ball bearings—nobody ever looks into them long.

"Let me help you with that," Morales said. "There was a bunch of baby-raping freaks, some kind of cult, making torture films. They fucked up a little kid, fucked him up real bad. And you know what this little kid did, Burke? He fucking killed a baby. *Killed* him, okay? Canceled his ticket, took his fucking life, all right? A little tiny baby . . . So we're talking to the DA's office. City-Wide Special Victims. Woman named Wolfe, maybe you heard of her?"

I kept my eyes on the middle distance between us, staying out of focus, not saying a word. Morales was hitting too close to home, and he'd never be cool enough to just leave it there.

"No, huh?" he sneered. "I guess fucking not. Anyway, we put it together. Put it together *slow*, see? Like we're gonna make a case, *prosecute* the miserable slime. But they disappear, just fucking vanish, okay? Now, they're *around*, way we understand it. Somewhere close. Turns out they were holed up in the South Bronx. In one of those rehabbed joints, right next to a burn-out. So we're ready to roll, just waiting on the warrants and all. And you know what happens then, Burke?"

I stayed in the middle distance, feeling him talk more than hearing, his gut-bucket voice climbing an octave as it got tighter and tighter.

"Yeah," he said. "*You* know. Somebody went into that house before we did. Blew the fucking front door right off. Couple of people at least, too much for one man. Maybe a whole fucking *team*, not that it matters. When they was done, it wasn't a house no more, it was a fucking crypt. Dead bodies. *Nine* dead bodies. A couple of splatter-jobs, probably with a sawed-off. One inside, one outside. The one outside had a long knife in her hand. The rest of them, all bullets. All nines, in fact. And, oh yeah, one had a broken neck. We found a whole video setup in the basement. Looked like they were gonna make themselves a snuff film . . . even had a little boy all tied up, ready to go. All kinds of that Satanic horseshit down there too.

The two downstairs, they was heeled, cranked off a few rounds. Didn't do 'em no good though—they both bought the farm."

"What's that got to do with—?"

"With *you*, motherfucker? With *you*? That's your work. Ain't a working cop in this town don't know that. Ain't the first time you went psycho like that either. We got a list, motherfucker. And you're on it, big-time."

"I don't know what—"

"You know what happens the next time you fall?" he asked, cutting me off. Like it was new information to me.

"Doesn't matter," I told him. "I'm not into anything."

"You been inside twice," Morales said. "Felony beefs. Hell, *armed* felony beefs. Don't you read the papers, asshole? Three strikes, you're in. One more, and you do the book."

I just nodded, like he knew the score. But he was off the mark—once you put ten years between your last prison sentence and your next conviction, they can't run them wild to habitch you into a down-forever, no parole never, life sentence.

"You wouldn't recognize things inside anymore. It's all changed, Burke. Face it, you're getting old."

"You know what's getting old, Morales? This shit you're putting on me. What do you think, you're gonna clear every homicide in the city by rousting me?"

"This ain't no roust. You see a squad car anywhere? You see any backup? I'm undercover," he said proudly, as though any fool couldn't make him for a cop at a hundred yards.

"What is it, then?"

Morales pulled the lapel of his jacket back just far enough for me to see the shoulder holster. "Assume the position," he growled.

I turned around, my back to him, hands on the trunk of my car. I felt his hands patting me down. When he got to the side pocket of my jacket he reached inside, took out what he found there. I knew what it was—a tiny box of wooden matches. A white box with a black bull's-eye on one side, an address and phone number on the other, with the name of the nightclub in black letters: TARGETS.

I felt his hands putting the matchbox back, felt him continue all the way down to my ankles. When he stepped back, I turned around, eyes still not meeting his.

"How come you ain't saying nothing about Probable Cause?" he sneered.

"Doesn't matter," I told him. "I'm clean."

"Clean? You'll *never* be clean, motherfucker. You know, I could understand a man doing a murder. Shit happens, right? Man gets up in your face, disrespects you, threatens you, tries to steal your money, fucks with your wife . . . anything. But a contract hitter, that's the scum of the planet."

Maybe Morales was slicker than I thought. It's an old cop technique—telling you how much they *understand* some crime they think you committed, get you talking. A legacy from his old partner, but he didn't have McGowan's honey-Irish voice. On Morales, "Have a nice day" sounds like a death threat.

But if he was playing that tune, he was in the wrong country. Down where I live, it's not the amateurs who lose their heads who get the respect, it's the ice-men: enforcers, torches, contract killers. I hadn't gone into that house of beasts alone. Max came down from the roof—that was the broken neck. And it was the Prof's scatter-gun that cut down the last of them, the woman with the long knife. The rest, that was me. But even a lunatic like Morales wouldn't believe I'd give up my own family to make a deal. I'd kill *him* first, right where he stood. But this wasn't the time. . . .

"What's that got to do with me?" I said.

"Look, pal, don't waste my time. I know you had something going with McGowan. He was a stone sucker for kids. So he let you slide a few times. Tell me you don't remember that massage parlor just off the Deuce. Tell me you didn't scam me and McGowan so you could total that karate freak. You think I forgot how you Pearl Harbored us that time? Well, you need to know this, punk—McGowan pulled the pin. Retired, understand? Moved down to motherfucking Florida so he could go fishing all the goddamned time. You ain't got a friend on the force anymore, Burke. Too bad too—from where I sit, you could use one."

"You volunteering?" I asked him, meeting his eyes for the first time.

"I'd suck every cock on an AIDS ward first," he snarled, subtle as ever.

As I pulled away in my Plymouth, I glimpsed Morales in my side mirror. Writing something on a pad.

I hadn't forgotten that massage parlor either. Morales never forgave me for that one. Not for the killing—he would have done that one himself, on the house—he just never forgave me for the double-cross. He's been on me ever since, laser-sighted on my heart, just waiting for a clear shot. I knew he was around, but I didn't know he was that close.

I didn't spot the red Stealth again. But I did spot Roxanne, on Eleventh Avenue near Thirty-ninth, standing with a pair of other hookers—one black with a red wig, the other white, sporting a Dolly Parton blond job. As I cruised up, Roxanne waved, bending forward at the waist, licking her lips. It looked about as sexy as a cow chewing its cud.

I slid the Plymouth to the curb, hit the power-window switch for the passenger side. She leaned into the open window, said, "You looking for a date, honey?"

"Mojo Mary said you wanted to talk to me," I answered.

"You're . . . ?"

"Yeah."

She opened the door, climbed inside. A white girl, maybe twenty-two, already sagging from The Life. The combination of cheap overdose perfume, body powder, and stale sweat was overpowering. I turned the AC up a notch as I pulled away. Noticed the blonde standing hip-shot, watching over her shoulder.

"Where do you—?" I asked her.

"There's a parking lot on Thirty-seventh," she said. "Just pull in near the corner. The guy lets us use it."

I found the spot, backed in so the nose of my Plymouth was facing out. Roxanne curled up on the front seat. "This way, if anybody's watching, they'll think it's a head job," she said.

"Okay," I told her, impatient with all this. "What's the deal?"

"What did Mojo Mary tell you?"

"Girl, you think I'm gonna sit here and play games with you? Your time is money, right? So's mine."

"I'm sorry," she whispered. "I told Mary that I was having trouble with my man, okay? I know you . . . do that kind of thing. So I figured, I could get to meet you that way, like with her introducing us."

"Okay, it worked. Now tell me the rest."

"My man, he's into all kinds of stuff. Powder, mostly. He works me hard, and he treats me hard too."

"So?"

"So he's in jail now. For a little while, then he'll be out. I got to make my move. Now, while he's still inside."

"Talk straight," I told her. This broad could have gangbanged every liar in Congress in the time it took her to get to the point.

"I heard you could get it done . . . inside. You got friends there. I want you to . . . take him out, okay?"

"No, it's not okay. I don't do that."

"Listen to me," she whispered harshly, her voice urgent, "he does kids too. Little kids. And he gets money for it. *Lots* of money. If you do it, it's all yours."

"You've got the wrong man, girl. The wrong man on both ends, it sounds like."

"How much would you want? Up front? If I paid—"

"It's not me," I told her. "I don't know what you heard, but you heard wrong. And you damn sure didn't hear it from Mojo Mary either."

"Look, it'd be easy. I know exactly where he—"

"Not now, not ever," I told her, starting the engine. She was still gabbing away when I pulled over at the same spot where I picked her up. The same two hookers were there. As she walked over to join them, the one with the Dolly Parton wig put her arm around Roxanne's shoulders, pulling her close, and walked off with her. The way it looked, soon as Roxanne found someone man enough to snuff her pimp, her next one wouldn't be a man at all.

It wasn't my problem. I cranked the wheel over, headed back downtown.

It was only late afternoon, but already I felt tired—like I'd worked all night. I closed my eyes at a traffic light—I could always count on some impatient swine waking me up with a horn blast when it turned green.

I drove quietly, trying for smoothness, calming my center so I could think. A guy in a blue Camaro cut me off—I let him go, ignoring the middle finger he saluted me with. There's a lot of other things I could have done, but the Plymouth was a pro—nothing for fun, anything for money.

The Camaro almost T-boned a white Ford Taurus at the next intersection. The driver was *already* wearing one of those foam cervical collars they give you in the Emergency Ward when you have whiplash—I guess he was related to a lawyer.

Pedestrians crossed against the light, right in front of me, just about begging to get hit, every one on full ready-to-lie alert . . . "I crossed on the green, officer. I had the Walk sign all the way. That maniac just swooped down on me. I never saw him coming."

Down here, you show some politeness, they think you're intimidated. Down here, mercy is rarer than honesty.

New York may be a woman, the way some writers say. If she is, she's a low-class evil bitch. She wouldn't care if you killed yourself. Probably giggle at it. And sell the suicide note to the newspapers.

I hate it all so much—more now than ever.

Pansy was waiting for me, ice-water eyes watchful in her massive skull. She's a Neapolitan mastiff: a hundred and forty pounds of brick-brained muscle in her salad days, the beast was probably pushing one seventy by now.

"Glad to see me, girl?" I asked her. Pansy was probably the only living female on this planet who would answer me the same way every time—her tail wagged out of control as she made happy sounds deep in her throat. I walked over to the tiny refrigerator and took out a quarter-pound of raw hamburger. I patted the hamburger into a round ball. Pansy watched me steadily, drooling quarts but not moving. I finally said "Speak!" and tossed it in her direction. She snapped it out of the air with the immaculate precision of a striking cobra. It was gone in one gulp, and she looked at me pleadingly. "You've had enough, you fat pig," I told her.

If her feelings were hurt, she didn't show it, padding over to the back door and knocking against it with a raised paw. I once thought about installing a dog door so she could go in and out herself whenever she wanted, but when I measured how big a cut it would take I realized there wouldn't be anything left but the frame.

I opened the door and she worked her way up the fire escape to the roof, where she'd dump another load. I don't go up there much—the smell would gag a mortician.

When Pansy came back down, I made myself something to eat from one of the takeout cartons from Mama's restaurant, heating the concoction up on my hot plate. I spooned it down, mixing swallows with some ice water from the refrigerator. What I didn't finish, I dumped into Pansy's bowl, right on top of the dry dog food she can get for herself anytime she wants by pushing a lever with her snout. I don't use plates much—everything has to be washed in the bathroom sink. Anything Pansy won't eat, I just throw into a thirty-gallon plastic bag. When that gets near full, I wrap it up, take it downstairs. First Dumpster I pass, in it goes. I keep the place squeaky-clean, like I did my cell when I was inside—you let New York roaches establish a beachhead, it's the beginning of the end.

I walked around the office for a few minutes until I realized I was pacing. I'd taught myself not to do that—it makes you tense, exaggerates the limits of your surroundings. That's what you are in jail, surrounded. And it's not the locks and bars that make you feel so hemmed in, it's the lack of choices. It basically comes down to two in there—you live or you die.

Sometimes it's hard to tell the difference.

It's safe up here. Besides Pansy, I've got all kinds of security systems. The Mole fixed it up for me. He arranged it so I could use the telephone line of the aging hippies who live in the big loft just below me too. He even has my electricity wired into their line. Only thing he couldn't pirate was the cable TV—Con Ed doesn't care what's going on so long as it makes its money, but the cable TV people get big-time serious about piracy. I make do with a wire coat hanger for an antenna on my old B&W set.

I found a Mets game on TV. That collection of egotistical mal-adroits was blowing still another opportunity to climb out of the cel-lar. Somebody must have put a curse on them—no team is as bad as they were playing. They say baseball is a game of inches, but those suckers were a couple of yards off the mark.

Pansy growled her disapproval—baseball bores the hell out of her. I played with the dial until I found some pro wrestling. She snarfled her approval, settling down into a huge lump on the floor next to me. I closed my eyes, one hand absently patting her sleek head.

When I came around, it was dark outside. I let Pansy out one more time, promised I'd bring her a treat when I got back.

Rain slanted down through the polluted air, dirty-dancing in my headlights. The blue-dragon tapestry was in Mama's window. I drove right on past, found a pay phone, called in.

"It's me. You have visitors?"

"All gone now. Lady."

"Lady cop?"

"Yes."

"Anything else?"

"Man call. Say he from Targets. Say somebody looking for you there."

"Lady too?"

"No. Man. Angry man."

"Thanks, Mama. I'll see you later."

"Lady cop, she not have uniform."

"How'd you know, then?"

"I know," Mama said, and broke the connection.

was on the move early the next morning. I felt boxed. Not trapped yet, but close. I needed a place to think things through. Not my office—if they came there, the best I could do would be to hold them off for a while—I couldn't get out of there fast enough.

I aimed the Plymouth north and let it roll toward the Mole's junkyard, sensors on full alert. When I was in prison, when I was studying all the time, I learned about artifacts. When psychologists do a series of interviews with the same guy, they sometimes insert a piece of false information and wait to see if the guy feeds it back to them. That would mean the guy's faking the symptoms. Malingering, they call it. What else would you expect from a business where they say you're "in denial" instead of just calling you a fucking liar.

Artifacts work like verbal trip-wires. Doc told me about them. He was doing a pretrial screening interview with a guy they'd dropped on a couple of dozen rapes. This guy, he said he was a multiple personality. You know, it wasn't *him* who did it, it was the *other* one. So what Doc did, he left some of his notes lying around on top of the desk. He gets an emergency phone call and he runs out. The guy, naturally, takes a look. Doc's notes said the guy sounded like a multiple all right, but one thing was missing—all male multiples complain of bad toothaches even when there's nothing wrong. Some mumbo-jumbo about the nerve endings in the lower jaw. Pure bullshit.

Anyway, a couple of days later, the guy starts screaming in his cell. When the guards come, he tells them he's got this incredible pain in his back teeth. They give him a couple of painkillers, stand there and make sure he swallows them. Next morning, he goes out on Sick Call. Sees the dentist. They take X-rays. Nothing shows. They mark the guy down for a hustler, send him back to his cell. So the next time he sees Doc, he doesn't want to talk about the rapes—all he does is complain that his teeth are killing him and begs Doc to make the dentist look at him again.

The guy went from NGI—Not Guilty by reason of Insanity—to NFG—No Fucking Good—in that session. Last I heard, he was still Upstate.

That's where I got the idea. What I do is carry these matchboxes around. The fancy kind you get in some joints—wooden matches in shiny little boxes. Free advertising, I guess it's supposed to be. Only I've never been in Targets except for one time. It's a tiny joint over on the West Side—only open from six at night to two in the morning. The guy who works the bar, he's actually the owner. But he's got a felony fall on his sheet, so he can't be listed that way. I know him from Upstate. He knows how things work. We made a deal—if anyone comes around asking for me, he drops word to Mama. I call him back, get a description. It costs me five yards each time, but it's worth it for the safety net.

I didn't need the description this time—it had to be Morales.

Morales on one end, Belinda Roberts on the other. I went back far enough with both of them so it couldn't be an accident—I was in a vise.

Hunts Point—a giant open-air discount market, from slightly used car parts to very used whores. I stopped for a red light on Bruckner, glancing to my left, toward the shantytown squatting below the overpass. Even out there, in the middle of a war zone, the homeless felt safer than they ever would in one of the city shelters. They weren't wrong, either.

As soon as traffic stopped for the light, the street was filled with young Latino men, all brandishing some form of sign. AUTO GLASS was the most common. They're all commission salesmen, shilling for one of the nearby body shops. You need a new windshield for your Chevy? Why pay four bills when you can get it done at the Point for one and a half, tops. The Point is an all-cash economy, everything's negotiable.

Everything. The Point is so dangerous, it can kill clichés. Down here, things *are* as bad as they seem.

I drove through slowly, staying smooth at the wheel—erratic movements in this neighborhood, they're like a fish going belly-up . . . the predators are always next on the scene. The Point—

where the feral dogs fear the feral children, and even the STOP signs are bullet-pocked.

You get a flat tire around here, you just keep driving on the rim until you're over the border.

Terry opened the back gate at the junkyard. I docked the Plymouth in the space he pointed to. We walked back to the Mole's bunker together. Terry was getting his growth. Filling out some too. No point in wondering who he'd look like when he was done—his bio-parents sold him to a kiddie pimp when he was small—all he remembered from them was the pain. He was the Mole's son now. The Mole's and Michelle's.

That's the way it happens down here. Somebody always picks up the strays. Most of the time, they're just table scraps for freaks. Terry, he got lucky. But he paid heavy for that luck before it came to him.

I half-listened to the kid going on about some experiment he and the Mole were doing—I already knew from experience I wouldn't understand it even if I focused on every word. The dog pack swirled around us, not herding so much as flowing along with us.

"Where's Simba?" I asked Terry. Simba was the pack leader, a mixed-breed murderer who'd held his position against all comers for years. Usually, he'd be the first one up when a stranger came through the gate.

"He's down at the other end," the kid said. "With a girl . . . Remember Orchid? The white pit bull? The one who had puppies last year?"

"Yeah."

"Well, the next batch of puppies, Simba's going to be the father," Terry told me proudly.

The Mole's deck chair was standing by itself in the afternoon's slanting sunlight, a cut-down oil drum with a cushion on top. But there was no sign of the Mole himself.

Terry saw me looking, asked: "You want me to get—?"

"No," I interrupted. "I'm okay. I just wanted a quiet place to be by myself for a bit, all right?"

"Sure," the kid said. He turned around and started back the way we'd come.

I sat on the Mole's chair, lit a cigarette, eyes half-closed, centering myself, dropping down in my mind to where I could do the work. I finished the smoke, breathing shallow. After I tossed it away, I swept the grounds until I saw a piece of chrome bumper from a derelict car. It was glinting in the sun, a spark in shadow. I focused on the spark, narrowing my vision, converting all the street sounds to white noise. I got quieter and quieter inside. When I closed my eyes, I could still see the spark of light. I went into it.

Morales hated me. Hated me for scamming McGowan—had me marked for that house of freaks in the Bronx too. Maybe some other stuff. He was a grudge-loving dinosaur pit bull. He'd stay on the case forever. And once he got his jaws locked, he'd never drop the bite.

If it was an accident that he ran across my path, why would he muscle over to Targets? What did he want to know?

That was one gap.

Belinda. She'd been on my case for a long time now. Calling, leaving messages. But she wasn't pushing it. Until now. Coming by Mama's joint, letting me know what she knew. Why? Why now?

Another gap.

The gaps were too big for me to fill with logic, so I let my other side work, trying to feel what I couldn't calculate.

What it felt was bad. Treacherous bad.

The Mole has a super-safe phone down in his bunker. He tried to explain it to me once . . . something about a blue box into the 800 loop and then back out. I never did understand it.

I walked over to the entrance of the bunker, called "Mole" softly. The Mole looks harmless but he's so smart that he's crazy with it— you don't want to spook someone like that.

After a minute or so, he appeared at the top of the stairs, his skin as underground-pale as always, eyes unreadable behind the thick Coke-bottle lenses, his form shapeless under a dirt-colored jumpsuit. He answers people who call his name the same way he answers his phone—with silence.

"I need to use the phone for a few minutes, okay?"

He didn't answer. Just turned his back and started down the stairs. I followed. The underground bunker was illuminated with diffused lighting, like an aquarium. The Mole went to his work-bench, started fumbling with some small vials of liquid. The phone was near the wall. I picked it up, got a dial tone, tapped out the number for Targets. The phone made a whirring sound, then a series of rapid-fire beep-tones as it worked its way into the loop and then back to Manhattan. It rang four times before it was picked up.

"Targets," a woman's voice said.

"Can I speak to Nate, please?" I asked the voice.

"Who should I tell him—?"

"A friend. From Upstate."

It was maybe half a minute before I heard Nate's voice. "What?"

"It's me," I said. "I got your message. About somebody asking for me."

"Yeah. Right. So when do I get—?"

"It's on the way. You'll have it tonight. What can you tell me about the guy?"

"Big man. Not tall, he *walked* big, understand?"

"Yeah."

"Latino. P.R. maybe, who can tell? Big chest. No neck. Growls when he talks."

"What'd he want?"

"Do I know you? You been around? You come there a lot?"

"He say my name?"

"Yeah. He flashed the tin, didn't make no secret of it."

"He leave any kind of message?"

"Yeah. Said he'd be back. I told him I take care of the captain—I'm not supposed to get no street rollers coming around. He just laughed. Only not 'ha ha,' you understand?"

"Yeah. Thanks, Nate."

I hung up on his "When do I—?"

I called Mama's. "It's me," I told her when she picked up my pay phone in the back of the restaurant. "Can you tell Max I need him to drop off five small at Targets? The guy's behind the bar. Named Nate. Fat guy, going bald."

"Where Targets?" she asked.

I gave her the address. Then asked, "Mama, this lady cop, what did she say?"

"Say very, very important. You call her."

"The same number she's always leaving?"

"Yes. Same number. Say anytime after four o'clock."

I looked at my watch. Seven-fifteen already. "Four o'clock when?" I asked.

"She not say. Walk out, fast."

"Thanks, Mama."

I crossed back over the Triborough into Manhattan, thinking how badly things had changed. Used to be, when I was leaving a place like Hunts Point, I could feel the muscles in the back of my neck relax as I crossed the border into safer territory. No more. Now the muscles stay tight—all the time. There's no safe harbor in this city, no neighborhood where anyone really feels secure. There's a thin vicious mist over the city, the whole place poisoned by that red-zone aggression-terror mix. That's another reason I don't carry a gun any-more—it makes you too brave. I know what being brave costs—I'd emptied that account the same time I emptied that last clip . . . in the basement of blood I walked away from in the Bronx.

I took the FDR downtown, darkness coming now. I found a parking spot on Lex, walked a couple of blocks until I got to the building I was looking for. The entranceway was deserted. I pushed the button for 11-G, my mouth near the intercom in case they were going to screen the clients. Nothing came out of the intercom, but the main door buzzed open.

I took the elevator to the eleventh floor, walked the length of the threadbare carpet to the last apartment on the right. The door was painted matte black, its flatness broken only by the letter "G" in gilt and a heavy steel plate surrounding the lower lock, protecting the deadbolt. I pushed the tiny pearl-white button on the door frame, heard chimes ring inside.

I stood back a couple of feet to give whoever was working the peephole a good look at me. The door was opened by a short, skinny man wearing a black suit with red suspenders over a white shirt. A wispy mustache made him look even more weasely.

"Can I do something for you?" he asked.

"I'm here to see Mojo Mary," I answered.

"You have an appointment?"

"No."

"She know you?"

"Yes. Name's Burke."

"Chill," the man said, closing the door in my face.

He was back in another minute. This time he stepped aside, waved me to a white Naugahyde couch in the front room, facing the door. I sat down, waited. The man disappeared to my left. A tall brunette in a peach-colored teddy walked across the room on my right, heading for another door. She winked at me, gave her hips an extra shake—a reflex action. I knew her—by reputation, anyway. Word is she was fired from her job as a porno actress because she couldn't memorize the lines.

The man came back with Mojo Mary in tow. She's half Cajun, half Lao—on any given day, she'll tell you a different story about how that happened. Her skin is a rosy bronze color, her glossy black hair long and straight; her teeth are so white they don't look real. She was wearing a man's red pajama top with the top buttons un-done. It fell to mid-thigh, showing off the fishnet stockings she wore with red spike heels.

"Hello, stranger," she said, smiling.

"How you doing?" I responded, getting to my feet.

"Come on with me—I'll tell you all about it," she said, holding out her hand.

I took it, followed her down a carpeted corridor. All the doors were closed except the one we went in. It was a bedroom, all pink and white, dominated by a king-size bed with an elaborate head-board. A bathroom door stood open to my left.

Mary closed the door behind us, stepped around me and sat on the bed, crossing her legs.

"It's seventy-five for a half-hour—a buck and a quarter for an hour. You feeling strong today?"

"I just want some answers," I told her, taking a roll of bills out of my jacket. "Here's the seventy-five—I'll be out of here in a few minutes. And here's your tip," I said softly, handing her another hundred.

"Ummm," she said, licking her lips. "Money makes me hot. You sure you don't want me to—?"

"Roxanne. That girl working the West Side, near the Javits Center—how'd you meet her?"

"Roxanne . . . ? I don't know if . . ."

"She gave your name. When she called me. Said she had a problem. White girl. Looks kind of used."

"All those tire-biters look used, honey—that's a rough life out there."

"She used your name, Mary. I know you got paid. Just tell me what you know and I'm out of here."

"Square business?"

"Square business. I got no beef with you. Just run it down—where, when, like that, okay?"

She looked up at me, dark eyes glinting over high cheekbones. "Look, honey, all I did was what I do, okay? I mean, I figured she had a job of work, she pays me to get word to you. After that, you're on your own, right?"

"Right."

"And, the way I figure it, if you make out good on the job, maybe you'll come by, take care of Mary."

"I just did that, take care of you. You don't like the way I did it?"

"Come *on*, honey. You know that isn't what I meant. It's just . . . you sound like you're mad at me for something."

"Mary, I came to your place, didn't I? I was mad at you, I wouldn't come here, give everybody a good look at me, would I?"

"I . . . guess not."

"And I came alone, didn't I? Showed you respect?"

"Yes . . ."

"So give it to me, girl."

She got up off the bed, walked over to a night table, knocked a cigarette out of a pack, tapped the filter against one long thumbnail. "You got a match?" she asked, coming over to where I was standing.

I cracked a wooden match into flame. She cupped my hand in both of hers, taking the light. "Sit down," she said. "You're making me nervous."

I took an easy chair near the foot of the bed, lit a smoke of my own. Mary walked in little circles, gesturing with her cigarette. "This Roxanne chick, she called me. Here. We're not supposed to get personal calls here, but Rudy—you know, the guy who let you in—he doesn't ride too hard. Anyway, she wanted to meet me. Said there was good money in it. I met her in Logan's. You know that bar on—?"

"Yeah."

"Okay. Anyway, that's a safe place. I mean, *I* picked it and all. And Rudy went with me. This Roxanne, I never saw her before. Not her friend either."

"Her friend?"

"Blonde girl. I think it was a wig . . . like too much hair for her face, you know? Kind of fat, you ask me. Too much makeup."

"She tell you her name, the blonde girl?"

"No. She didn't say much of anything. But I could tell it was her pulling the strings—this Roxanne, her motor's not hitting on all cylinders, you understand?"

"Yeah," I said, making a "get on with it" gesture with my right hand.

Mary took a deep drag from her cigarette, buying herself a little time. "Anyway, she said she was having trouble with her man. She wanted to jet, but she was scared of him. Happens all the time, right?"

"Sure."

"So I asked her, does she want to hire Rudy, take care of it? And—"

"Rudy? The skinny guy who answered the door out there?"

"Oh yes, honey. Rudy maybe can't bench-press fifty pounds, but he's quick as a snake with that blade of his. Quiet too."

"Okay. So . . . ?"

"So she says no. She wants you. Burke, she said. She knew your name. Said she heard you was real good at this. I told her, everybody on the street has peeped your hole card a long time ago—if it don't have nothing to do with kids, you not gonna do any heavy work."

Wesley flashed across my mind. Wesley, the maybe-dead ice-monster. The perfect killer, good for nothing else, but better at it than any man alive. Wesley telling me I had a bull's-eye on my back. A weakness. Kids. Get rid of it, he told me in his deadman's voice. I wish I'd listened then. I put the cigarette to my lips, making a smoke screen for my eyes. "So what happened after that?" I asked Mary.

"She said it *was* about kids, kind of. Anyway, she'd pay me to get word out to you."

I raised my eyebrows.

"Five yards," Mary said. "I figured, it must be big, she was gonna pay that much for just a message. Figured, you were gonna get paid big too."

"So she paid you how much up front?"

"The whole thing. Only, she didn't actually pay me—it was the blonde chick."

"And that's all you know?"

"That *is* all I know, honey. I even told her—I can get word to you, but I can't promise you'll do anything about it. She just told me where her stroll is, told me to tell you that."

"You'd know the blonde girl if you saw her again?"

"I . . . think so. Like I said, she didn't say much. And it's dark in there, so—"

"Okay, Mary. Thanks." I got up to leave.

Mary opened another button on the pajama top, flashing a smile. "You paid for some time, honey. You want me to earn it?"

"If you told me the truth, you just did," I said, reaching behind me to open the door, watching Mojo Mary all the time.

I drove back downtown, working it over in my mind. Coming up short again. That last bit stunk worse than aged sushi. Mojo Mary has a hooker's soul. She's all whore in her heart—no way she gives up pussy for free. But she didn't seem scared, the way she would if she thought she'd sold me out and I was still walking around. She was guilty all right, but lightweight guilty—figured she could work it off. Just didn't add up.

Only the white dragon was in Mama's window. I pulled around to the back, walked through and found my booth. Mama came over, clapping her hands for soup. This time, she didn't wait for the ceremony, just sat down across from me.

"What is all this?" she asked me, gesturing in a wide circle.

"I don't know, Mama. Mojo Mary gave my name to a street girl. Girl wanted me to ice her man, take him off the count. Mary knows I don't do that kind of work. . . ."

"Mary is street girl too?"

"Yeah. Only she works inside."

"So! Maybe she . . . *hear* something. From long ago . . ."

I kept my mind away from that, away from the past. Too many "Father Unknown" birth certificates—too many unmarked graves. Who knows what the pimps gossip about in their after-hours joints, where flash counts heavier than cash? Who knows what Mojo Mary heard? "Maybe you're right, Mama," is all I said.

I sipped my soup in silence, expecting Mama to go back to her cash register. But she stayed where she was, face composed, watching me.

"What?" I finally asked her.

"Why you not ask about lady police?"

"I already know her," I said. "Belinda. The same one who's been calling here all along, remember?"

"Short girl, kind of . . ."

"Plump?"

"No, not plump. Like . . . solid. Strong."

"Yeah, that's her."

"Blue eyes?"

"I don't remember," I told her. It was the truth.

"Blond hair?"

I looked up from my soup, paying attention for the first time. "No. It's kind of reddish-brown."

"This one blonde."

"You sure?"

Mama gave me a look of intense pity, clearly wondering how I got to be as old as I am despite being so stupid. "Yes," she said. "Sure. Blonde."

"Maybe she dyed her hair. Women do things like that, right?"

"Not dye hair," Mama said. "Blond wig."

I felt a hammer drop somewhere in my head. Maybe I *was* getting too old for this. Who strips a blow-job whore looking for a wire? That blonde girl, the one on the same corner as Roxanne . . . I tried to replay the image, but I couldn't get the screen to clear. Belinda? Belinda getting me on tape, agreeing to kill a man for money?

But I hadn't gone for it.

I was in a long corridor. A long mirrored corridor. I couldn't see the end. Just reflections. Images. I couldn't see, so I listened.

And all I heard was that special-ugly slammer-sound when the jailers rack the bars closed at night.

"Mama," I asked, "you still have that loft over on Mott Street?"

"Sure."

"Anybody staying there now?"

"No. Nobody till next month."

"Can I borrow the key?"

Mama reached in one of her kimono pockets, handed it over. "Take Max," she said.

I used the phone in the back to reach out for the Prof, came up empty. He wasn't at the gym. Not at any of his usual spots either. I left word.

Mama's is a good place for waiting. It's quiet and peaceful, the food is great . . . you can make a call or get one, read the racing form, take a nap if you want. Mama always keeps a stock of English-language international newspapers around. I opened one idly, glanced through it, enjoying the soup the waiter had poured into a thick coffee cup for me.

The paper had two full pages of escort services. One place said all their girls spoke at least three languages. Sure—French, Greek, and Missionary.

The classifieds were more interesting. An offshore bank was offered for sale: ten thousand, cash. Somebody was advertising a kidney for sale. His own. Cost you a hundred grand plus expenses, but if you needed a transplant, you wouldn't have to wait in line.

I dropped the international stuff and shifted to the local tabloids. A human on the Holy Coast fixed up his basement for his stepdaughter—soundproofed walls with a videocam set up on a tripod. Called it his War Room. He tortured the girl down there. When they busted him, he said he was trying to teach the girl right from wrong. That's what's wrong with kids today—they have no discipline. He was willing to plead guilty to child abuse, but not to any sex crimes.

It might have worked if the jury hadn't seen the tapes.

I turned the page. A man and woman—a male and female anyway—got all embarrassed about the woman's condition. She was about to give birth, but the baby wasn't his. So they took the baby home from the hospital and buried it in their back yard. Nobody knew anything about it until the woman got pregnant again . . . by the *right* man this time. A nurse asked her if she'd ever been pregnant before, and the woman said she had, but the baby had died. It didn't take them long to find the baby's body—the cops locked them both up.

When the man was produced for his arraignment the next day, his face was badly swollen. Some sanctimonious columnist wrote the story, smirking self-righteously about "jailhouse justice." Every time I read wishful-thinking garbage like that, I want to puke. I did time with a guy once—Mestron, his name was—he was a sex killer, and proud of it. None of the girls was over seven years old. The miserable freak would snatch the poor little things, take them back to the basement where he lived . . . grab their ankles, hold them upside down, then use his powerful arms to crack the little girls like wishbones . . . so he could slide in on the blood. I know the details because he told them to anyone who would listen. Over and over, doing it again in his mind.

Mestron was a short guy, maybe five foot six, tops. He weighed about two hundred and thirty pounds, all of it muscle. He was good with his hands and better with a shank. And he wasn't in population two weeks before he raped a bank robber—hundred-and-twenty-pound bank robber who couldn't bring his gun to prison with him. And Mestron? That baby-killer did *good* time—righteous indignation doesn't stack up too high against homicidal muscle. You want to see jailhouse justice? Just spend some time in a jungle . . . and pray *you're* not the prey.

The scumbag on the Coast, the one who tortured his step-daughter—my hope for him was that he'd have something worth killing for in prison. It wouldn't take much.

I stopped reading the paper—I don't know why they call it "news." I got up from my booth, bowed a goodbye to Mama, and got back out into the world.

The next day was Friday. Still no sign of the Prof. I figured I could catch him at the fights, so I picked Max up and we drove over the Manhattan Bridge to the BQE, exited on Queens Boulevard and motored along, watching for the turnoff. All along the strip, the topless bars and storefront churches coexisted, each crew deluding itself it was competition for the other. I found the turnoff, followed the Prof's directions. The joint was off Skillman Avenue, an old arena that hadn't been big-time since World War II. We circled the area half a dozen times before Max spotted a parking place. I pulled in, secured the Plymouth.

"We're with one of the fighters," I told the guy at the door. "Where's the dressing rooms? I got a boy going tonight."

"Him?" the guy at the door said, nodding his head in Max's direction.

"Not this time," I told him.

"You're not gonna work the corner, you gotta pay like everybody else," he said.

I gave him a fifty for two ringside seats. "First come, first served," the guy said, gesturing toward the ring standing in the middle of the auditorium surrounded by rows of folding chairs.

One of the cable networks was setting up a trio of heavy cameras on massive tripods. I saw the lights had already been strung, the network's logo was firmly in place near the ceiling. They tape all the fights, but the four-rounders only make it to the screen if the main event ends early.

We walked around the perimeter until I found the entrance to the back rooms. The locker room was crowded with fighters—they were all in the one room, but separated by invisible lines, surrounded by handlers and hangers-on. The place smelled of fresh sweat and stale hopes. I spotted the Prof standing over to one side, saying something to Frankie as Clarence carefully wrapped the fighter's hands in tape.

"It's the first bout for the other guy too," the Prof was saying to Frankie, "but he's a Golden Gloves winner—they looking for you to be a sheep for the creep. But ain't the way it's gonna play, okay?"

Frankie nodded attentively, not speaking.

"You got to be quick, babe," the Prof continued. "Get off fast—don't let it last. On TV, KO is all they know. You ready?"

Frankie nodded again.

"We're up first," the Prof said to me. "Got about a half-hour." He turned to Frankie. "Just lie back, son. Relax. Don't bother trying to break a sweat until it gets close to game time."

Frankie obediently lay back on the table, closed his eyes.

"I got to ask you something," I said to the Prof, drawing him aside.

"After the bout, schoolboy. This is business now."

"Okay," I agreed, staying on his topic. "You know anything about this boy Frankie's going to fight?"

"Sure. See that guy over there? The one against the lockers? That's him. Jermaine Jenkins."

I looked over. Jenkins was a black kid, looked about nineteen.

He stood about six four, looked like he weighed maybe two thirty. A real big kid. Big all over. He was admiring a neon-blue robe with his name on the back, rapping to a couple of guys in suits.

"We can take him easy," the Prof said, smiling. "Boy's got a nice wardrobe. Slick moves too. But his punch don't crunch. Only reason we got the date is they glommed Frankie's weight. We should be fighting cruisers, but there ain't no cash in the off-brands."

"What corner they give you?"

"Blue," he replied. "True blue."

"Frankie's ready?"

"He'll be on that pretty-boy like a ho' on dough, bro—nothing to it."

I walked back over to where Frankie was lying down. Noticed Clarence had placed a clean white washcloth over the fighter's eyes. "Be yourself," I told him, giving his shoulder a pat.

"I will," he said quietly.

Max and I went out, found seats near the blue corner. The place was filling up. I spotted a crew of dope gangstahs through the ropes, all sitting ringside. One of them was talking on a cellular phone, making a production out of it. A dark-haired man in his fifties in an expensive-looking midnight-blue suit sat a few places over to my left, his arm around the waist of a sharp-featured bottle-blonde about a foot taller and thirty years younger than him. Most of the crowd was local—blue-collar whites and flashier-dressed Latins. A group of Orientals sat by themselves, occasionally glancing over at the black gangstah crew. Hard looks, returned with interest.

The announcer stepped to the center of the ring, a middle-aged man with an elaborate hairdo wearing a bright-red tuxedo jacket with black shawl lapels. He held a microphone in one hand and a large index card in the other. Then he did the usual bit about welcoming us to the fabulous arena, announced each of the three judges by name, identified the State Boxing Commissioner and a bunch of other people. Then the referee. In the middle of his spiel, the two fighters walked toward the ring from opposite directions. Jenkins was resplendent in his pretty robe, surrounded by half a dozen different guys. Frankie's robe was wide black-and-white vertical stripes, like an old-time convict's uniform. Jenkins' handlers held the ropes for him to climb in the ring—Clarence did the same for Frankie. The cornermen removed their fighters' robes. Jenkins' blue trunks were a perfect match. Frankie's were striped the same as his robe too.

The referee called the fighters to the center of the ring, mumbled something. Jenkins looked much bigger than Frankie, a menacing scowl on his face. He glared at Frankie—Frankie gave him a blank stare back. The referee said to touch gloves. Frankie held his two hands out—Jenkins brought both fists down hard, said something I couldn't catch. The fighters went back to their corners, sat down.

Frankie opened his mouth for Clarence to insert the white rubber mouthpiece. The Prof leaned close to Frankie's ear, whispering something.

The bell rang.

Jenkins trotted out of his corner, circled to Frankie's left, up on his toes, firing a series of pretty jabs that Frankie caught on his gloves. Frankie shuffled forward methodically, working from a slight crouch, occasionally pushing a weak jab out.

"Let your hands go!" the Prof screamed.

Jenkins continued to circle, drawing cheers from the crowd with each flurry. Frankie cut off the ring, bulling Jenkins into a corner. But Jenkins spun away, slapping a glove to the back of Frankie's head as the crowd laughed.

Jenkins pop-pop-popped more jabs, then crossed with his right, catching Frankie flush on the jaw. Frankie stepped back, but quickly lowered his head and came on again. The bell rang with both fighters in the center of the ring throwing punches—Jenkins outspeeding Frankie by an easy three-to-one. Jenkins raised both hands over his head as he strutted back to his corner.

Clarence took the mouthpiece from Frankie, held a sponge to the back of the fighter's neck. A girl in a gold thong-back bikini pranced around the ring in matching spike heels, holding up a white card with a red 2 on it.

The Prof was saying something in Frankie's ear—I couldn't make it out.

The bell for the second round sounded. Jenkins was off his stool quickly, covering most of the distance between the fighters before Frankie took a single step. Jenkins flicked the jab. Frankie didn't move his feet, but he dropped his right shoulder, shifted his weight way over and exploded a pair of right hooks to Jenkins' ribs. Jenkins staggered backward, hands up to protect his face. Frankie threw another right hook, legs spread apart, feet planted for power. The crowd screamed as Frankie came on, hooking with both hands now. Jenkins dropped to one knee. The referee started to count. Jenkins was up at eight. The referee asked him if he was all right. Jenkins nodded, held his hands up to show he was ready. The referee wiped off Jenkins' gloves on the front of his white shirt, waved Frankie in.

Frankie shuffled forward as Jenkins retreated behind his flicking jab, maintaining distance. It didn't work—Frankie swallowed the jabs, a flash of white showing at his mouth. Either a smile or a snarl—I couldn't tell.

Jenkins still had his hands up, elbows against his chest, armor-plated. Frankie pounded away at what he was offered, smashing blow after blow to his opponent's forearms. Jenkins backed into the ropes. Frankie threw a left just below Jenkins' elbow, then followed with an overhand right to the temple. Jenkins lost his legs—his knees wobbled as he tried to pull Frankie into a clench. The referee separated the fighters, pushing Frankie back a few feet.

It didn't help. Frankie drove a right into Jenkins' kidneys and the other man went down—this time he didn't get up. A doctor came into the ring as Frankie walked slowly back to his own corner.

Max and I found Frankie back where he'd started the night. He had just stepped out of the shower and was toweling himself off.

"Good job," I told him.

The kid kept his head down, mumbled "Thanks." The Prof pulled himself up onto the table, used it for a chair as he spoke to Frankie. "You got to get off *first*," he said to the fighter. "You was all warmed up before you went out there. What happened?"

"I . . . dunno," Frankie replied.

"That boy was all flash," the Prof said. "He couldn't hurt you with a fucking tire iron, right?"

"Yeah."

"Look, kid, you don't want to get a rep as a slow starter. You can't be giving away the first round every time—that makes the other guy brave."

Frankie's head came up, looking the Prof full in the eyes for the first time. "I know," he said.

A smile broke across the Prof's handsome face. "You hear that, schoolboy?" he said to me. "My man's got a plan. The other boy raps, *my* boy sets the traps. Beautiful!"

"You cannot be defeated, mahn," Clarence said to Frankie, as gravely as quoting the Bible.

Max tapped Frankie's shoulder to get his attention. Then he mimed throwing a right hook, bowed to Frankie. Frankie returned the bow. "How do I tell him thanks?" he asked me.

"You just did," I told him. I turned to the Prof. "You about ready to go?"

"I want Frankie to see the rest of the fights, all right? Only a fool cuts school."

We all went back outside, just in time to see another four-rounder come to an end, this time with both fighters standing. When the decision was announced, one of the fighters leaped into the air, waving a gloved fist in triumph—the other made an emphatic gesture of disgust. The crowd booed them both.

Frankie sat to my left, Max to my right. The Prof and Clarence went off somewhere, probably to arrange Frankie's next fight. Or to collect some bets.

We watched some paunchy heavyweights waltz around the ring to the thunderous boredom of the crowd. It was so bad that the ref tapped one of them on the shoulder when he wanted to cut in. I knew cable TV was desperate for product, but this was obscene—if it wasn't for the 10-point-must system, the sorry bout would have ended up a 0–0 double-draw loss. The crowd booed and hissed at the decision, disgusted that either of the slobs won. Like New York voters, wishing there was a Fuck-All-a-Youse choice on the ballot.

Finally, they announced the main event. Frankie sat up straight in his chair, taking it all in.

The Golden Boy was black. Twenty-one and zip, with seventeen KOs. He was as sleek as an otter—all smooth, rubbery muscle under glistening chocolate skin. He wore royal-purple trunks with a white stripe under an ankle-length robe in matching colors, his name blazing across the back: Cleophus "Cobra" Carr.

Tonight he *was* the main event, a ten-rounder. Middleweights, they were supposed to be, but they called Carr's weight out at one sixty-four.

There was a lot of betting in the mid-priced seats just past ring-side—betting how long the fight would go before Carr stopped the other guy.

Nobody knew the opponent—he was the last-minute replacement for the guy Carr was supposed to fight. He walked to the ring by himself, wearing a thin white terry-cloth robe. His trunks were black.

The announcer pointed to the opponent's corner first. Manuel Ortiz. Dragging the last name out way past two syllables—*Orrrr-Teeese!* Ortiz was fifty-six and sixteen, with thirty-two KOs. Originally a welterweight, he'd go up or down . . . wherever there was work. They had him at one fifty-nine tonight.

Maybe he had dreams for this once—now it was a part-time job.

I knew his story like it was printed in a book. He got the call the day before, finished his shift at the car wash, got on the Greyhound and rode until he got to the arena—I could see it in his face, all of that.

Carr was twenty-two. He'd gone all the way to the finals at the Olympic Trials before turning pro two years ago. They said Ortiz was thirty, shading it at least a half-dozen. The guy who managed him worked out of a phone booth in a gym somewhere near the Cal-Mex border. His boxers always gave good value—they wouldn't go down easy, didn't quit, played their role.

The fighters stepped to the center of the ring for their instructions. Carr had three men standing with him, one to each side, the third gently kneading the muscles at the back of the middleweight's neck. Ortiz stood alone—the cornerman they supplied him with stayed outside the ring, bored.

Carr gave Ortiz a gunfighter's stare. Ortiz never met his eyes. That was for younger men—Ortiz was working. I could feel the pachuco cross tattoo under the glove on his right hand. . . . I knew it would be there.

The referee nodded to the fighters. Ortiz held out his gloves the way Frankie had, just doing as he was told. Carr slammed his right fist down against them. The crowd cheered, starting early.

The bell sounded. Carr snake-hipped out of his corner, firing a quick series of jackhammer jabs. Ortiz walked forward like a man in slow motion, catching the jabs on his gloves and forearms, pressing.

Carr danced out of his way, grinning. I dropped my eyes to the canvas, watching parallel as Carr's white leather boxing shoes ice-skated over the ring, purple tassels bouncing as Ortiz's black lace-ups plodded in pursuit.

Deep into the first round, Ortiz hadn't landed more than a half-dozen punches. He kept swarming forward, smothering Carr's crisp shots, his face a mask of patience. Suddenly, Carr stopped backpedaling, stepped to the side, hooked off his jab and followed with a smoking right cross, catching Ortiz on the lower jaw. Ortiz shook his head—then he stifled the crowd's cheers with a left hook to Carr's ribs.

The bell sounded. Carr raised his hands, took a quick lap around the ring, like he'd already won. Ortiz walked over and sat on his stool. His cornerman held out his hand to take the mouthpiece, splashed some water in the fighter's face, leaned close to say something. Ortiz didn't change expression, looking straight ahead—maybe the cornerman didn't speak Spanish.

Over in Carr's corner, all three of his people were talking at once. Carr was grinning.

The girl in the gold bikini wiggled around again, holding up the round-number card. The crowd applauded. She blew a kiss.

Carr was off his stool before the bell sounded, already gliding across the ring. Ortiz stepped toward Carr, as nervous as a gardener. Carr drove him against the ropes, firing with both hands, overdosing on the crowd's adrenaline. Ortiz unleashed the left hook to the body again. Carr stepped back, drew a breath, and came on again, working close. Ortiz launched a short uppercut. Carr's head snapped back. Ortiz bulled his way forward, throwing short, clubbing blows. Carr grabbed him, clutching the other fighter close, smothering the punches. The referee broke them.

Carr stepped away, flicking his jab, using his feet. The crowd applauded.

The ring girl put something extra into her wiggle between the rounds, probably figuring it was her last chance to strut her stuff.

Halfway through the next round, the crowd was getting impatient—they came to see Carr extend his KO record, not watch a mismatch crawling to a decision.

"Shoeshine, Cleo!" a caramel-colored woman in a big white hat screamed. As though tuned in to her voice, Carr cranked it up, unleashing a rapid-fire eight-punch combo. The crowd went wild. Carr stepped back to admire his handiwork. And Ortiz walked forward.

By the sixth round, Carr was a mile ahead. He would dance until Ortiz caught him, then use his superior hand speed to flash his way free, scoring all the while. When he went back to his corner at the bell, the crowd roared its displeasure—this wasn't what they had come to see.

A slashing right hand opened a cut over Ortiz's eye to start the next round. An accidental head-butt halfway through turned the cut into a river. The referee brought him over to the ring apron. The house doctor took a look, signaled he could go on. The crowd screamed, finally getting its money's worth.

Carr snapped at the cut like a terrier with a rat. Ortiz kept playing his role.

Between rounds, Carr's handlers yelled into both his ears, urging him to go and get it. Ortiz's cornerman sponged his cut, covered it with Vaseline.

The ring girl was really energized now, hips swinging harder than Carr was hitting.

Carr came out to finish it and drove Ortiz to the ropes, firing a quick burst of unanswered punches. Ortiz came back with his trademark left hook, but Carr was too wired to get off-tracked, smelling the end. A right hand landed flush on Ortiz's nose, a bubble burst of blood. Ortiz spit out his mouthpiece, hauled in a ragged breath and rallied with both hands. A quick look of surprise crossed Carr's face. He stepped back, measuring. Ortiz waved him in. Carr took the challenge, supercharged now, doubling up with each hand, piston-punching. Ortiz's face was all bone and blood.

The referee jumped in and stopped it, wrapping his arms around Ortiz.

Carr took a lap around the ring, waving to the crowd.

Ortiz walked over and sat on his stool.

The announcer grabbed the microphone. "Ladies and gentlemen! The referee has stopped this contest at two minutes and thirty-three seconds of the eighth round. The winner by TKO, and *still* undefeated . . . Cleophus . . . Cobra . . . *Caaaarrrr!*"

The crowd stood and applauded. Carr did a back flip in the center of the ring.

Ortiz's cornerman draped the white robe over the fighter's shoulders.

Ortiz walked back to the dressing room alone.

"That's a real warrior," Frankie said to me.

"Carr? He's nothing but a—"

"Not him," Frankie said. "The Spanish guy."

That's when I knew for sure that Frankie was a fighter.

We followed Clarence's green Rover sedan to the Bronx, where they'd drop Frankie off near Arthur Avenue. Through their back window I could see Clarence driving, Frankie in the passenger's bucket seat, the Prof's head between them, probably doing all the talking.

"Meet you at the gym, Slim," the Prof called out his window as the Rover pulled away.

The Prof had a key. Inside, the gym was deserted. Clarence

found the light switch. One wall was lined with gym mats. I leaned against one, offering the Prof a smoke before he could snatch one out of my hands.

"You remember that Belinda girl?" I asked him. "The one who Clarence made for a cop in Central Park?"

"Yeah, his pick was slick—and he got there quick. Pulled your coat in time, too. What now?"

"She's been calling. For a long time now."

"So?"

"So she calls Mama's direct, not to the bounce number. Letting me know she knows where to find me."

"What's she want?"

"I don't know. But whatever it is, she's been after it for a while. Anyway, Mojo Mary gave me the word—some street stroller had a job for me. I go to meet her. What she wants me to do is drop her pimp."

"Total him?"

"Oh yeah."

"Damn, man. That old rep died a natural death. Long time ago. Even the players don't be saying it. The street's got its own wire. . . . Some little girl might knock on the wrong door, hear some bullshit rumor, but Mojo Mary . . . fuck! The ho' is a pro, she knows you don't do contracts."

"Yeah. Anyway, I meet this girl. And she makes her pitch. I blow her off—tell her I don't do work on people. So she throws in some tripe about how her man is doing some kids."

"She read the book, knows the hook. They can call, but you won't fall. What's so strange?"

"Couple of things, Prof. When I go to drop her off, I see another hooker close by. Chunky girl, blonde. I figure, maybe the two are hooked up. You know pimps—that girl-girl stuff really spooks them. Maybe the guy they wanted me to do is really macking them both. Anyway, next, I brace Mojo Mary. She comes across like Little Miss Innocence—she's just trying to toss a job my way, looking out for the commission, okay? Tells me this little girl makes a date, meets her in Logan's. And the blonde hooker is with her. They don't say Word One about me icing her man, just want Mary to pass the message."

"It don't take no rocket scientist to be a ho', bro—all you need is the lips and the hips. Her story's weak, but it don't sound freak."

"How about this? I pay Mary for her time, right? Toss another yard at her for a tip before she even opens her mouth, okay? Then, *after* she gives up the information, she offers me a free ride. And when I talk to Mama about Belinda, turns out she was there. In the restaurant. In person. And she's wearing a blond wig."

"Bitch wanted you on tape," the Prof said quietly.

"Sure. She has a tape like that, I have to dance to her tune. Especially because that fucking Morales, he's still on my case."

"That last clue is true, brother. Morales, he's got a memory like a damn *herd* of elephants. Bad business, you get on the bad side of that roller. And he ain't got no good side."

"How does it scan to you?"

"Got to be this, schoolboy: this Belinda bitch, she's working with Morales, setting you up on a conspiracy rap, leverage you into dime-ing everybody on that old stuff. You go back a long way with that blue coat. . . . Hard to see him working with a woman, though. He's an old East Harlem head-breaker, that's more his style."

"His partner's gone now. So maybe he's—"

"No way to tell," the Prof mused. "Hell, maybe it's just the broad. Maybe she's got something she wants you to do. Something off the books."

"I'm gonna meet her," I said.

The Prof just nodded, covering it all.

It was 5:05 a.m. when I punched Belinda's number into a pay phone on Canal Street. She answered on the third ring.

"Hello?"

"You wanted to talk to me?" I said, gentle-voiced.

"I sure do," she said, recognizing my voice too quickly for someone who hadn't heard it in years . . . and never over the phone. "I've been trying for—"

"Tomorrow night okay with you?"

"I don't get off work until after two in the morning."

"How about if I pick you up there?" I asked, like I didn't know what she did for a living.

"Uh . . . no, that wouldn't work. I need to take a shower, change my clothes, put on some perfume. . . ."

Or a body mike, I thought. But I told her, "Whatever you say. How about five in the morning, that suit you?"

"That would be great. I'll meet you at—"

"I can come to your place," I said innocently.

"No, that's okay. I could meet you at the restaurant. You know, the one where I—"

"It's closed by then," I lied smoothly. "How about the corner of Canal and Mulberry?"

"It's a date," she replied.

I hung up the phone, putting the lies on Pause until we could do it again in person.

I had almost twenty-four hours to set things up—I wouldn't need them all. I stopped in an all-night deli on Broadway and cruised the aisles like a lunatic in a gun shop, looking for something to catch my eye and speak to me.

A slightly built kid with an olive complexion and a long ponytail was restocking shelves—he was already on the last aisle. The kid's ears were covered with stereo headphones plugged into a tape recorder hooked onto his belt, his lips moving in silent-sync to the lyrics pumping through his head. On a low deep shelf I spotted a flat tray of dark-chocolate-covered coconut bars. I reached in and took three of them from the front. A young woman dressed in head-to-toe *I'm Serious* black gave me a pitying look before she reached all the way to the back of the shelf to take some for herself. Her glance said it all—any idiot knows they stock the shelves with the freshest goods at the back so they can move the stale stuff first.

Maybe in Iowa. In this city, the hipper you think you are, the easier you are.

I picked out an assortment of cold cuts, a loaf of rye bread, and a half-dozen bottles of Ginseng-Up, then walked it all over to the register. Behind the counter was a whole wall of glass, designed to display the refrigerated collection of .40-caliber malt liquors. The oversized bottles are best-sellers. The kids take one of the baby cigars—Philly Blunts are the favorite—razor it open, load it with marijuana, and mix tokes with sips. The big booze brand is called Crazy Horse. Real classy, like naming a vodka after Chernobyl.

When I got back to my office, I shared the food with Pansy. All except the soda—she hates the bubbles.

For dessert, I cracked one of the coconut bars—it was as fresh as a just-burst rosebud. I hoped the hipster chick didn't crack one of her expensive caps on the ones she bought.

After supper, me and Pansy each got a handful of Dismutase tablets. One tab's the equivalent of about a quart of wheat sprouts. Vets give them to dogs who've had broken bones—they say it's the best thing for arthritis. Pansy's a long way from being a pup—sometimes her bones give her trouble, especially in the winter. I tried some on her—in a few weeks, she was moving a lot easier. No way a dog reacts to a placebo, so I figured the stuff had to be doing the job. I have trouble with my hands—the right one's been broken too many times and I can feel cold weather right through it. Since I've been taking the Dismutase along with Pansy, they don't hurt as bad.

I measured out the dose. You start with one tab per twenty pounds of dog, then switch to one tab per forty pounds as maintenance. We're both on maintenance now. We weigh about the goddamned same, too—she's really packed on the poundage the last couple of years.

While she was up on her roof, I fiddled with the TV set. Once I got a channel to come in, I kicked back on the couch, eyes closed. Pansy came back downstairs, walked over and put her massive head on my chest. She does that sometimes. I got her when she was a tiny puppy, not even weaned. I had to let her nurse from a baby bottle. When you first pull a pup from the litter, it's a good idea to wrap a towel around a wind-up clock and put it next to them—the ticking makes them think of their mother's heartbeat and they sleep better, safer in their minds. I didn't have one of those clocks, so I slept on my back with Pansy on my chest. Seemed to work pretty good. Every once in a while, I don't know why, she wants to hear my heartbeat again. I scratched behind her ears until she settled down. She took her head away, curled up on the floor to watch TV with me, making that noise that sounds like a downshifting diesel truck to show she was about to relax.

After a few minutes of product-pushing perjurers, I got lucky—an old episode of the Andy Griffith show—one I hadn't seen before. There was this guy, came to Mayberry from some other place. And the townspeople, they really treated him like shit, like he was a foreign spy or something. Finally, Sheriff Andy read them all the riot act . . . about how they should be flattered that this guy *picked* Mayberry to be his home town . . . how most folks don't have a choice. Kind of like the difference between adoption and birth.

I don't have a home town. New York isn't anybody's home town. It's different in other places. If you're a Chicago boy or a Detroit girl, the local papers treat you special. You're home-grown, and that counts for something.

Not here. In this city, PTA groups are more worried about the metal detectors' working than whether their kids are learning to read. Confidence is crumbling faster than the infrastructure. People with options flee this city—then they sit around in the suburbs whining about how much they miss the "energy."

When I got out of prison one time, I went over to Two Dollar Dominick's to get a haircut. I don't why they called it that—there never was a guy named Dominick there. It was a little two-chair shop. Full service, though—you could get a manicure, your shoes shined, bet on a horse, borrow some cash . . . the works. Anyway, a haircut always used to be two bucks, but I'd been away a long time. When Angelo was finished cutting my hair, I asked him, "How much does a haircut go for now?"

The old man hadn't seen me for five years or so. He just looked me in the eye, said, "For you, it's still two bucks."

That was the closest I ever felt to having a home town.

Angelo, he's gone now. To the one retirement community where everybody gets the same pension.

I slept in late the next morning—I knew I'd be up a long time once it got dark. I had breakfast with Pansy, then I went over to the restaurant to find Mama debriefing Max about last night's fight. The Mongolian was showing her each and every move, acting it all out. Mama's eyes had that glazed-over look people get when they're stoned on boredom, but Max was relentless. I never saw Mama so glad to see me.

"Burke! Our boxer won, yes?"

"Did it easy," I told her.

"How much money we make?"

"Mama, we didn't make *any* money. The whole purse was only a thousand dollars and—"

"So! A thousand dollars. How many investors?"

"No, Mama, that's not the way it works, okay? We have to pay the training expenses . . . like for the use of the gym and all. And we have to keep getting Frankie money so he can pay his rent and eat and all. This isn't any part-time gig with him—he has to be in training all the time. He's gotta go a long way before we can start taking money out."

"But what if he wins championship? That is worth millions, yes?"

"Sure. But that's a long dark road to walk. And it's booby-trapped too—if he keeps winning, the other guys won't want to fight him. You need connections to move up in that business."

"Boxing is crooked?" Mama asked, as though shocked by the very possibility.

"Sure. The big thing is, you gotta know people, understand?"

"Oh yes, understand. I know people too." She smiled.

I shook my head sadly. Mama knew money was the grease that lubed the gears of government, but she was used to Hong Kong style, where a bought politician *stayed* bought—that kind of honorable corruption doesn't play down here. "It's pretty tricky, Mama," I told her.

"Oh, okay," she said happily. "You fix it, yes?"

"I'll do my best," I promised.

I explained what I needed from Max, but he acted like I wasn't coming through clearly. I tried to change channels on him—he wasn't going for it. He kept it up until I signed we could go up to the gym. . . . All of a sudden, he was reading me perfect.

I wasn't sure Frankie would be back to work so soon after last night's fight, but as soon as I spotted Clarence at the door, I knew he was.

"We got another bout. Two weeks," the Prof said, watching Frankie spar against a big, flabby Latin guy. The gym was quieter than usual, most of the fighters watching the action in the ring. Frankie wasn't as quick as you'd think for his size. He was only a few pounds over the cruiserweight limit, but he slogged along like an out-of-shape heavy. The Latin guy was leaning all over Frankie, smothering him with his bulk, crowding away Frankie's punching power.

"Give him angles!" the Prof screamed. Frankie stepped to his left, dropped his left shoulder, but instead of the left hook the Latin guy figured was coming, Frankie looped his right hand over the top, catching the Latin flush on the chin. The Latin guy grinned to show he wasn't hurt, opening his hands wide to invite Frankie in. Frankie accepted the invitation . . . and stopped in his tracks when the Latin flashed a quick left to the heart. Frankie's knees trembled, but his body kept moving forward. Both fighters were still punching when someone rang the bell.

The Prof stepped to one side of Frankie, me to the other. "That's enough rounds for one day," the Prof said to the kid. "Three is the key."

"One more round, *blanquito*?" the Latin yelled across the ring.

"What's that mean?" Frankie asked.

"Means 'pussy,' " the Prof said before I could tell the kid the truth.

Frankie came off his stool, gloved hands fumbling with the chin strap to his protective headgear, pulling it off his head. He spit out the mouthpiece halfway across the ring. "Come on, bitch!" Frankie shouted.

The Latin launched off his stool, spit his own mouthpiece to the floor as the crowd started cheering. He was probably forty pounds heavier than Frankie but his hands were faster. He caught Frankie two quick ones to the face—blood blossomed around Frankie's mouth, his teeth flashing white underneath. Frankie drove the bigger man backward with a relentless barrage of punches, finishing with a vicious shot just below the belt. The Latin went down cupping his groin. Frankie loomed over him, right hand cocked, not retreating to a neutral corner. Half a dozen people jumped into the ring, but Max was first, throwing his body between Frankie and a pair of Latins who wanted to pick up where their pal had left off. Max wrestled Frankie back to his corner, and then out of the ring entirely. The warrior kept his grip on the kid, walking him over to a bench against the far wall.

Clarence dabbed at Frankie's face with a rag that smelled of peroxide.

The kid was breathing easily, but his eyes were still wild. "Nobody calls me a—"

"He didn't," I interrupted. "*Blanquito* just means 'whiteboy.' It ain't no gesture of respect, true enough, but it's a long way from 'pussy.' "

"So why'd the Prof—?"

"To see if you went lame when they called your name, fool," the Prof said over my shoulder—I hadn't seen him come back.

"You got to—" the Prof started, then stopped when he felt Max's paw on his shoulder. The warrior stood in front of Frankie, making sure he had the fighter's attention. Then he pointed at me, flattening one hand so he could sign without the kid seeing what he was doing. Max made one of the few universal gestures, the kind that you don't need either sign language or speech to understand—he gave me the finger, hidden behind his other hand. Then he nodded rapidly and stood back. Max and I were facing each other so Frankie was looking right between us.

Max held up his index finger. One. Then he nodded at me again. I shot Max the finger—he responded by cowering, covering his face as if in terror. After a few seconds, he shook his head from side to side. NO.

Max held up two fingers. Two. He nodded at me. I repeated the finger gesture—Max leaped forward, snarling, perfectly miming a man out of control. Then he shook his head again. NO.

Then Max held up three fingers, but this time the warrior turned to face Frankie flush, extending his right arm as far forward as it would go, one finger pointing out from his closed fist. Then he did the same with his left arm, two fingers pointing out in that direction.

Max took a small step backward, bringing his two hands together in a flowing gesture of harmony. When his hands were precisely in the middle of his body, he crossed his wrists, holding three fingers out from each hand.

"You get it?" I asked Frankie.

"I . . . think so. He's saying it's no good to be afraid when you fight. And no good losing your fucking temper either."

"Right. Max is telling you about being centered. It's somewhere between the two. A peaceful place. You *use* the adrenaline, see? But your mind is calm . . . like the eye of a hurricane. You can't get mad in a fight—it knots your muscles, slows you down, stops you from thinking."

"You know how to do that?" the kid asked. "What with him teaching you and all?"

"He only *told* me, Frankie," I said. "He didn't *teach* me. The best teacher in the world can't help you if you're not ready to learn."

"You was a fighter?" he asked.

"Schoolboy could hit a little bit, back when we was inside," the Prof conceded reluctantly. "But he just put up a show—he wasn't no pro."

Max thrust his way forward, searching Frankie's face. The kid returned his gaze, calm, not aggressive. Max smiled. Bowed.

The kid bowed back.

I sat next to Frankie, asked: "Last night, just before you touched gloves, what'd the other guy say to you?"

"Said he was gonna fuck me *up*." Frankie grinned.

"What'd you tell him?"

"Told him he was too late."

I watched the fighter's face. Caught the fineness of his bone structure, the slightly off-center Roman nose, the blue eyes with their little deep dots of banked fire.

Fuck, I thought to myself, maybe the kid *could* make it happen.

I was at the corner of Canal and Mulberry by four-fifteen in the morning, the Plymouth safely docked, me alone in the front seat, a cellular phone at my side. I always hated the damn things—they work off radio waves and too many geeks stay up nights in their rooms, monitoring the phone traffic the way they used to eavesdrop on CB radios. But the Mole told me he had the whole thing wired so they all worked off the same encryption device. If your unit wasn't keyed to the encoding, all you got was static when you tried to listen in. We had four of the phones, passed them around on an as-needed basis. We didn't worry about the billing either. All you need is the serial number of a legit phone—any phone, it doesn't matter. Then you can reprogram the chip in your own phone to match that serial number . . . and some chump gets a bill he can't *begin* to explain. The Mole does it all the time, switching them every few weeks. There's a guy who works in an electronics store in Times Square. What he does, he checks the numbers on the new phones, before they're even sold. Takes him a few minutes, and he gets fifty bucks for each one. Pretty stupid to be an armed robber these days—there's so many easier ways to steal.

Canal and Mulberry is a border crossing—Chinatown to one side, Little Italy to the other. The border is constantly shifting, with the Orientals taking more and more territory every year. It was still a bit early for the Chinatown merchants to open up, but I knew they were busy behind the closed doors.

Time and people passed, at about the same speed. I know about that—in my life, I've killed some of both. I learned something too—killing time is harder.

The cellular phone purred. I picked it up, said "What?" in a neutral voice.

"Here she comes," the Prof said. "Walkin', not talkin'."

The Prof was stationed on the northeast corner of Broadway and

Canal. If you looked close, all you'd see would be another soldier in the homeless horde of discharged mental patients that blanket the street in the early-morning hours, grabbing those last few minutes of peace before they had to go to work. Some of them vacuum garbage, looking for return-deposit bottles. Some beg for money. Some threaten for it. There's still guys who try and clean your windshield with dirty rags. And there's those who don't know where they are. Or why.

Belinda was a few blocks away. On foot. And alone, far as the Prof could tell. Okay.

I spotted her before she saw me. A medium-sized woman who looked shorter than she was because of her chunky build. Wearing a baggy pink sweatshirt over a pair of dark jeans, white running shoes on her feet, a white canvas purse on a sling over one shoulder. She walked with a beat cop's "I can handle it" strut, hands swinging loose and free at her sides, chestnut hair tied behind her with a white ribbon.

I slipped out of the Plymouth, closed the door quietly, the cellular phone in my jacket pocket. Then I crossed the street to intersect her path. She saw me coming, waved a hand in greeting.

I closed the gap between us, eyes only on Belinda, as if I didn't even consider the possibility she wouldn't be alone.

"Hello, stranger," she said, flashing a smile.

"We can walk it from here," I replied.

A puzzled expression flitted over her face. Then she shrugged, holding out one hand. I took it—a soft, chubby hand, the pad of her palm a deep, meaty slab.

We walked along in silence for a minute, not in a hurry. Couple of lovers coming home after a late-night downtown party, it might look like.

The question was: who was looking? If the cellular phone in my pocket rang, I'd know we had company—maybe Max can't talk, but he can punch numbers on a keypad. And in this part of town, he was even more invisible than the Prof.

"I tried—" she said.

"Later," I told her, tugging just a slight bit on her hand. She came along, not resisting.

The loft was on the third story of the building on Mott Street. I know Mama owned the whole building—that story about renting it as a crash pad for visitors was just her way of maintaining the façade. You ask Mama, she'd tell you she was poor, didn't know *what* the hell she was going to do in her old age. I used the key she lent me to open the downstairs door, made a sweeping gesture with my left hand to show Belinda she should go up the stairs ahead of me. She put a lot into the effort—hard not to admire those fine flesh-gears meshing. A woman who can't look good climbing a flight of stairs doesn't have a chance on level ground.

At the second-floor landing, I made the same gesture . . . and watched the same way. The stairwells were lit with low-wattage bulbs in little wire cages—just enough to see by.

On the third floor, we came to an orange steel door with some Chinese characters painted in black in a narrow band down the left side. I used the downstairs key to open the door, ushered her inside.

"Good morning," a lyrical voice greeted us. Oriental, with a faint trace of a French accent. Immaculata was calmly seated in a straight chair of black lacquered wood standing between a matched set of end tables of the same material. She was dressed in her Suzie Wong outfit: red silk sheath with a Mandarin collar, slit all the way up to mid-thigh, dragon-claw fake fingernails in a matching shade, heavy stage makeup. If Belinda was like most Europeans, she'd never recognize Mac's face if she ever saw it again.

"Good morning," I greeted her, bowing slightly.

If Belinda was taken aback, she gave no sign, standing silently to one side.

"Come with me," I told the lady cop, walking across the gleaming hardwood floor to a closed door. I opened that door, and Belinda followed me inside.

"Have a seat," I told her, gesturing toward a black leather easy chair. She sat down. So did I, in a matching chair a few feet away. Nobody ever really slept here. Mama had designed the negotiation suite herself—no one could gain status by claiming a certain piece of furniture—every piece had its twin.

"The reason I—" she began.

"Don't say anything yet," I stopped her. "Just listen, okay? Don't waste my time. This isn't about a date. I may not know who you are, but I know what you do. For a living, I mean. And I know this much too: you're a woman. A prideful woman. This was about a date, you would have stopped calling a long time ago."

"It was, at first. Then I—"

"Let me finish, tell you what the rules are down here. I don't do auditions for the police, understand? You want to talk, I got to know you're the only one I'm talking to."

She made a face, tossed her canvas purse over to me, and crossed her arms into a good imitation of a push-up bra. I stood up, walked over to a flat table in the corner. The table was covered with black felt. A telescoping wand held a white quartz bulb. Mama's guests used it to examine jewelry—it would work just as well for this.

I took a pair of thin white cotton gloves from a flat drawer inside the examining table and slipped them onto my hands. Then I emptied the purse onto the table and flicked on the observation lamp.

First, a chrome cylinder of lipstick—Rose Dawn, it said on the bottom. I uncapped it, cranked the soft pink tube all the way out, shook it to see if it rattled. No.

Next, a dark-brown leather folding wallet. Inside, an NYPD gold shield—a detective's badge. The photo ID confirmed it.

A ring of keys—looked like car, apartment, couple of others . . . storage locker maybe? safe-deposit box?

Some crumpled bills, less than a hundred total. Subway tokens. A pair of sparkling earrings for pierced ears—probably CZ—no way to tell without a jeweler's loupe.

An orange pencil-stick of eyeliner.

A blue steel .38. S&W four-incher. I popped the cylinder, turned it upside down to catch the cartridges as they spilled out, set them aside.

A cellophane packet of tissues, half-empty.

Three condoms in individual foil packs, lubricated.

A brown plastic vial with a child-proof top—no label. I tapped the contents into my palm. No mistaking the telltale green-and-white capsules even without the name and dosage on each one—Prozac.

"How many of these you take every day?" I asked her, holding up the vial so she could see what I was asking about.

"Two," she replied in a flat voice. "One when I get up, one around noon. Okay?"

I nodded. It was the right answer—a forty-milligram dose was the usual maintenance weight, and you shouldn't take that stuff before you go to sleep. Whatever was depressing her, she'd had it for a while. Had it deep.

A picture postcard showing a sandy beach, palm trees, a smiling golden-skinned little girl waving at the camera, naked from the waist up. On the back, in a childish scrawl: "You should have come with us!" Signed: "Love, Gaby. From Baby Beach, Pattaya."

A notebook with a white vinyl cover, complete with attached ballpoint pen. I leafed through it. Nothing but names and phone numbers—I didn't see mine. In the back of the notebook, a calendar. None of the dates were marked.

I put everything back, tossing it in the way I'd found it. "It looks okay to me," I told her. "But what we're gonna do, just to be safe, I'm gonna put this in a box. Outside the room. Come on, I'll show you."

She followed right behind as I went back into the main room, where Immaculata waited. The box is about the size of a thirty-gallon aquarium only it's made of steel. I opened the lid to show her that the walls were a couple of inches thick. The lid itself was padded too. I dropped her purse inside, closed the lid, and threw a toggle switch on the side of the box. A red LED glowed.

"What's that mean?" Belinda asked.

"It means that it's working. Even if you had a recorder inside the box, all it would pick up is interference noise, understand?"

"Yeah!" She grinned. "Pretty slick. You do this kind of thing a lot?"

"Enough," I told her. No point explaining why Mama had a use for such devices in her various businesses.

I walked back into the room I was using, closed the door behind her.

"Okay," I said. "That takes care of the purse. But there's one more thing. . . . That's why Rosita is out there."

"Rosita? The Chinese woman?"

"Her mother was from Brazil. Dad from Macao," I said, embroidering the lie to give it some texture.

"Oh. So what . . . ?"

"You go in the other room. With Rosita. And you take off your clothes. All of them. You leave the clothes there—she'll give you a robe to put on. Then, when you come back in here, I'll know you're the only person I'm talking to. See?"

Belinda stood up, started walking over to me, hauling the pink sweatshirt over her head in one motion. Underneath she had on one of those workout bras, black jersey with X-straps across her back. She unzipped the jeans, tugged them down over her hips. Then she bent forward from the waist, untied each sneaker, pulled them off, stepped out of the jeans. Her panties were the same black jersey material as the bra, only their waistband was white.

"This far enough?" she challenged.

"No," I told her. "You sure you don't want—?"

She lifted the bra past her breasts, pulled it over her head in one flowing motion, and dropped it on the floor. Then she hooked her thumbs in the waistband of the panties, pulled them all the way down. She stepped out of them with one foot, used the other to hold the puddle of black and flicked it away with a half-kicking motion. Her body was thick, muscular, breasts rounded but not meeting in the middle, stomach slightly washboarded. Her thighs looked as hard as marble. She stood without a trace of self-consciousness, eyes on mine.

"You want the socks too?" she asked, a sarcastic smile on her face.

"Yeah."

She stood easily on one foot, pulled off one white sock. Did the same with the other. Then she held her hands high over her head, turned slowly one full rotation. A port-wine stain showed on her right hip, a dark mole under her left shoulder blade. Her buttocks were wide and deep, with a sharply cut definition just where they met her upper thighs. It was the first thing Clarence had noticed about her . . . the last good thing.

"Seen enough?" she asked.

"It's not about seeing," I told her. I took the white cotton gloves off, put them aside. Then I sprinkled some baby powder over my right hand and pulled on a latex surgeon's glove. I slapped a tube of K-Y jelly on the tabletop, looked over at her, waiting. Bright circles of red broke out on her cheeks. "You—" she started to say.

"I'm not playing," I said quietly. "Someone's gonna check. You want me or you want Rosita?"

She spun on her heel and padded out of the room, slamming the door behind her.

I was halfway through my third cigarette when the door opened again. Belinda entered, wearing a jade silk kimono. Immaculata was right behind her, nodding to me that it was all clear.

"Sorry about that," I said to Belinda as she sat down, pulling the kimono closed around her breasts with one hand. "I had to be sure."

"You're a very cautious man, Mr. Burke," she said, tossing her head to throw some of her chestnut hair out of her eyes.

"But not a disrespectful one," I replied, warning her. "Now, tell me what you want."

"Could I have one of your cigarettes first?"

I stepped over to where she was seated, handed her the pack. She shook one loose, put it in her mouth. I snapped a wooden match alive, held it down to her. She dragged deeply, holding the kimono closed tightly in front of her. I could feel her eyes, checking where I was looking—not where she'd guessed. Didn't know if she'd recognize where I *was* looking—if you haven't looked there yourself, you wouldn't recognize it—the middle distance.

I put a small milk-glass ashtray on the arm of her chair, went back to where I'd been sitting.

She puffed on the cigarette like she expected more out of it than she was getting, eyes slitting slightly from the smoke. I watched those eyes—watched for that nobody's-home flatness. I didn't see it.

"There's a man," she said slowly. "An innocent man. He's in prison—for a crime he didn't commit. I want to get him out. I want to set him free."

"Hire a lawyer," I told her, uninterested.

"He *has* a lawyer. A good one. Raymond Fortunato. Maybe you know him . . . ?"

"I've heard of him," I said, not giving anything away. Fortunato was a mob lawyer, specializing in disappearing witnesses and juiced juries . . . not the guy you'd want if you needed a strong appellate brief. He cost too. Cost big.

"It was a one-witness ID. Not the victim . . . a woman who lived in the same building. She said she saw him going out of the apartment."

"After he did what?"

"He didn't *do* anything. That's what I'm trying to tell you."

"Spare me the violins, all right? You want to play it cute, that's okay. But tell me what happened to the victim."

"She was murdered."

"Ah."

"Not just murdered," Belinda said, leaning forward, forgetting about keeping the kimono closed. Or maybe not. "She was splattered. All over the walls."

"Shotgunned?"

"A razor. A straight razor."

"The woman on University Place. About a year and a half, two years ago?"

"Yes. You read about it in the papers?"

"Sure," I replied—it was close enough to the truth.

"She'd been raped. First. Then the killer . . . cut her up."

"And they made a homicide against this guy with nothing more than somebody seeing him coming out of her apartment?" I asked, letting an organ stop of sarcastic disbelief creep into my voice.

"There was more . . . I guess. His . . . fingerprints. But he said he knew the woman—he'd been inside the place before. A few weeks before. When he picked her up. In a bar. Right around the corner."

"And . . . ?"

"And there was a . . . 'signature.' At least that's what they called it."

"If they were talking signature, there had to be more than one."

"That's just it! They didn't have more than one. Just that woman. They didn't have any more until . . ."

"What was the signature?" I interrupted, trying to get her focused.

"A piece of ribbon," she said. "Red ribbon. Nothing special. The kind you could buy in any dime store."

"And the killer left this with the woman? On her body? What?"

"He left it . . . inside of her."

"And they found some of this ribbon when they tossed this guy's place?"

"Yes! But it's a common type—you can get it anywhere. It doesn't mean anything by itself."

"Sounds shaky to me. What happened, the jury didn't buy his story?"

"He didn't get to *tell* his story. He didn't have Fortunato then, he had a Legal Aid. He had priors."

"But not for sex cases?" I asked her.

"No."

"What then?"

"Assaults, like. He was . . . crazy, once. He was 730'ed out years ago. They said he tried to push a woman onto the subway tracks."

Every working cop knows about 730 exams. The court can force any defendant into a psych evaluation, not to see if he's crazy—that wouldn't be any big deal—but to see if he's competent to stand trial. "If he was found unfit, they couldn't use that later," I said.

"I know," she answered. "That was only that one time. But there were a couple of other times too. And then he *was* found guilty. On other things. Before he went into the hospital. But he's been okay for years. *Years!* There was a perjury rap too . . . something about a corporation he was in charge of. . . . I don't know too much about it."

"So what makes you so sure he was bum-beefed on the homicide? He don't sound like any prize package to me."

"Since he's been away . . . there's been other murders . . . two others. But he was never charged with them . . . how *could* he be?"

"Two more murders?"

"Two more murders. Two women. Both raped. And, listen, both with the *same* signature. So how could—?"

"Copycat crimes," I interrupted.

"Burke, the signature, it never made the papers."

"A red ribbon . . ."

"*Inside* them," she said, watching me steadily, hands on her knees.

"So why don't you . . . ?"

"I can't," she said flatly. "I can't do anything. The other murders, they're in an open file. You ask the detectives who caught it, they'll tell you it's still working. They've got two homicides. Linked, you understand? You know the way the Department does it—three all-the-same crimes, it's a Pattern Case. Three *big* crimes, then the papers give the guy a name . . . like the Silver Gun Rapist or the Subway Stalker or some other bullshit thing. And then the fucking brass calls a press conference and appoints a task force, just so the public thinks we're *serious* all of a sudden."

She was good at it, mixing truth in with the lies, making you swallow the whole pie if you wanted a taste. "When did these others happen?" I asked.

"Why?"

"Just tell me."

"The first one was right after he was arrested. Maybe two, three weeks later. The next one was a few months later. Before he came to trial."

"So why didn't the Legal Aid—"

"They didn't *know,* I'm telling you! By the time I found this out, he was already sentenced."

"So tell Fortunato. He can subpoena—"

"Burke, I did. I did that. And you know what he found when he looked in the file? *Nothing!* Not a thing. The whole business? About the red ribbons? It was gone. Wiped out. Far as NYPD's concerned, it was different guys, understand?"

"No. I *don't* fucking understand. Why go to all this? I know how the Man works. . . . They pop some chump for one burglary, they throw every damn Unsolved they got on the books at him, right? He pleads to the whole mess, they go light on the sentence, everybody's happy. But they can't do that here—the crimes happened *after* he was inside, right? No way he got bail on a rape-murder."

"That's right. He didn't make bail. And I don't know *why* they're doing it—I just know that they are. And I know George didn't do it."

"George?"

"George Piersall. That's his name. I know . . . a lot about him now."

"Because . . . ?"

"Because I've been visiting him," she said, tilting her chin up defiantly. "At the prison. In New Jersey. I told him—"

"Hold up a minute. If the crime took place here, how come he's locked down in Jersey?"

"For assault," she said, her head cocked, listening to my breathing, checking if it changed. "*Sex* assault, all right? It was across the river, just the other side of the Tunnel. At a truck stop. The . . . victim was a hooker. She said George took her to a motel. That's where it . . . happened."

"So she *saw* him, right?"

"No. I mean, she couldn't make a positive ID. It was a shaky case. The woman was buzzed at the time, on downers, before it . . . happened. And she had a long sheet herself. Extortion, badger game, you know?"

"Yeah, but how—?"

"He pleaded guilty, all right?" she said, her tone somewhere between hostile and defensive. "He had a lousy lawyer. And they offered him a plea bargain. He only got three years. The lawyer told him he shouldn't gamble on the trial. He'd be out real soon that way—it wasn't worth the risk."

"So . . . ?"

"*So* . . . no murder, no red ribbon. But after Jersey nailed him, *then* New York got brave and charged him with the murder on University Place. He waived extradition. I mean, he knew he didn't do it, so . . ."

"But he was—"

"Yes. Convicted, like I told you."

"What'd he get?"

"He got it all," she said, chin tilted up again, this time like she was ready for a fight. "The Book. Twenty-five to Life."

"So when he's done in Jersey . . . ?"

"That's right. They slapped a detainer on him. When he wraps up in New Jersey, they're going to bring him over here. Forever."

"So you go over there to visit him? What'd you tell him?"

"I told him the truth—that I was investigating the cases. He was glad to see me. He'd be glad to see *anybody* now."

"He knows you're a cop, right? Didn't he think you were working him for more evidence?"

"We got that straight in front. I told him, if he wanted me to really look into it, he'd have to do something for me first—take a lie-detector test."

"You got that done? Inside?"

"Sure. His lawyer got a court order. And you know what? He *passed*. With flying colors, the examiner said. He's the wrong man. And the *right* man, he's still out there."

"Go to the papers," I suggested. "Hell, go to one of those trash-TV shows. They'd be glad to jump on it. Nothing they like better than a man falsely accused of rape . . . unless it's an innocent child-molester."

"I tried. They don't care. . . . One of them told me psychopaths pass polygraphs all the time. Without the red-ribbon evidence, it's nothing."

"Look, I . . ."

"I want *you* to do it," she said, her eyes aiming somewhere above mine, stitching a line of rivets across my forehead. "Find the killer. That's the only way George's going to get out. I talked to a couple of private eyes. They both said they weren't going to take on NYPD—they were on the job once themselves. And they know what would happen. Those guys live on leaks—they go ahead on something like this, the faucets all get turned off, you understand? You know how hard it is to work without a friend on the force? You need somebody to run a plate for you, check a file, all that stuff. You work PI too, right? Off the books, I know. No license, all that. But I can fix it. Fortunato says anyone can work as a PI if they're working for a lawyer. He says it would be okay for you to be working for him. He'd cover for you and everything."

"It's not my kind of thing," I told her.

"There's money. Real money. George has a trust fund. He's got nothing to spend it on now."

"I'm not interested," I told her in a door-closing voice.

She sat back in her chair. Straightened her spine, took a breath. "Are you interested in what Morales is trying to set you up for?" she asked.

"I don't know any Morales," I shot back, lying with the natural smoothness of a man who learned it—*had* to learn it—when I was just a little kid.

"Yes you do," she said. "I know you do—and I know he's got plans . . . plans for you."

"Still doesn't ring a bell," I told her. "And what's in it for you, anyway?"

"An innocent man—"

"I look that pure fucking stupid to you?" I interrupted. "You want me to buy this 'justice' bullshit, you can tell your story walking."

She took a deep breath. My eyes never left her face. "It's . . . personal, okay?"

"I don't give discounts for *personal*," I told her. "You don't want to tell me the truth, you take the risk, understand?"

"Just take a look," she said, leaning forward. "One look, okay? Let me show you what I've got. You'll get paid. Just for that, you'll get paid. And if you do it, win or lose, you'll have a friend on the force, how's that?"

A friend on the force—where had I heard that before?

"I'll ask around," I told her. "No promises. One week. A whole week. And I don't leave the city, understand? Just cover the old tracks down here. Costs you five grand. Say Yes or say No."

"Yes!" she breathed at me, so happy she almost popped right out of the kimono.

After Belinda left, I sat and smoked a sociable cigarette with Immaculata, waiting to hear where the lady cop went once she left the building. I wasn't worried about her marking the loft—I'd never be there again in life.

"What did you make of her?" I asked Mac. It wasn't a pass-the-time question—Immaculata had been a superb therapist for years . . . and a survival expert since the day she was born.

"There's something . . . *coarse* about her," Mac said. "I can't put my finger on it. Not yet, anyway—I'd have to see her a few more times."

"Coarse . . . ?"

"Yes. That's the only word I can think of. When I . . . examined her, she acted . . . I don't know . . . flirtatious? When my finger was inside her, she . . . responded in some way."

"Maybe she's gay?"

"I don't think so. Even if she was, the circumstances were so clinical, you wouldn't think . . . It was more as though she was trying to test me in some way."

"She's a cop. You know how they always look for a weak spot—it's their nature."

"That wasn't it. I can't tell you more than what I said. It's too . . . muddled. But she has that one-note-off thing—you know what I mean?"

"Yeah."

"Something else. It may mean nothing, but . . ."

"What?"

"In the pocket of her jeans, she had a little flat metal box. Like aspirin used to come in, remember?"

"Sure. And . . . ?"

"And inside the box, there was maybe three inches of clear Scotch tape. With a paper tab on the end. You know what that could be?"

"A fingerprint kit," I told Mac. "You never took the gloves off around her?"

"Never. And I never took my eyes off her either."

"Good."

"Are you going to—?"

"I don't know yet," I lied, segueing into "How's Flower?" to get her off the subject.

"She is quite wonderful," Mac said formally. "She loves school, especially art—she draws all the time. She can imitate Max's chop perfectly."

"I know. I saw her do it once, when Max brought her over to the restaurant."

"Yes. Mama is already concerned about a proper match for her when she is old enough."

"That's jumping the gun a bit, isn't it?"

"Oh yes." She smiled. "But you know how Mama is—she thinks Flower will need a *dowry*, can you imagine?"

"Sure. Mama thinks you can't get anywhere unless you pay your way. I guess she's not so wrong, when you think about it."

The phone in my pocket buzzed. I pulled the flap open, said "Go."

"The cop didn't make no stops." The Prof's voice. Belinda had gone straight back to where she'd started from, alone.

"Can I drive you back over to your place?" I asked Mac.

"I'll stay awhile," she said. "There's another way out of here—through the basement. And I want to change first. If she has people around, they won't see anything."

"Thank you," I said, bowing slightly.

"You are my brother," she replied.

Halfway through talking to Belinda, I knew who I needed for this one. Morelli was off the set now. After years and years at ground zero, he'd finally hit it big. A hardcore reporter from the old school, his copy was always gold, and he's been covering the Mob for so long they probably ask *him* for advice. Anyway, he wrote a book and it caught fire. He's been on the Holy Coast for a while now, tending the harvest.

But a pro like Morelli doesn't move on until he's trained some new recruits. J. P. Hauser was his choice. I remember when Morelli first told me about him.

"I ask him, go over and see this guy, supposed to be an informant, staying in some rat-trap over in Times Square," Morelli told me. "This guy, his story is that he's got a bad ticker, so he wants to make his peace with God, give me all the inside dope on a muscle operation Giapietro's crew is running out at the airport. So I tell J.P., get me everything, all right?" Morelli smiled, taking a sip of his drink. Years ago, it used to be Cutty Sark and Lucky Strikes. Now it's red wine and he doesn't smoke at all. What the hell, at least he doesn't drink mineral water and pay his bills over a modem.

"Okay, so, a few hours later, I get this frantic call from the informant. He's screaming blue murder. Said J.P. goes up there, tosses the place worse than any parole officer ever did. J.P., he takes the serial number from this guy's clock radio, looks at the labels in his coat, checks his shoe size. Then he whips out one of those blood-pressure things . . . you know, the kind you slip over your finger? Wants to see if this guy's *really* got a bad heart, you ever hear anything like that? The kid doesn't just take notes, he's got a tape recorder. And *another* tape recorder in his pocket too, just in case. Makes the guy go over his story a dozen times, out of sequence, backwards, you know, the whole bit. The *federales* could take lessons from old J.P. I mean, the man takes it *all*. He's a fucking vacuum cleaner, you understand? He's gonna pull the dirt out until they pull his plug. I fucking *love* this kid."

I worked with Hauser myself a couple of times since Morelli split. Any twit with a street thesaurus and an active imagination can write a newspaper column—but Hauser, if he's got a God, it's The Facts. And I learned this much about him too: he's got a set on him so big that, if you added one more and painted them gold, you could hang them over a pawnshop.

Early on a Sunday morning, I figure Hauser's probably at home. He lives on Central Park West, somewhere in the Nineties. But he keeps a dump of an office in the garment district. Doesn't matter where he is—I know how his phone system works.

I drove up Eighth Avenue until I found a parking space a few blocks south of Port Authority. I slid in and punched the number into the cellular.

"You have reached the voice mail of J. P. Hauser," the tape said. "Leave a number and a time to call. I'll get back to you."

I waited for the beep, hit 333 on my phone, waited again. Another beep-tone. This time, I hit 49. Waited again while the phone rang.

"Burke?" Hauser's voice came through.

"I got something," I told him. "Meet you . . . where?"

"How about my office? Give me half an . . . no, make it forty-five minutes, okay?"

"You got it," I said, and cut the connection.

That's one of the beauties of cellular phones—you call from where you're supposed to meet someone, you're already there—no time for the other guy to set up a welcoming committee. Not that I distrusted Hauser, but if I let my old habits die hard, the same thing could happen to me.

I was at the curb when I spotted Hauser through the windshield. He's medium height, with reddish-brown hair and a trim beard to match, but it was his walk that drew my eyes. He was coming fast, like he always does. You stop to smell the roses in this neighborhood, you'll need a stomach pump.

I climbed out of the Plymouth, fell into step with Hauser. He used his own key to open the outside door—the security guard doesn't work weekends. Not a big loss either. One time I came to see Hauser during the week, signed the register "Deputy Dog." The guard never looked at it. Never looked at my face either.

We went up in the freight elevator, stopped at the fourth floor. Hauser unlocked his office and we both went inside. He walked around turning things on. As the screen on his computer was blinking into life, he pulled a couple of sheets of thermal paper out of his fax machine, glanced at them once, tossed them in a wire basket on his desk. He sat back in an old green leather swivel chair behind his desk, tipped his hat back on his head, said, "What's the story?"

To Hauser, that's the meaning of life.

I moved some files off the couch onto the floor and took a seat. Lit a smoke. Hauser didn't move, didn't reach for a notebook, didn't do anything. Okay, I called the meeting—it was my move.

"You know about a guy called George Piersall?" I asked.

"Sex killer," Hauser replied in his level newsman's voice. "He pleaded guilty to some kind of sex crime over in Jersey, then they charged him with a homicide in the Village. He came back to court here for that one. Rolled the dice, drew the max. So?"

"You follow the trial?"

"No. When it comes to rape, there's always the same three defenses: one, it never happened; two, she consented; three: SODDI. What's the big deal?"

SODDI. Some Other Dude Did It. That's a Legal Aid expression, but I figured Hauser could have pulled it from anywhere. It's Top of the Charts on Riker's Island—number one with a full clip of bullets.

"I'm not arguing about the Jersey one," I told him. "That's a closed coffin. But when it comes to the murder on University Place, I got someone who says Piersall's innocent."

Hauser raised an eyebrow, a classier version of a sneer, but I plunged ahead. "Not 'legally' innocent," I said, making little quote marks with my fingers, "innocent for real. This person says there was a signature to the murder . . . to *three* murders. A red ribbon."

"So there's a signature. . . . Why couldn't it be *Piersall's* signature?"

"For the one on University Place, I guess it could have been. But I said *three* murders, not one. And this person says the other two happened *since* Piersall's been locked down. Same MO. Same signature."

"What's the punch line?" Hauser asked, leaning forward.

"The punch line is a two-parter," I told him. "One, the cops never released that piece of info, so it can't be a copycat. Two, the cops working the open cases, they're not looking *backward*, see? If they drop someone for the new crimes, it isn't gonna do Piersall any good."

"This . . . 'person' of yours . . . how reliable are they?"

"I don't know. But I can tell you this much: the person is a cop. A detective, on the job right now."

"What's their interest in this?"

"Personal. At least I think so—I wouldn't swear to it."

"If *you* wouldn't swear to it, it has to be pretty shaky."

"Thanks for the vote of confidence," I said, giving him a half-smile to show I wasn't taking offense. "The question is . . . are you interested?"

"What's in it for me?" he asked. An honest man's question in our part of the world.

"The usual, I guess. Whatever you reporter guys usually want. Exclusive this, exclusive that . . . you know."

"Will this . . . 'person' talk to me? Even off the record?"

"Sure. I can make that a condition. Only I don't need to tell them what you do, okay? I can just say you're working with me."

"No," Hauser said. "It has to be straight up—the truth from the beginning. If they want to spring this Piersall, they have to know the media could be a help."

"Maybe. But they wouldn't just want a lot of noise made, you understand? It'd have to be the real thing."

"Meaning?"

"Meaning it was a stand-up conviction, far as I can tell. He's got a lawyer now. Raymond Fortunato."

"Oh," Hauser said, taking a breath. "It's like that, huh?"

"I don't know what it's like," I told him truthfully. "No way Fortunato's gonna do this without he gets paid. The person who came to me, they said Piersall has a trust fund. A nice-sized one."

"Well, I guess he can't spend it in prison, huh?"

I looked at Hauser for a minute, drifting back inside with my thoughts. Maybe he'd never really understand, but there's one thing about Hauser—he'd try like all hell. "There's plenty of uses for money behind the Walls," I told him. "There's a maximum amount you can have on the books—it's probably changed since I was inside, but it still won't be much. You can buy cigarettes with it. And you can trade a couple of crates of smokes for any work you want done, understand? You got money in there, you don't have to eat Mainline. If you're weak, or if you don't have a crew, you can buy protection. Enough cash, you can buy bodyguards. There's other things too: you can take care of the hacks—get them to look the other way when you have a visit. . . ."

"So stuff could get smuggled in?"

"That, sure. There's sex too."

"You mean . . . other prisoners?"

"Yeah, some of them go on the whore inside. But that's not what I meant—if you're connected right, you can get it on right there."

"In the Visiting Room? In front of everyone?"

"Handjobs, maybe . . . I was talking about the real thing. They use the bathrooms for that. You take your visitor in there, do what you want. Inside, everything runs on juice—you got it, you can use it. Next time you read about a stabbing on Riker's Island, look close—you'll see it was nothing personal. Just turf strutting—mostly on the pay phones. Everyone's supposed to form a line, wait their turn. When your time's up, you're supposed to move on. You got cash on the books, you can pay for more time. And if that don't fly, you can buy some muscle, get you the same result, understand?"

"Yeah," said Hauser. I watched his face as he made mental notes. Hauser was an insatiable info-maniac—if it was out there, he wanted it.

"When you hear about a gun turning up inside, you can bet it was the guards," I told him. "Same for drugs, for serious weight, anyway—there's only so much stuff a visitor can mouth-carry. It's a special economy in there—the prices are real, real high. The guards, they're just people. Some of them go for the gold."

"You think that's what this Piersall may be doing?"

"I don't know." I shrugged. "It's too late for jury-juice now—Fortunato took it on appeal."

Hauser took off his glasses, polished them on a piece of cloth he took out of the pocket of his blue work shirt. His wrists were much thicker than you'd think from looking at his build. I saw a quick flash of a heavy steel chronograph as he polished. Without the glasses, his eyes had a harsh, tight-focused glint as he looked over at me. "Meaning he needs something spectacular . . . 'newly discovered evidence,' like that, right?" Hauser said.

"Right," I agreed.

"So how come this 'signature' stuff wouldn't do the job for him?"

"According to this person, the one I spoke to, Fortunato subpoenaed the whole mess, files and everything. And there's no record of the red ribbons."

"The ribbons were tied around their necks?" Hauser asked. "You're saying some beat cop pulled them off?"

"No," I said, watching the reporter's eyes, now steady behind the glasses. "That couldn't be. See, the red ribbons, they were *inside* the bodies. Way inside. You wouldn't find them until you did the autopsy."

"Unh," Hauser grunted, half to himself. "So you're saying the ME's office is in on this?"

"*I'm* not saying anything," I reminded him. "It's this cop who's saying it."

"You know which of the MEs did the autopsies?"

"No. I don't have any of the paper. I guess I could get it. Or copies, anyway."

"You have a read on this? A personal one?"

"No. Me, I'm clueless. Somebody's playing, but I don't even know what the game is."

"Why me?"

"You're Morelli's legacy, right? I figure, you can check some places I can't go—I can go places you can't too. We put it all together, maybe I crack the case and you get a hot story," I told him, playing the PI role to the hilt.

"That's all?" Hauser asked, his face a study in skepticism.

"Everything," I promised him, back to lying.

"There's nobody you're protecting? Chips fall where they may?"

"You got it."

"And what we *know*, actually *know*, not *guess* . . . what we know is that this guy Piersall did something to some hooker in Jersey, pleaded guilty, and he's doing a short stretch for it, right?"

"Right."

"And he got tried for a sex murder here in the city, and he got convicted of that too?"

"Right."

"And there was a red ribbon inside the woman who got murdered . . . but not inside the woman who got beat up?"

"Yeah. Nothing inside the New Jersey woman, the only red ribbon inside the New York woman, the one who died."

"And you got a source *inside* NYPD that says there are two *more* sex murders . . . ?"

"Right."

"With red ribbons inside both of them . . . ?"

"Right."

"But that the ribbons don't show up on the autopsies?"

"That's it."

"So either the cop's lying, or someone removed the ribbons . . . ?"

I just shrugged, waiting.

Hauser pretended to be thinking it over, but I knew it was no contest—he was a bloodhound, and he had the scent. Finally, he looked over at me. "I'll take a look," he said. "No promises."

"It's a deal," I said.

The first step was to check my back-trail. Belinda hadn't been wired—I could tell that as much by the dialogue as the body search—you could replay our whole conversation for a grand jury and I'd still be as safe as a Kennedy in Massachusetts. But it didn't ring true, none of it. Mojo Mary offers me sex *after* she got paid. And Belinda doesn't even flash a smile when it might have cut her some slack. I never worry about what side I'm on. It's always the same one—mine. Sometimes that side's in the middle . . . and what I care about then is staying out of the crossfire.

The obvious answer was a crew of cops, working me for those mad-dog homicides in the Bronx a couple of years ago. But they didn't have a thing on me. And I haven't carried a gun since.

Don't misunderstand. I'm not crazy—I know the guns didn't do the killing—I know it was me. The guns just made it easy. So easy. Shooting, it's a different head than stabbing, especially with a high-tech piece like the Glock I used that time, so silky smooth it was like squirting death out of a hose. Close-up work, that takes a different mind. It's messier, more involved. Riskier too. The drive-by boys, it's like playing a video game to them. Not real. Electronic beeps sound in their sociopathic minds. The targets they shoot, they aren't human—they're little two-dimensional objects. You hit one just right, it falls down.

Technology changes things—the closer it gets to the street, the higher the body counts. Today, when one high-school kid bumps into another in the hall, one of them says, "I'll see you after school." But it's not a fistfight they're talking about. Not knives or bicycle chains either. Today, even the worst wimp can deliver a full-clip message. It's techno-magic—bang, the other guy's dead.

But why would Belinda warn me about Morales if she was working with him? Besides, I couldn't imagine Morales working with any partner but McGowan. Morales is a surly, hair-trigger straight arrow—not the kind of partner anyone in NYPD wants. A fucking thug for justice, that's Morales. I'd always figured he had everything a good manhunter needs except for one thing . . . patience. But maybe I'd underestimated him.

I couldn't do anything until tomorrow anyway. I stopped back by the office, grabbed Pansy and took off for the Bronx.

"You are surely one beautiful girl," Clarence said to Pansy, remembering her from a long-ago day in Central Park. Pansy doesn't understand words, but she reads tone of voice perfect—she rubbed her big head against Clarence's pants leg, purring deep. I left the two of them and went looking for the Prof.

"Sit *down* on those punches," the Prof was barking at Frankie. "This ain't no fencing match—*drive* those shots home. Come *on!*"

Frankie circled a thick-bodied black boxer in the sparring ring, stalking, not punching much. The other guy was so relaxed he looked almost sleepy, slipping Frankie's punches with practiced ease. Somebody rang the bell, and both fighters returned to their corners. The Prof was up on the ring apron in a flash, talking urgently to Frankie.

"You too light for the fight, boy? This ain't no aerobics class. *Box* the motherfucker, understand? Box him in. Punches in bunches, that's the ticket here. Now, go out there and *dump* that chump!"

Frankie nodded, never taking his eyes from the other guy, who was also seated, joking with his cornermen. When the bell rang, Frankie lumbered off his stool toward the center of the ring, holding out one gloved hand for the other fighter to touch. "This ain't the last round, stupid!" one of the black guy's cornermen yelled.

"It is for you, sucker!" the Prof shot back.

Frankie bulled his way forward. The black guy backpedaled to the ropes, leaned against them easily, his sleek upper body glistening with sweat as if to emphasize how slippery he was. Frankie fired a left hook, grunting with the effort, then doubled with the same hand. The black guy slid away, but Frankie's overhand right was already launched. The black guy turned his head and the punch caught him on the neck. He stumbled once, and Frankie was on him like spandex, legs spread, knees locked, pounding hard enough to drive railroad spikes. The black guy tried to clutch Frankie but he was too late—the uppercut lanced between their bodies—the black guy's eyes rolled up and he went down face-first. Frankie turned away and came toward his corner, exposing his wrists so the Prof could take off the gloves.

Nobody bothered to count.

Frankie was breathing hard on his stool, but I could see he wasn't exhausted, just pumped up. The Prof kept up a steady patter of reassuring nonsense—Frankie didn't seem as though he was listening. He hit the showers. The Prof came over to where I was standing.

"Boy hits like a jackhammer, don't he?"

"Sure does," I agreed. "It's like a switch goes off in his head."

"Yeah, that's the trick. That's what makes him tick. You trip that switch, he's one mean sonofabitch."

"You know where the button is?"

"No. Sure don't, son. I thought it was a race thing when we first got started. But when Frankie goes on full boil, I don't think he sees color at all."

"What, then?"

"I glommed his act, and that's a fact," the Prof said. "The kid would have been glad to have *your* father."

"I never knew—"

"Right," the Prof cut in, his tone closing the door. "Look, school-boy, Frankie's about ninety percent hate and twenty percent mean, but he only goes off inside the ropes. At least, now he does."

"You think he's bent?"

"He ain't no saint, but that don't mean he's gonna start stomping citizens. I think he's okay. Far as I can tell, anyway."

"You got another TV fight for him?"

"Yeah. Over in Jersey. At one of the casinos. Another undercard thing, but the exposure's great."

"You got a minute, talk about something else?" I asked.

"We're off the yard, but I'm still on guard," the little man said. "Run it."

I was almost through the entire rundown when Frankie came outside to where the Prof and I had been sitting on the loading dock—it's not a good move to smoke inside a working gym.

"Am I . . . ?" Frankie let his voice trail away.

"You're cool, kid," the Prof said. "Me and schoolboy here was just discussing old times."

"How far back do you go?" Frankie asked.

"To the beginning," I told him. "When I met the Prof, I was doing time. It wasn't a big thing to me—I'd been doing it all my life, since I was a kid. The Prof showed me the ropes, showed me how I could get out. Stay out, too. Before I met him, it was just the jailhouse or the graveyard—that was my whole future."

"He taught you all that?" Frankie asked, his face close to mine, really wanting to know.

"More," I assured him.

"I was inside," he said quietly. "How'd you get past the . . . race thing? I mean, inside, you can't . . . ."

"I come from a different generation," I said. "When I was inside, you measured a man by what he did on the bricks. What his fall was for, right? And how he did his time. That's what you looked at. I don't mean there wasn't racial stuff. You got that out in the World too—it's always around. But the Prof had . . . I don't know, status. He was respected. A professional. He was the only one to really look at me. The only one who could see what I was."

"It's different in there now," Frankie said.

"I know," I told him. "It doesn't matter—I'm not going back."

"Me neither," the kid said quietly.

"You was mad at that boy?" the Prof asked Frankie. "Your sparring partner?"

"No," Frankie said, honestly puzzled.

"Then what set you off?"

"I . . . don't know. It's always something. I see . . . colors, like. Bright colors. Not with my eyes, inside my head. When that happens, I *feel* the blood in me. Only it's not like blood, it's like . . . acid or something."

"It's okay," the Prof reassured him. "Inside those ropes you can do anything you want. Except lose. There's no room for that, honeyboy. You get jobbed on a decision, you get flattened, it won't matter—the blame's the same. You lose and we can still get you fights, but then you're just working for a living, getting beat on. I don't tell lies, we want the prize. The big thing, see? One *real* score, then we don't need no more."

"What would I do if I didn't—?"

"Fight? Fuck, what do I care? Take up fishing, go into group therapy. Find a good woman and have a dozen kids. Join the motherfucking Peace Corps. It don't matter what you do, you'll have *choices*, see? That's what it's about. That's your trip ticket, Frankie. First day you walk out of the joint, freedom looks as fine as a brand-new Cadillac, don't it? But that kitty ain't going nowhere 'less you got the gas money, right? The honey's in the hive, son—ain't no way you get nice without paying the price. You with me?"

"Yeah," Frankie said slowly, nodding his head, a heavy lock of black hair falling over his forehead. He looked closer to sixteen than twenty-six.

"We fight this Cuban guy next," the Prof said. "Montez. Big stupid fuck, got a whole bunch of KOs against patsy setups. Fights like a schoolyard bully—looks for the fear in your face. And he can't hit backing up. But he's got a nice record, maybe eleven straight. We take him out, the next one's for real cash, see? Do him in one, and the deal is done, got it?"

"I got it, Prof," Frankie said.

"Go run your sprints," the little man replied, turning back to me.

"**S**prints?" I asked the Prof. "I thought fighters did road work."

"That's all bullshit," he responded. "It ain't no marathon the kid's training for. He runs fifty yards full tilt, then fifty half-speed. Then he jogs for a couple of hundred, then he starts again. What you need in the ring is not to get tired, but this ain't no footrace—the other guy's *hitting* you, all right? Frankie's got to be able to go in *bursts* . . . full-tilt, all-out, pedal-to-the-metal. And he's gotta be able to do that every round. He does that and, sooner or later, the other guy goes to sleep. I been studying this all my life—I know what I'm doing."

"Did you ask Max—?"

"I ain't asking that Mongolian misfit *nothing*, understand? I'm training a fighter, not a fucking Zen Buddhist."

"Okay, Prof, don't get worked up. I was just—"

"Flapping your gums," he finished for me. "How many times I saved your sorry ass, schoolboy?"

"Too many to count," I acknowledged.

"And now you come around asking me to do it again, right? And you're gonna give *me* advice? Fuck a whole bunch of that!"

"Hey, I'm sorry, Prof. I was just trying to help."

"You want to help, stay on the shelf. I'll handle Frankie."

"Okay," I surrendered. Then I went back to telling him about Belinda.

"**W**hat the fuck is *that*?" I heard a voice asking just as I turned the corner to the doorway area of the gym. I took another couple of steps and saw a Latin bantamweight with a kit bag in one hand. He was facing Clarence, who was seated at the front desk, one hand idly scratching behind Pansy's right ear. Pansy eyed the Latin like she had a taste for Mexican food, but she didn't make a sound.

"This is a pit bull, mahn," Clarence told him, straight-faced.

"There ain't no pit bull in the world that big," the Latin guy challenged.

"This is a *West Indian* pit bull," Clarence told him, embellishing the lie to give it texture. "Direct from the Islands."

"Damn!" the Latin guy responded. "You know where I could get one?"

"No, mahn, that is not possible. Listen to me now. It is not enough that you go *to* the Islands, you must be *from* the Islands, understand? These are very, very special dogs. . . ."

The Latin eyed Pansy dubiously, indecision all over his face. "You . . . fight him?" he asked.

"That is not done," Clarence said, his tone dead serious, not bothering to correct the Latin's gender error. "On the Islands, these dogs are not for fighting other dogs. We love our dogs."

"Yeah, but—"

"These dogs only fight people, mahn. Understand?"

"I guess . . ." the Latin said, walking past me, shaking his head.

I took a seat on the desk, looked at Clarence. "A West Indian pit bull?" I asked.

"I think that is probably true, mahn," Clarence replied, deadpan. "You see how royally she stands. You see the pride in her carriage. That is nobility, mahn. It does not matter where she came from, Pansy is a West Indian in her heart. I know this."

"Yeah, okay," I agreed, being reasonable.

But Clarence wasn't going for it. "I can prove it, Burke. You watch this. Watch close now." He reached into one of those little iceboxes that look like tool chests, came out with something that looked like a fat dumpling. Pansy immediately started salivating, eyes almost spinning with rapture. "May I tell her the word, mahn?" he asked.

I nodded. Clarence said *"Speak!,"* tossing the dumpling in Pansy's general direction. She snapped it out of the air like an alligator—a perfect one-bite chomp.

"That, mahn, was a Tower Island beef patty. Pure Jamaican. I tell you something else, too. Pansy, she *loves* Red Stripe. You see, her natural diet is West Indian."

"You might be right," I acknowledged, not bursting his bubble. Truth is, Pansy would eat damn near anything—she has a digestive system like a trash compactor and no taste buds. I snapped the lead on her collar, threw Clarence the clench, and got back into the Plymouth.

I was up early the next morning. Called Mama from a pay phone. Two messages. One from Hauser, the other from Belinda. I dialed Hauser. "It's me," I said.

"I got into the morgue at the *Daily News*," he said. "Got all the clips, right from the beginning. When are you going to have the other stuff?"

"Maybe today," I told him. "I'll call you back. Where are you gonna be?"

"My office," he said, and hung up.

Belinda grabbed her phone on the first ring, said "Burke, I was hoping—" before I said anything.

"Do you have the—?" I asked.

"Yes! I went by your place earlier, but . . ."

"But what?"

"Maybe I went to the wrong address. I mean, it looked like it did before, but—"

"Where did you go?" I asked her, wondering what the hell she was talking about.

"The place on Mott Street. You know, the—"

"I don't have a place on Mott Street," I told her quietly. "If you want to see me, use the telephone, understand?"

"Okay. I just thought—"

"That's enough," I interrupted. "You don't want me coming to your place, don't come to mine."

We made the meet for eleven, in the park behind the Criminal Court. That's where she wanted it—maybe out in the open so she could have her people watch better than they did last time. It didn't bother me. The park is really part of Chinatown—I could get the job done there too.

I walked up Broadway, past the giant Federal Building, which houses everything from Social Security to the FBI. The building's biggest business is Immigration—the hopefuls start lining up hours before the place opens.

On the wide sidewalk in front of the building, dozens of merchants had set up shop, selling everything from jewelry to perfume to bootleg videocassettes. Different kinds of food, pastries, fresh vegetables. Children's books, street maps, umbrellas. They were packed so close together it was hard to move along the sidewalk. All cash businesses, every single one. And right behind them, the IRS slumbered, unaware and uninterested, too busy terrorizing honest citizens to care about the outlaws.

Belinda was already there when I rolled up, sitting comfortably on a metal cross-brace to some permanent outdoor exercise equipment. The park is a monument to filth, full of pigeons rooting around for the take-out food tossed onto the ground every day. At night, the homeless take over. And rats replace the pigeons.

She waved when she saw me. Or maybe the wave was to tip off her backup—no way to tell.

I walked closer, changing my stride enough so she'd know I'd seen her. She bounced off the exercise bar, landing lightly on her feet. "Where's that big dog of yours?" she asked. "What's her name again . . . ?"

"Betsy," I told her, not missing a beat. The difference between a professional liar like me and a garden-variety bullshit artist is that I always remember the lies I tell.

"That's right." She brightened. "Betsy. I really liked her. She liked me too, didn't she?"

"Sure did," I replied, doubling up on the lie. "You have that stuff with you?"

"In my purse," she said. "I thought we could go someplace. Inside. You live around here?"

"No," I said. "But if you do . . ."

"I'm not ready for that yet," she said, watching my face too closely.

I didn't push it. "I know a restaurant," I said. "It's a little early, but maybe it's open. . . ."

"I'm game," she replied. "Let's try it."

We walked slowly through the twisting back streets, heading for Mama's. The white-dragon tapestry was hanging in the window, alone. Belinda's expression didn't change, like she'd never been there before. Okay. I opened the front door, ushered Belinda inside. Mama looked up from her cash register, asked "How many, please?"

"Just us," I told her.

"Sit anywhere," Mama said dismissively, going back to her ledger book. Anytime I come in the front door, she knows something's up. There's a button under her cash register. She pushes it and a light starts flashing back in the kitchen. A red light.

I led Belinda to one of the middle tables, staying away from my booth in the back. A waiter came out after a few minutes, silently handed us each a plastic-coated, fly-specked menu, the kind they give tourists. Mama has a lot of businesses, but selling food isn't one of them—the last thing she wants in her joint is repeat customers.

Belinda told the waiter what she wanted. He gave her a mildly hostile look, said something in Cantonese. "They don't speak English here," I told her. She finally pointed to the menu, ordered the #2 combination plate: pepper steak, fried rice, egg roll. The whole package cost $4.95, a bargain on the surface.

I knew what kind of bargains Mama served up, so I just ordered a plate of fried rice.

Belinda wanted a Coke—I asked for water.

The waiter left. I lit a cigarette. "At least he seemed to understand 'coke.' " Belinda smiled.

I nodded, editing out a half-dozen stupid comments I could have made. I felt the tip of Belinda's sneaker tapping at my ankle. It didn't feel like she was playing—or that she was nervous either. I kept my face empty, put my left hand under the table. Belinda met me halfway—handed me a thick envelope of some kind. I took it from her, left it on my lap.

The waiter brought the food, slapping it down on the Formica table with sullen indifference. I checked out Belinda's combination plate. The green peppers looked soggy, the steak was a suspicious two-tone chocolate color, age-ringed like an old tree. And the fried rice they gave her didn't resemble what was on my own plate.

Belinda didn't seem to notice. "I didn't have breakfast," she said by way of explanation as she dug into the food. I ate my rice in silence.

"Ugh!" she said suddenly. "This Coke is flat."

"This water's no bargain either," I told her.

"Why do you come here, anyway?" she asked.

"I live in a hotel," I told her. "No cooking facilities. Better the devil you know . . ."

She flashed another smile. "It's all there," she said quietly. "Some of the photocopies aren't that good—I didn't have that much time."

"I'm sure it'll be okay," I told her.

We finished the meal at about the same time. The waiter dropped a check on the table, face-up. It came to twelve bucks and change—bogus addition is another way Mama keeps her customers from coming back. I left a five and a ten on the table. Unless Belinda had the digestive system of a goat, she was going to pay *her* share later on that day. As we passed by the cash register, Mama said "Come again," with all the passion of an embalmer.

The envelope felt heavy in my inside jacket pocket as we strolled back to the park. Belinda let her hand rest on my right forearm, her soft rounded hip occasionally bumping me as we walked. "Are you already working on it?" she asked.

"Yeah."

"You want to tell me—?"

"No."

"Okay, don't get hostile. We're on the same side, right?"

"Me, I'm doing a job," I told her. "We had a deal—I'm living up to my piece of it."

"Is that a subtle way of asking for the money?"

"It'll do."

"I don't have it," she said. I clenched my fist so the muscles in my forearm tightened, giving her my response. "But I'll get it," she finished quickly. "It has to come from . . . George. Like I told you, the—"

"Trust fund," I put in, just the trace of sarcasm in my voice.

"It's *true*," she said, in a pouty girl's voice. "You can check it out for yourself."

"What I want to check out is five thousand dollars. Like we agreed. One week, five G's, right?"

"Right. What I'm trying to tell you, if you'll just give me the chance to *say* something, is that *I* don't have it . . . but Fortunato does. I already spoke to him. You can go by his office anytime, pick it up yourself."

"He's gonna leave a package for me at the receptionist's desk?"

"Stop being so mean," she said. "He wants to talk to you—what's so strange about that?"

"Which means I got to call him, make an appointment, all that, right?"

"Well, I guess . . ."

"Guess again, sister. If you think I'm gonna work this job for you on spec, you need therapy. I work the same way Fortunato does. You know how it goes: money in front, all cash, no big bills. And no refunds."

"That's okay. I mean—"

"Here's what *I* mean," I told her quietly. "I already started this thing. And I still haven't seen any money. I'm not gonna spend a week chasing this lawyer. Call him. Tell him I'll see him today. Anytime he wants. But *today*, understand? I don't get the money today, I'm out of this."

"Okay, okay, *okay*," she spit out rapid-fire. "I'll call him. You'll get the money today, I promise."

"Not *the* money," I reminded her. "*My* money."

"Fine," she said with a sniff, taking her hand off my forearm. "Give me an hour. I'll leave you a message."

"See you around," I told her. I walked away, leaving her standing there. When I got as far as Worth Street, a pair of Chinese kids in matching red silk shirts under fingertip-length black leather jackets nodded an "okay" at me. I nodded back to show them I understood—I hadn't been followed.

I went over to my office, patted Pansy for a minute, opened the back door so she could get to her roof. Then I spread the contents of Belinda's envelope out on my desk. Everything was on that cheap flimsy paper they use in government copiers. Nothing but DD5s, the Complaint Follow-up form they use to keep track of investigations. Three women. Three bodies. All cut to pieces, first stabbed to immobilize them, then sliced for fun. Sex crimes for sure, every one of the women razor-raped. The report was in Cop-Speak: "On the above date, the undersigned Detective Oscar Wandell, Sh#99771 of the Manhattan Homicide Squad, entered the premises known as 1188 University Place Apt 9B at approx. 09:45 hours. . . ." Whoever prepared it had just X-ed out any typos he saw—cops don't use Wite-Out.

All the homicides were south of Midtown, west of Fifth. All inside the victims' apartments. Somebody they knew? Bar pickups? No way to tell. All the victims were white. The youngest was twenty-nine, the oldest thirty-six. The killer was working a narrow band—maybe they were all targets of opportunity?

I took a yellow legal pad from the desk, started working on a chart. The dates synched with what Belinda had said: One of the murders—the woman on University Place—went down before Piersall had been popped over in Jersey. The other two came while he was being held without bail. No indication that the cops had linked the crimes in any way.

I went back to the different reports. Some were more detailed than others. One detective had really done a job—even included a diagram of the apartment's floor plan, an outline to show where the body had been found, an inventory of the victim's medicine cabinet. I checked the signature box at the bottom—I couldn't make a name out of the scrawl. But next to it was a box for the detective's name to be typed.

Morales.

Fuck!

Being in a box is bad enough—it turns to all kinds of holy hell when you don't know where the walls are. Or what they're made of. I folded up the reports, stuck them in my pocket and split.

I hit the switch for the garage door, nosed the Plymouth out onto the street behind my building. Once I got the car rolling uptown, I hit the cellular, reaching out for Hauser.

"It's me," I said. "Now a good time?"

"*Very* good," he said. "Come on up."

I couldn't find an open meter, so I settled for an outdoor parking lot. The attendant looked at the Plymouth with distaste, but he gave me a claim ticket without a word.

I knocked on Hauser's office door—he doesn't have a bell or a buzzer. He opened it quick, a phone with a long cord in his hand. Hauser motioned me over to the couch, made a "just give me a minute" gesture and went back to his conversation.

"Of course it's sourced," he said into the receiver. "No way I'd write it otherwise."

He listened impatiently to whoever was on the other end of the line. Then he said, "Look, here's the deal. I'll let you see the stuff, but there's no way you can talk to my source. You want to do it that way . . . okay. If you don't, I'll just—"

Hauser listened again, this time nodding his head in satisfaction. "I'll be there," he said, hanging up the phone.

"Great-looking boys, aren't they?" he said to me, pointing to a framed color photograph on the end table next to the couch.

"Yeah," I agreed. "Yours?"

"All mine," he said, a broad smile on his face. "The big one's J.A., the other one's J.R. You want to hear something absolutely fucking incredible," he went on without taking a breath, cluing me to one of those stupidass cutesy-poo stories all parents tell . . . like it's a big deal if their kid smeared jam on the wall or something. But I wanted something from him, so . . .

"Run it," I said.

"Okay. Last night, I'm reading J.A. a bedtime story. 'Goldilocks and the Three Bears.' Now, he's heard this one before, see, but it's one of his favorites. You remember how it goes, right?"

"Sure," I said, to prevent him from telling it to me.

"Okay, when you get to the part about the Papa Bear saying, 'Someone's been sitting in my chair,' J.A. pops up and asks me, 'How would he know?' I was gonna brush him off, finish the damn story so he'd get to sleep, but then he pipes up again. 'It's a *hard* chair, Dad. See? in the picture? So you couldn't tell by *looking*, right? So how would the bear *know*?' And it just knocked me out. You see it?"

"Yeah. The kid figured it out, right? How's a little girl gonna make a dent in a chair that holds a goddamned *bear.* That's amazing," I said, not lying now.

I guess a minute or two passed. Hauser was staring at my face. "What is it?" he asked.

"Nothing," I told him, shaking my head to clear it, feeling wetness on my face. Thinking about Hauser's kid being a genius so early, how Hauser adored that kid, how he must have hugged him and kissed him and been proud of him. Thinking about another kid, a little kid who questioned what he was told. Thinking about the vicious slap in the face, the ugly curses. Thinking . . . Ah, fuck this! I didn't need Hauser poking around in *my* life. So I pointed at his kids' pictures, asked him, "What's all those initials stand for?"

"Same as mine—nothing."

"You wanted to name them after you, how come you didn't just call one of them Junior?"

"Jews don't do that," he told me in a serious tone. "You only name a child after someone who's dead."

"Okay, I kind of knew that, I think. But I thought only Southerners named their kids with initials."

"There's Jews in Atlanta." Hauser smiled. "Now, how about showing me what you got?"

I handed over the reports. Hauser put them on his desk, pulled a few sheets of paper from his wire basket, laid them side-by-side with what I gave him. I smoked a couple of cigarettes while Hauser browsed around in the paperwork.

"Nothing here," he said finally, looking up from the desk.

"Nothing?"

"Nothing that would support the idea that it's the same killer."

"The signature—?"

"There *is* no goddamn 'signature,' " Hauser said. "It's not there. Take a look for yourself."

He shoved the sheaf of papers across the desk to me. I sat down to read, then stopped as soon as I saw AUTOPSY centered at the top of the first page. "How'd you—?" I asked.

His answer was a shrug, just a hint of self-satisfaction at the corner of his mouth.

The language of the reports was as cold as the corpses. They all ended the same way.

MANNER OF DEATH: HOMICIDE.

"Check where I marked," Hauser said.

Portions of the reports were covered with a yellow highlighter. But I didn't need it to pick out the red ribbon Belinda told me about—the woman on University Place had one stuffed inside her, just a little piece trailing out. But the two later ones—after Piersall was locked up—there was no ribbon mentioned. What the hell . . . ?

"So this one woman, the one in New York, that's the only place they found the red ribbon?" I asked. "What about the one in Jersey—the one who survived?"

"They didn't *need* any red ribbon there, Burke. I did a NEXIS spin too. This cop pal of yours, he didn't happen to mention DNA, did he?"

"No," I said, already getting it, wondering if I could possibly be as stupid as Belinda must be thinking I was.

"The investigation they did—the one in Jersey, not here—they introduced DNA-fingerprinting evidence on top of the ID. The woman had enough of Piersall's flesh under her fingernails to make it open-and-shut. No question about it—they got the right guy."

"You're . . . sure?"

"A dead match," Hauser told me.

"So why wouldn't the ME report on the red ribbon in the other killings?"

"You got me," Hauser said. "It's the same coroner's office, true enough, but they used a different doctor for each one. I don't see anything suspicious in that—whoever's around, that's who gets to do it. And I read it *close*, too—no red ribbon, no trace of red fibers, no nothing."

"So there's no way this guy is innocent?"

"Not of the Jersey crime," he confirmed. "That DNA stuff is dynamite. I've been reading up on it. Even checked with an expert. There's some people in the forensics field who claim it can get screwed up pretty easy—wrong samples, not enough differentiation fields to work with, poor tagging procedures . . . all that. But the bottom line is that it's still being used—you got people being convicted with it every day—people getting *out* of jail with it too. They use it for paternity tests too—when the regular blood test isn't conclusive enough for the court."

"So you're off the job?" I asked him.

"Not a chance," he replied. "*Something's* going on here. Maybe not what you—or that cop friend of yours—think. But something. Let me know what happens, okay?"

"Yeah."

I called in to Mama's. "Same girl," she said, as soon as she recognized my voice. "No wig this time."

"It's starting to get messy," I told her. "Any other calls?"

"Lawyer call. Say his name: For-too-not-toe. He say, he have your material. Six o'clock tonight."

"Thanks, Mama. Nothing from the Prof?"

"No. Maybe busy with fighter?"

"Maybe. I'll call you later."

I ran through it in my head, showering and shaving on automatic pilot. Copycat crime, it's a fact of life. But most of the time, they copy the style more than the deed. There's no such thing as a first-time crime—humans have been on the planet too long for that. But once the media *names* a crime—like when the newspaper jerks started calling gang rape "wilding"—it becomes the hot ticket and every punk wants to play.

Take carjacking—nothing new about it except the name. But once the name catches on, the crime catches fire. It's all grapevine stuff: no way there's a nationwide group of mutants united in a giant conspiracy to hijack cars. It's a moron-move all the way—you risk life in the pen for a used car. But as soon as the media names it, the twenty-four-karat dumb-fuck imbeciles have to go and do it. Starts in D.C., spreads to New York. Then over to L.A., back to Chicago, down to Miami. You ask one of those idiots why they do it, they couldn't tell you. A whole battalion of sheep, following the herd, armed and stupid.

The latest craze is so totally retarded I almost couldn't believe it when I first heard about it—now they're robbing toll booths on the bridges. The G.W., the Triborough, the Whitestone . . . you name it. They just drive up to the booth, stick a gun out the window, and demand the cash. Incredible. Start with armed robbery, throw in a string of other crimes, and you're risking a dozen years Upstate before you can even *dream* about the Parole Board. All for what? A few handfuls of change and a bunch of tokens you'd have to sell at a discount. That's why prison never changes anybody—you can convince a man to be honest, but there's no way to make him smart.

Of course, the people who collect the tolls, they're demanding the right to carry firearms. There's a pretty picture—some self-righteous loon who watched too many cop shows blazing away in the middle of rush hour.

The real answer would be to eliminate the toll collectors entirely. They could train chimps to do it, but the chimps would probably get bored and swing off the job.

You see it everywhere. Somebody says they found a syringe in their can of Pepsi, next thing you know, tampered cans are showing up all over the country. Sure. Good thing they don't make you pass an IQ test before they accept you into prison—most of the joints would be empty.

A pattern crime, one with a *signature,* that's custom-made for copycats. That's a fact of life in this cancer ward of a city. But who could be copying something he never heard of . . . ?

I finished shaving, still no closer to an answer. Time to go to work. I know how to look like a lawyer. All you need is a dark pin-stripe suit, a dress shirt with a monogram on the cuff, any necktie that looks expensive. The younger breed goes more for the Italian look, more silk, more slouchy—the older guys stay closer to tradition. They wear their hair different too. The older guys go for blow-dried razor-cuts—the younger ones wear their hair longer, go heavy on the gel. They both display flashy wristwatches and leather attaché cases—slim ones, so they don't get confused with the 18-B guys, who have to haul files around with them. And the look is indispensable: superior, snotty, arrogant, with a distinctive weasel-tint to the eyes.

I didn't bother with any of that to go see Fortunato. He knows what I do. And I know what he is. I put on a pair of carpenter's pants over steel-toed work shoes. Then a black sweatshirt under an old leather jacket. Lots of pockets, lots of room . . . I didn't need an attaché case.

Fortunato makes most of his scores downtown, from the pits on the first floor of Centre Street to the tower in Foley Square, but he wasn't a Baxter Street type of guy—his office was on Forty-second, between Madison and Lex.

His name was in large gilt letters, standing guard over the double doors to the office. I stepped inside, into an empty reception area. The sliding glass window to the receptionist's desk was standing open. I reached my hand in and rapped on the top of the desk. A guy in his twenties came around a corner. He was wearing a white shirt with the sleeves rolled up. His tie was pulled loose from around his neck. He looked pressured.

"Can I help you?" he asked, an undercurrent of annoyance in his voice.

"I'm here to see Fortunato," I told him. "Name's Burke."

He turned his back on me, walked away. He was back in a minute, said "Come in," and hit a buzzer to release the inner door.

"Last one on the left," he told me.

Fortunato's office was bigger than the whole reception area, a corner spot with two exposures through large windows. He was sitting behind his desk, a kidney-shaped monster—its left lobe held three separate telephone mini-consoles—the right had a smoked-plastic stack of trays loaded with various documents. The broad expanse in the middle was empty, gleaming like it had just been polished. I walked in, took the middle of three identical leather chairs facing the desk.

"You're Burke?" he said by way of greeting.

"Yes."

Fortunato leaned forward, elbows on the desk. He didn't ask for identification, didn't offer to shake hands. He reached into one of the plastic stacked trays, extracted a white envelope, held it in his hand for a few seconds. Then he slid it across the slick surface toward me. I caught it, pocketed it without looking inside.

"You have any questions?" he asked.

"The way I understand it, this guy was dropped behind some DNA fingerprinting, right?"

"That was one of the factors," he said cautiously. "There were others."

"So what's his play on appeal? How do you get around that?"

"An appeal isn't usually about the evidence," he said smoothly. "It's about the law, not the facts. Let's say the police find the murder weapon in the trunk of a guy's car. But let's say it was a bad search—no warrant, no probable cause. They can't use it in court, understand?"

"Yeah, I do. But they wouldn't need a warrant to take a blood sample."

"It's all in how you look at the evidence," he said. "The DNA . . . Wait a minute, are you saying they got DNA samples from the New York case?"

"Well . . . yeah, I guess so. I mean, I knew they had it in Jersey, and I thought—"

"There was no DNA taken from the body on University Place," he said flatly.

"None at all? How could that be?"

"Look, maybe you don't have all the facts here," he said, ticking off the points on his fingers. "One, the DNA they got in Jersey was a *tissue* sample, understand? From fingernail scrapings—the woman scratched, she fought hard. There were fragments of skin under her nails. Two, the woman in New York, the one on University Place? Her fingernails were smooth, like she just had a manicure. Nothing under them at all. Three, there was no sperm in the body."

"You telling me they found *different* DNA in the other bodies?"

"There were three bodies," Fortunato said, ticking them off on his fingers, one-two-three. His manicure was perfect. "Three murders," he said. "And *all* of them in New York. And the assault, the one in Jersey—I already explained that one, right? The woman on University Place—there was no sperm—they never made a match. The other two—the other two murders, I mean—there was no sperm either."

"You sure that's right? No sperm at all? Sometimes, a guy isn't a secretor . . ."

"I know that," he said, looking up sharply. "No sperm, period—*that's* what they found. And they didn't find any in the other two, the ones that happened after he was in custody."

"So let's say he didn't do the last two—hell, that would make sense. He was inside, right? But there's no question about the first pair."

"One of them," Fortunato corrected. "The one that lived. That'll stand up, no question. But the woman on University Place, he may have been in her apartment, he may have fucked her a couple of times—hell, he *admits* all of that—but there's no real hard evidence that he *killed* her."

"Sounds like a dead loser to me," I said. "What's the point? Without proof that the ME pulled the red ribbon out of the other bodies—and you gotta admit, *that* sounds ridiculous—you got nothing."

Fortunato shrugged, watching my face. "Sometimes," he said, "you take a case as a favor. Even if it doesn't look good. You never know what can happen. . . ."

"Okay," I said. It was like I'd thought—if Fortunato had a scheme, it didn't have anything to do with the law books.

He reached behind him to where a shelf was built in below the window line, brought out a small wood humidor. He reached inside, took out a long dark cigar. "You mind?" he asked.

I shook my head. Shook it again when he turned the humidor in my direction, offering me one. He clipped the end of the cigar with a little silver guillotine, flicked a wafer-thin lighter into flame. He made a ceremony out of it, rolling the cigar in his lips, making sure it was fully lit. He finally got it going to his satisfaction, leaned back in his chair.

"You're an interesting man," he said. "I've heard a lot about you."

"People talk," I told him. "I don't."

"I understand. You have a very strong reputation . . . in some circles."

"And your point is . . . ?"

"My point is that this job, it doesn't have anything to do with family business. You following me?"

"Sure."

"Julio used to speak well of you," he said. I could feel his eyes through the cigar smoke.

"Used to?"

"He's dead," Fortunato said. "You didn't know?"

"How would I know? Was it in the papers?"

"Just a little squib," he said. "Old man sitting on a bench just off the water by La Guardia. Watching the planes come in, it looked like. Only his neck was broken."

I gave out a short grunt of surprise, with a question mark at the end.

"The cops have it down as Unsolved," Fortunato answered. "They never made an arrest."

"You want me to look into it?" I asked, flat-faced.

"No, that's okay," he replied. "We know who did it."

"Then you're telling me because . . . ?"

"I just thought you'd be interested. I know you were tight with the old man once."

"Inside I was. I didn't see much of him once I was out."

He nodded as if that made sense. "Your record . . . it's long, but it's old. You ever think of going for a Certificate of Release from Civil Disabilities?"

"What's that?"

"It's like a pardon. Not really a pardon . . . I mean, you still have your record, but you can do things you couldn't do before."

"Like what?"

"Well, you could vote. Open certain kinds of businesses . . ." he said, the sly hint of suggestion in his voice.

Telling me he knew about me owning a piece of Frankie? "How much does it cost?" I asked him, no sign of real interest on my face.

"Well, that depends. Different lawyers charge different rates. You know that. Me, I could get it done. Guaranteed."

"How much?" I asked again.

"I could do it as a favor. No charge."

"That's too high a price," I told him.

He took another hit off the cigar, blew a perfect smoke ring toward the ceiling. "The offer's still open," he said. "You change your mind, let me know. Anytime."

"I'll do that," I told him.

On the way back to my office, I tried to put it together. Fortunato as much as told me he knew I was involved in Julio's murder. Was he threatening me, or offering me a way out?

I wasn't afraid of Fortunato. Inside his pretty office, he was strong and confident, but he was only a messenger—he couldn't deliver the payload. A mob lawyer might get involved with homicide for money, might even set it up, but he wouldn't do the work himself. Guys like that, they stay between the lines, trying to widen them by pushing from the inside.

But Julio . . . it was a long time ago. A family quarrel the newspapers called a Mob War. One side hired Wesley, and Wesley got it done, delivering the bodies like he always did. But then Julio's crew stiffed Wesley on the fee, and Wesley starting taking them out, one at a time. Julio, the old alligator, had been screaming for Wesley's blood—even promising me the earth if I could lure the ice-man into a trap. But it was Julio who got trapped . . . by a flame-haired witch named Strega who licked her lips as she watched him die.

What was Fortunato telling me? Wesley was a shooter—the best there ever was. But Julio had died of a broken neck. Just like one of those freaks in the Bronx house of beasts.

I got back to my car and headed downtown. I left the West Side Highway at Chambers Street, heading for the Brooklyn Bridge. I took the on-ramp before the span. It was the tail end of rush hour, but the bridge was clogged. I looked ahead, saw one of those orange signs: LEFT LANE ENDS 500 YARDS. I was in that lane, and I wasn't getting much play from the middle lane, so merging right wasn't all that easy. I didn't get worked up about it—I wasn't in a hurry.

In some cities, the citizens have actually mastered the art of staggered lane merging—one from the right, one from the left, until it's all done. It'll never happen here—if you're in the lane that needs to merge you don't hope for courtesy, you watch for weakness.

A tired old black Buick finally came up on my right, laboring and sputtering along, an elderly Hasid at the wheel. Everybody was cutting him off, jumping ahead of him—he was acting so unaggressive he became fair game. Just before the left lane ended, I tapped my brakes to let him pull ahead of me, then slipped in behind. He chugged on ahead, reaching his left arm out the window to wave a thank-you to me. It felt good. I *like* that kind of stuff. If motherfuckers would just let me be, I swear I would be a polite, respectful man.

Then I heard the angry blare of a horn, glanced in the mirror. A white Nissan sedan had been behind me, but it got pinched off when I let that other guy in.

So what? I worked the middle lane for a piece, saw my opening, and rolled once more to the right, setting up for the exit to the BQE. The white Nissan pulled up on my left, running parallel. The driver and the two in the back seat were black males—there was a black woman in the front passenger seat. She rolled down her window. I hit the switch to drop mine too.

She leaned out her window, screamed "You fucking Jew bastard!" at me just as the Nissan pulled away, obviously concluding she'd been the victim of still another Zionist plot.

I thought about how much fun it would be to lock her in a room with old Cline-as-in-Patsy.

After I completed all the necessary loops, I climbed onto the BQE, heading for Queens. As I passed the Flushing Avenue exit I spotted a congenital defective driving a Cadillac in the left lane. Driving slow. Posting up so everyone had to pass in the middle lane and then cut back in. Nobody did it calmly—some of them shot the finger, others waved fists. One cut back in so close the Cadillac had to stand on its brakes.

I dialed my mind to calm, waited for my shot, then swept around the fat Cadillac. I got back into the left lane and settled in, punched the button for the all-news station, half-listened as I drove. The news came out in little blips:

Down South, another anti-abortion maniac gunned down a doctor going into a clinic. An equally freakish misfit killed two nurses and a secretary somewhere in New England. Good thing there's no waiting period for buying a handgun—makes it so much easier to act on impulse.

A nine-year-old girl writes an essay for school. "Daddy Raped Me," it was called. She gets an A on her paper—nothing else. Months later, the scumbag gets himself arrested for some other stuff—turns out he has AIDS. Some group promises a protest.

Another baby killed in another crossfire. The only difference between certain neighborhoods in this city and Bosnia is that we're better armed here.

The New York weather report: cold and vicious.

I switched to FM, punched the oldies station. They were playing music from the '70s, as impossible as that sounds.

I slammed in the one sure cure: a Judy Henske tape. That broad's got enough rich, dark juice for a grape arbor, every word dripping with promise. I had a scheme to meet her in person, years ago. It worked out the same as most of my schemes.

Traffic crawled once we got over the Kosciusko Bridge—the halfass government was doing something stupid to the highway again. I grabbed the LIE eastbound, still in no hurry. Just before the

Elmhurst Tanks, I spotted a downed Lincoln Continental in the right lane. I wasn't the first to see it—one of the vulture vans that cruise the city expressways looking for crippled cars was already on the scene. A pro team was at work—one guy had a hydraulic jack under the back wheels while his partner had popped the hood. Give them a half-hour, they'd turn a wounded car into a corpse.

I exited at Woodhaven Boulevard and worked my way toward Forest Park. I found a quiet spot. Pulled over to a roadside pay phone and punched a number in.

"What?" came the rust-bucket greeting.

"You been looking for me?" I asked.

"ID me something," the voice demanded.

"Baby Pete," I said.

"More."

"I found him. Where you said he couldn't be."

Baby Pete. Big Peter's grandson. Kidnapped, held for ransom. Big Peter never went near the Law. Paid in full. Never got the boy back. After that, he reached out for me. I found the little kid. In the basement of Big Peter's next-in-line. Found his ashes and a few bone fragments—the furnace hadn't finished its work. The next-in-line was impatient, but he needed a war chest before he made his move. Big Peter hadn't called the Law about that one either.

"Ask the question again?"

"You looking for me?"

"If I wanted to find you, I would," he said softly. "I know how to do that."

"Yeah. That's what I figured. I just wanted to make sure you didn't have some problem—"

"With you?" he interrupted.

"Yeah. Some strange stuff is happening. And I heard a name today. . . ."

"Say it."

"Julio."

"Oh." The line was quiet for a few seconds. Then he said, "Come see me."

"Where?"

"At the house."

"When?"

"Now. I'll wait."

"Twenty minutes," I told him, and hung up.

The house was a simple wood-frame two-story in Ozone Park. Only the chain-link fence looked serious. The gypsy cab dropped me off in front. I walked around to the side of the house and rang the bell.

Big Peter opened the door himself. He stood about five feet four, weighed maybe a hundred and twenty pounds. There's a number of stories about how he came into his name—none of them are pretty.

"Sit," he said, pointing at a kitchen table with four padded chairs.

He took the chair opposite me, looked me over, nodded his head. Said, "So?"

"I got a case," I told him. "There's this guy doing time. A sex killer. There's this cop hired me to look into it, claims he's innocent. I went to see the guy's lawyer, the one he got for the appeal. Raymond Fortunato. This Fortunato, he asks me, would I maybe like a favor done? I tell him No. So he pays me the money that was promised . . . for this case. To look into it, all right? Then he says Julio always spoke well of me. I say, I haven't seen him in a long time. Then Fortunato says, Julio's dead. I ask him: When? How? . . . like that. He tells me, says they *know* who did it. The way he looked at me, I couldn't tell if he was selling wolf tickets or what. So I thought I'd ask you."

"You ain't afraid of Raymond fucking Fortunato," Big Peter said. A flat statement, not a question.

"I'm afraid of you," I told him, just as flat.

"I would never hurt you," he said. "I would never let anyone hurt you. I would never forget what you did. For me. Too late for my grandson," he said quietly, one knuckle to his eye like he was expecting a tear. "I shoulda listened to you first. I wanted to trust . . . and I got my grandson dead."

"He was gone from the moment they took him," I said. "He was a smart kid, would've ID'ed them in a minute."

"Yeah . . ." The old man stayed quiet for a minute. Forgiving himself, tricking me . . . no way to tell. Finally, he looked up. "You're not afraid of me either," he said. "That was true, you wouldn't come here. Unless you was wearing a wire."

I stood up, started to unbutton my shirt.

"Sit the fuck down, okay? I was just jerking your chain. You want something from me, there's something I can do for you, just ask."

I looked down at my cigarette, at the long ash, realized I hadn't dragged on it at all. I snubbed it out in the glass ashtray, deciding. I could hear my heart—I slowed it down, took a deep breath, and plunged in. "There's a cop, brought a case to me. It's a woman, a lady cop. I met her a while ago, when I was doing something else. She never told me she was a cop—I found out by accident. She's been calling me ever since. I never returned the calls. Then she turned up the pressure. Came to . . . a place where I hang out sometimes. Something else . . . She got a hooker to offer me a job. A homicide job. I turned it down, but . . . it's starting to look like a box."

"So walk away," he said. "What's the problem?"

"There's another cop," I went on like I hadn't heard him. "He's been on my case forever. We had some dealings—he didn't like the way they turned out. Now he thinks I'm connected to a bunch of murders—I don't know why. He's been around, watching. Turns out he was one of the investigators on one of the rape-murders this guy—the guy the lady cop says is innocent—is doing time for. It's all too coincidental for me to buy it. Fortunato, he's all mobbed up, right? Julio's gone, sure . . . but the family's still in business. I thought you might . . ."

"What? Call off the dogs?"

"If that's what it is."

"That's *not* what it is. Fortunato's a worm. The family may know something about how Julio got done, but not a one of them cares. You know better than that. Why would they care? For *honor*?" he sneered.

"I don't know," I told him. "But why would a mob mouthpiece like Fortunato take this kind of case?"

"Don't make a big thing out of it," he said. "It's all about this"—rubbing his thumb against the first two fingers of his right hand, a money gesture. "There's really only two families now. One deals with drugs, the other does the unions, gambling, puts money on the street—all the old stuff. Fortunato, he's nothing—a dealer, not a lawyer. If they didn't fix the juries for him, he's nothing. And he knows it, see? This is all about greed, that's all. But if you want, I could have somebody talk to him. . . ."

"I don't know. . . ."

"Don't get cute," he said. "I'm not going to talk you into it. You want it done, it's done. If not, no. *Capisce?*"

"Yeah."

"And . . . ?"

"Do it," I told him, "And thank you."

The next morning, I shaved extra carefully before I put on my lawyer outfit. What I needed was a look at the court file they'd have on Piersall. Not the criminal file—Fortunato would already have all of that for the appeal—what I wanted was over at the Surrogate's Court. A look at that trust fund.

They kept me waiting almost forty-five minutes before I got into the office. Not the judge's chambers, the office they gave his law secretary. "Law secretary" isn't what it sounds like—they're all lawyers themselves, and they don't do any typing or filing. What they do depends on the judge, whatever the judge wants. And they get their jobs the same way the judges do—the right person taps them on the shoulder and they're made. Kind of like the Mafia would be if the feds made them swallow Affirmative Action.

This one was a skinny guy with a prominent Adam's apple, hair cut real short. He was wearing a white button-down shirt and black suspenders, sleeves rolled up like he'd been hard at work for hours.

Sure.

"My name is Rodriguez, sir," I introduced myself. He looked up impatiently, not offering to shake hands. "This concerns a client," I continued. "George Piersall. What we need is some information regarding Mr. Piersall's trust fund. . . . I understand it came about as a result of a bequest. I wonder if it would be possible to look through the file. . . . ?"

"You *are* a lawyer, Mr. . . . ah . . . Rodriguez?" he asked, just this side of snide. If I'd told him my name was Anderson, he wouldn't have asked.

"No sir," I replied. "I apologize. I should have made that clear. I am a paralegal—I work for Raymond Fortunato."

The weasel's face shifted. Not a lot, but I'd been looking for it. He was a mid-list ass-kisser—he did it on the way up, and he expected those below him in the political food chain to treat him the same way. But he wouldn't risk offending someone of Fortunato's weight.

"Will you excuse me a moment?" he asked. "I need to make a phone call."

"Certainly, sir," I said, backing out of the room. I took a seat on the polished wood bench in the corridor, one hand stroking my status-appropriate attaché case.

In less than five minutes, the weasel poked his head out of his den, motioned for me to come back.

"Here's the file," he said, handing me three thick folders, holding about half a ream of paper each. "There's a lot to go through, I know, so, if you want, you could use this empty room we have down the hall."

"I would appreciate that," I told him.

He led me to the room. It was bare except for a long wooden table and six matching chairs. I sat down at the table, thanked the weasel again, put on a pair of reading glasses and started to work.

"When you're done, just let me know," the weasel said.

"Thank you, sir," I replied.

As soon as he left the room, I put the reading glasses off to one side. I don't need them—the prescription is for someone with a radical astigmatism. I'd leave them behind . . . accidentally. It's the same thing I do with the matchbooks—if the weasel ever had to prove I was there, he'd whip out the reading glasses triumphantly . . . and they wouldn't fit.

Most of the papers were the kind of boilerplate legalese you expect from people who get paid by the hour or by the pound. I finally got to the meat: the guy who left all the money was Morton L. Capshaw, last listed address was on Park Avenue. There's a key to finding the cross streets for any avenue address in New York—what you do is take the number, cancel the last digit, divide by two, then add or subtract another number, depending on the avenue. For Park, it's a +34. Park Avenue runs all the way from Gramercy to Harlem. I did the math—Capshaw lived in the Seventies . . . big-bucks territory.

I kept reading. He died at Sloan Kettering, the cancer hospital. Age seventy-three when he cashed out. The trust fund was huge—more than seven million. The way it was set up, Piersall got the income only, not the principal. There was a long list after that, all next in line. I counted seven names. Once I sorted it out, it was easy to see what Capshaw had done. Piersall got the income from the trust for as long as he lived. When he died, the next name on the list took over. When they all died, the principal went to something called the Adelnaws Foundation. I read through the rest of it, but couldn't find anything more. The Adelnaws Foundation was a 501(c)(3) corporation—not-for-profit. Its stated purpose was "social research"—you know, what the reverend told the cops he was doing in a whorehouse.

The trustee was a white-shoe law firm with a whole hive of WASPs on its letterhead. They were to pay the interest "monthly, quarterly, or annually, at the election of the beneficiary," and the instructions were to invest in "prudent instruments, the goal being preservation of capital." Commodities, options, and precious metals were specifically excluded from permissible investments.

I went back to the beneficiary tree again. Something about it . . . Yeah—none of them were named Capshaw. So that meant . . . Sure enough—I found what I was looking for in the last folder—a will contest. Capshaw's ex-wife, a sister, and a cousin all brought suit, challenging the will on grounds of "undue influence" and "lack of testamentary capacity." Meaning, somebody got to the old man when he was dying, or he was out of his head when he made out the will.

But it was no go. Most of those things get settled out of court, but this one went to the wall. The relatives got zilch—they were completely shut out, even on appeal. The trustee law firm did a little better—they billed for $477,504.25, and the Surrogate allowed them every penny, pulling it right out of the principal.

I looked at the list of beneficiaries again—just the names, dates of birth, Social Security numbers—straight ID stuff. All the beneficiaries were approximately the same age—there wasn't ten years' difference between the oldest and the youngest. The list was the only thing in the whole file that varied from the kind of air-pumped filler you find in any document lawyers get their hands on. I copied it onto my yellow legal pad, checked it again to be sure I had it right.

On my way out, I stopped by the weasel's office to thank him for his courtesy. He wasn't at his desk.

I carried the money I'd gotten from Fortunato over to Mama's. As I was crossing Lafayette Street, a tall slender Chinese girl shot by on Rollerblades, her long black hair flying behind her. She was a pro at it—had a backpack strapped on, a whistle on a chain around her neck, and black kneepads against a possible spill. A pair of business-dressed guys saw her too. One told the other the girl had another use for the kneepads. His pal laughed in appreciation. I figured the guy who made the crack was an expert—probably on his way to do the same thing to his boss.

Anytime I forget how bad I hate this place, somebody's always good enough to remind me.

When I handed Mama the money, she didn't react with her usual happiness as she extracted her cut. When Mama doesn't smile around money, it's a storm warning. I gave her a look, waiting for it to hit. But she just sipped her soup in silence. Patience is one of my few virtues, but I knew better than to try outwaiting Mama.

"What?" I asked.

"You like this woman?" she answered my question with one of her own.

"What woman?"

"Girl with wig. Police lady."

"No," I told Mama. "I don't like her."

"Why you work, then?"

"For money," I responded, playing the one card that Mama always recognized as trump.

"This money?" Mama asked, holding up the bills I'd just handed her, a disgusted tone in her voice.

"Yeah."

"Not much," Mama said. "You have money. From . . . last time, yes? I know." She *did* know. Hell, she was holding most of it. "Balance," she continued, looking at me straight on. She held out her hands parallel to the tabletop, palms up, raising first one, then the other, imitating a scale.

"Yeah," I told her. "I'm impressed. You gamble all the time yourself," I said, thinking of her endless fan-tan games and her love of lotteries.

"Gamble with money, sure," she said, shrugging her shoulders to show that was of little consequence. "Horses, cards, dice. Even buy a fighter, yes? All you lose is money. Always get more money."

I knew what she was saying. Hell, any professional thief knows the odds. You measure risk against gain, and take your shot. A B&E in a slum neighborhood is easy—not much chance of the cops' even coming around, much less dusting for prints and all that techno-stuff. Only problem is, the score's going to be low. Try the same stunt on Park Avenue, you raise the chances of being caught—but the take is a lot better if you pull it off. And you don't just look at the score, you look at the penalty too. You stick up a grocery store, you're probably looking at some serious time Upstate. If you're lucky enough to get out of there alive, that is—every self-respecting *bodeguero* has a gun somewhere under the counter. But if you embezzle a million bucks out of some widow's estate, you're probably looking at probation and community service.

You have to pick out the right scores too. If I was going to rob someone in Grand Central Station, I'd stick up a beggar instead of a guy in a business suit. I asked a beggar there for change of a five once, and he pulled out a roll thick enough to choke a boa constrictor. All I'd probably get from the suit would be an ATM card.

"You think there should be more money?" I asked innocently.

"Not enough money for this," Mama said, her tone serious, unrelenting. "This woman is bad. Immaculata, she say that too."

"This is . . . what? Woman's intuition?" I smiled at her.

"This is truth. You do something because you like a woman, it is not wise."

"I wouldn't—"

"You do it before," she interrupted.

I didn't need Mama to remind me. I still hurt for Belle—for what happened to her. My fault, all of it. Mama wouldn't have used such a heavy hammer on me unless she was scared about something.

"Mama, I don't like this girl. That's the truth. I think I'm in a box, and I think she's part of it. There's no way I can hide from her. I have to go down the tunnel, look around for myself."

"Take Max," she suggested.

"Maybe. Maybe later. I have to see first, okay?"

Mama nodded her head, reluctantly agreeing.

When I checked in later, Mama told me I had a message from Belinda. "That woman," Mama called her. It wasn't much of a message—just an address in the Village and a time.

The address Belinda left was on Van Dam, a few blocks south of Houston, just off Sixth Avenue. Ten o'clock, she said. I left my car on Fifth, just north of Washington Square Park, figuring I'd walk the rest of the way.

When I was a kid, I used to come here a lot. By myself. There was always something to see: the chess hustlers on the permanent playing boards, folksingers trying out new stuff, pretty girls walking—gentle, safe stuff. I was so young then that I thought the sun had something to do with it—that all the bad stuff only happened after dark.

Or inside houses.

Even a kid wouldn't believe that anymore. The sun burned fresh-butter bright, but it didn't mellow the shirtless man wearing a heavy winter hat with flapping earmuffs, viciously arguing with a schizophrenic inner voice. And it didn't have any effect on the drug dealers and assorted lurkers. It didn't calm the nervous citizens looking over their shoulders.

An open-top, pus-yellow Suzuki Samurai slowly prowled past, a boom box on wheels, aggressively smashing its hyper-amped sound violence at hapless citizens in a scorched-earth assault. The latest city ugliness—the sonic drive-by.

A long-haired white man in a denim jacket with the sleeves cut off strolled by, pushing one of those metal shopping carts they give you in supermarkets. The homeless love those carts—they pile all kinds of stuff in them and wheel them around the streets. The carts are stainless steel—they don't break easy and they never rust. They're real expensive too, and the supermarkets hate to lose them. In fact, they have a contract with a business that gets a flat rate for every one they recover.

The stroller wasn't homeless, he was a thief. There's a guy works out of a vacant lot off Houston on the East Side—he's got a standing offer to buy all the carts you can bring in.

On MacDougal, the precious-special shops looked depressed, pounded into near-submission by the sidewalk vendors. It was prime-time out there for cruising, but I didn't see many tourists. A man urinated against the side of a building. A woman sat on the curb, picking at her head, her blackened fingernails no match for the lice. Another boom-box Jeep rolled by, this one full of young men all decked out in brand-name gangstah-gear. Even the scavenging pigeons looked more degenerate than usual.

I stopped at a corner, right behind two guys on bicycles. They were pro messengers—you could tell by their gear. Not the Speedo pants or the fingerless gloves or the whistles on cords around their necks. Not even by the crash hats—open-weave padded leather fit-ted tight over their heads. No, what gave them away was the heavy combat chains wrapped around the base of the bicycle seats, always ready. One of them had his chain in his hands, talking urgently to the other.

"Motherfucker tried to *door* me, check it out! I laid it down, but when I come up swinging, pussy decides to bail!"

The other messenger high-fived his endorsement of biker self-defense as I stepped around them to move on. Three black youths approached, spread out in a fan across the sidewalk, blocking the way. One wore a T-shirt with "Back The Fuck UP!" on the chest. Another had a picture of Mike Tyson silk-screened on it, with "I'LL BE BACK!" below. I guess that was a political statement—Tyson gets convicted of raping a young girl and all of a sudden he's Emmett Till.

I gave way to them, stepping into the street, ignoring the sneering hiss one threw in my direction. When I was their age, I wouldn't have stepped aside. I was stupid then, and I paid what stupid people pay.

The sidewalk was clogged, but I wasn't in a hurry. I stopped at a bakery, bought myself a French bread, scooped out the inside and dropped it in an overflowing garbage can, and munched on the crust as I moved along.

On the next corner, a dressed-for-success woman was telling a tall man—her husband? boyfriend?—some miserable story. . . . I could see it in her stance.

"You know, you kind of expect this over in the *East* Village," she said, pointing a finger at a decrepit gray-haired man huddled in a doorway, his pants down around his ankles, calmly dumping a load as people stepped out into the street to avoid him.

"I know," the tall man commiserated. "Just the other—"

"I hate them," the woman interrupted. "The fucking *homeless*. I can't help it. I really *hate* them for what they've done to this city. You can't even use an ATM machine in peace anymore—they're always there, standing around with their hands out, like a pack of filthy doormen."

The dangerous ones, you won't see their hands, I thought to myself. I never considered sharing my professional knowledge with the woman—New York isn't that kind of place.

Once I crossed Houston into Little Italy, it got quieter. I wondered how long that would hold—in this city, there's no border invaders won't cross.

I found the place easy enough. The sign on the door said: RING BELL AND STEP BACK! I knew what that meant, so I wasn't surprised when I saw a second-floor window open and Belinda lean out. "Catch!" she said, tossing down a thick wooden stick with a key attached by a loop of wire.

I used the key to let myself in, then climbed a set of metal stairs to the second floor. Belinda was standing in an open doorway, wearing a baggy T-shirt that fell to mid-thigh. Her hair was lighter than I remembered, reddish highlights dancing in the reflected sunbeams from the window. As I stepped past her to walk inside, she put her lips against my cheek, a butterfly kiss so soft I couldn't be sure it had landed at all.

The place was furnished totally in Now and Today—which, from looking around, I guessed meant Retro. The joint was loaded with reproductions of old junk—a red-and-white Coke machine reprogrammed for diet soda, a Wurlitzer jukebox that spins CDs instead of 45s, and a painting that gave me a headache. I walked over, took a closer look. It was about twice the size of an eight-by-ten, done on white Crescent board. Supposed to be the Seven Dwarfs, near as I could tell, slapped on in a crude, amateur style, all in primary colors, right out of the tube. In the lower right hand corner: POGO in small block letters. I looked over at Belinda.

"An original," she said. "Before they made him stop signing that way."

I nodded, keeping my face expressionless—it wasn't the first time I'd seen Serial Killer Chic proudly displayed by moral midgets. The thrill-killers themselves have a rigid pecking order: if you want to qualify for celebrity status, if you want freakish disciples memorizing your trial transcripts like they were religious tracts, if you want erotic mail and money orders too, it's not enough to have slaughtered a bunch of people, there's other qualifications you have to meet. First, it really helps to have three names, like Westley Alan Dowd or Henry Lee Lucas. Then you need a high body-count—preferably in several states, so you can have serial trials to go with your serial killings. If you can lead the cops to some buried bodies, that's always good for a few more fans. But the most important thing is what John Wayne Gacy lacked—the secret ingredient that rocketed Ted Bundy to high-status serial killer even without a middle name. If you want to be at the top, you've got to kill females, the younger the better. Holding victims captive is a plus. So is torture. But it's all for nothing if you don't do it to females—male-victim snuff films always do lousy box office.

Belinda spread her arms wide, like a rancher showing how much land he had. "This is a perfect place," she said. "All the other lofts are empty—the owner bought them out. He wants to convert the place to condos. This is the last one."

"Very nice," I said, still thinking about the Gacy painting.

She walked over and perched on a big white plastic cube—it must have been stronger than it looked. The only other seat was a leather director's chair, with "Jon" written in embroidered script across the back panel. I took it, settled in, waited.

Belinda leaned forward. "Did you . . . find out anything? I know it's early, but . . ."

"Yeah," I told her. "I found out some stuff. DNA."

"That isn't foolproof," she said so quickly that she must have known. "They only got that in Jersey, right? And the woman on University Place, George *knew* her, I told you. Before it happened, I mean. And there was no sperm in her anyway, remember? Just that red ribbon . . ."

"So he just caught a bad break, right?" I asked. "He had legit sex with her, then some maniac came along and wasted her before she got a chance to leave the apartment?"

"It's not the weirdest thing I've ever seen," she said. "One time, when I was working Vice, I—"

"Yeah. Okay, I got it—people are strange, sure. But here's the part that throws me—the woman on University Place, the other two victims, *none* of them had any sperm in them at all. How does that play with you?"

Belinda got up, started pacing in little circles. I noticed she was barefoot, her feet were tiny, too small for the rest of her. I watched her pace, not saying anything more. She walked over to me. Stopped and made a "come here" gesture. I got up. She put her finger to her lips, held out her hand. I took it, and she gently pulled me along a hall to a back room. A bedroom, it looked like, but only because there was a bed—the rest was all file cabinets and photography equipment.

"This isn't my place," she whispered into my ear. "But Jon lets me use it sometimes, when he's out on assignment. He's a video freak—I think he has the living room wired. There's something I have to tell you, but it's just for you, okay?"

I nodded Okay back, not saying anything.

"You want me to strip?" she asked. "So you can be sure there's no—"

"You're the only one talking," I reminded her.

"You sure you wouldn't want me to anyway?" she asked softly, more promise in her voice than in her eyes.

"Some other time," I said. "When I'm not working." *And when you're not either, bitch,* I thought.

"It's a date," she whispered.

I stepped past her, sat on the bed—there was no other place to sit in the little room. Belinda started her pacing again. Then she stopped, moved very close to me, bent down and whispered, "You don't have to talk. Just nod for Yes or No, okay?"

I nodded Yes.

"You looked at the autopsy reports, didn't you?"

I nodded Yes.

"And you saw . . . there was no sperm in any of the bodies, right? Not the one George went down for, not the ones that got killed after he was inside?"

I nodded Yes.

"So what does that tell you?"

I shrugged my shoulders, spread my hands wide in a "Who knows?" gesture.

"The killer . . . the *real* killer, I think he read the autopsy reports too. On the woman, the one George knew. I think he . . . the killer . . . figured it out. If he left any sperm inside the others, they'd know it wasn't George—the DNA would clear him. The way I figure it, he wore a condom."

I made a "So what?" gesture.

"I think the killer is crazy," she said. "Stark raving mad. And I think he killed those women, stuffed the red ribbons inside them . . . and then pulled them out of the dead bodies himself . . . later."

"When?" I asked her, tired of playing.

"When? What do you mean?" she said.

"I mean, when did he do it? What's so complicated? When would he get the chance?"

"Think about it," she said, no longer whispering.

I did. Inside myself, willing my face to go flat as my mind ripped through the possibilities.

Leaving only one.

"You're saying it's a—"

"Cop," Belinda finished my sentence. "Yes. And I think I know who it is."

I just looked at her—the name wasn't going to come out of my mouth. But I knew. . . .

"Morales," she said. "Detective First Jorge Ortega Morales. He killed the woman on University Place. He killed them all."

I didn't argue with her—what was the point? As soon as she dropped her bombshell, she sat back on top of a two-drawer file cabinet, hugging herself, almost squirming in the embrace. The look on her face—I'd seen it before. In England, just before I went over to Africa and into a stupid war. I saw that same look on the hard face of a woman who called herself Colleen—a woman who planted bombs in department stores. Not for the revolution—that was just her excuse—for the thrill. Colleen always wanted to be *close* to her work—close enough to bask in the fallout.

That was Belinda, the way I saw her then—playing with fire, close enough to feel the heat . . . the only heat that really made her hot.

"Why am I in this?" I asked her. "You got all this stuff, what do you need me for?"

"Don't you understand?" she said, leaning forward, holding my eyes. "This isn't about the truth. If that's all it was, this would be easy—*life* would be easy. The way I figure it, you don't have many choices. Morales wants you. You know it and so do I. He's not the kind of man that'll stop. That's what gives him so much juice—he's insane. Out-of-his-fucking-mind insane. Most cops, they *respect* that. That's his rep—an Officer Down goes out over the box, Morales is gonna be the first one on the scene every single time. And if you're outside a door—a *wood* door—and you know a bad guy's inside—a nothing-to-lose killer—one of those crazy young don't-mind-dying gangbangers, probably got his Tec-9 stuffed with Teflon bullets so even your vest won't save you, okay? Well, Morales, he's going *in,* you can bet on it. He's been shot on the job. Twice. Couple of years ago, he caught a round in the chest taking down a dealer in Washington Heights. And he dropped the shooter . . . just blew him away. He's got more CCRB complaints than anyone working—any detective, anyway—but they keep cutting him slack because he's a cops' cop, you know what I mean?"

"Yeah, I know," I told her. "He may have a screw or two loose, but nothing you said about him makes him into a sex psycho."

"There's more," she said. "You remember McGowan, his old partner? The guy who worked the pimp detail?"

"Sure."

"Well, let me tell you something you *don't* know. McGowan pulled the pin last year. Retired. That was the price."

"The price for what?"

"McGowan always hated pimps—specially the kiddie pimps. You knew that. Everybody knew that. Morales knew it the best of all. Anyway, McGowan got this little girl to talk. Not just to him, to a grand jury. They finally had enough to take out this guy named Remington. You ever hear of him?"

I shook my head No—another lie.

"Okay, anyway, they go to this hotel where Remington was staying. In Times Square. Nobody knows exactly what happened, but Remington took off. He made it down the back stairs, into an alley.

That's where Morales shot him. In the head—he was dead before he hit the ground. And then Morales flaked him. With a throw-down piece—he always carries one. McGowan saw it all—he was standing right there. But he wouldn't testify against his partner. He didn't want to risk his pension either, not after so many years on the job. So he gave it up and went fishing."

"So Morales flaked a bad guy, so what? He's not the first, won't be the last. It don't make him—"

"Just *listen* to yourself," Belinda said. "You know McGowan how many years? A dozen? Twenty? Whatever, a long time, right? You ever know him to flake a perp? Even a live one? No. No you don't. 'Cause he never did it. But Morales, for him, that's a day at the office."

I knew that was true. I even heard Morales once threaten a pimp, *telling* the pimp that's what he was going to do if he didn't give up some information. That's what I was after too, so I told her, "I still don't get it," wanting to listen, not talk.

"The way I heard it, Remington had his hands up in the air," Belinda said, standing up and raising her own hands high enough to show me she wasn't wearing anything under the T-shirt. "Morales just walked up and smoked him. Cold-blooded murder. He put McGowan in a cross. The old man did the right thing—but Morales knows he made his own partner retire, and it's eating him up inside. He was always ready to go over the line—now he *lives* there."

Where I live too, I thought. "It doesn't add up," I said aloud. "Morales, he's a law-and-order freak, right enough—I can see him cutting some corners to make a case. But you got him *doing* the crimes without a—"

"Burke, I'm telling you, he's out of control. He's fucking *nuts.* That's why he's working solo now—nobody'll partner him. And I've got proof. . . ."

"What proof?"

"After the shooting, he saw a shrink. A Department shrink. You have to—that's the rule. They call it a trauma screen—it's just to see if you're dealing with it okay. The shrink made a report. And I got a copy."

"How?"

Belinda ran her tongue over her lips—doing it slow, watching me from under her long eyelashes. Working undercover as a whore must have been a piece of cake for her.

"This report, it says he's the killer?" I asked her. "Is that what you're trying to tell me?"

"Read it for yourself," she said, getting up and walking over to a blue gym bag in the corner. She bent from the waist, held the unnecessary pose an extra beat, letting the T-shirt ride high, still working undercover, until she finally fished out a few sheets of paper. She straightened up and walked back over to me, holding the papers in her hands.

"Here," she said. "Take your time—I've got another copy."

I stuffed the papers in my jacket without looking at them. "I want to talk to him," I said.

"Morales?"

"No. Piersall. I want to talk to him."

"We can do that," she said quickly. "I'm going down to see him on—"

"You, me, and this reporter I know," I told her.

"I don't know. I—"

"There's no 'I don't know' in this," I said. "Either I talk to him—my way, the way I said—or I'll work out the week and keep the cash. You want more, you're gonna have to go the extra mile."

"Let me think about it," she said, calm now. "Can you call me on—?"

"You know where to find me," I told her. "And it's your call. But the clock's running."

The psych report. Rigid, obsessive-compulsive. Superstitious. Guilt-ridden. All black and white, no gray areas. Unmarried. No significant peer relationships.

Q: What if you lost your job?
A: I'd eat my fucking gun.

Calvinistic. Angry. Feels he must keep tight hold on his emotions or he'll crack. Doesn't smoke, drink.

I returned Belinda's call, standing on the corner of Van Dam so I'd see if she went into action right after. She grabbed it on the first ring.

"Hi," is all she said, as if she could see through the telephone.

"You called me," I said.

"It's . . . okay. For the visit, I mean. The way you want it. I don't have a car. I usually rent one to go down there, but—"

"You don't need to do that," I told her. "Just give me your address and we'll pick you up."

"Ah . . . no, that wouldn't work. I'm working a split shift. And Tuesdays are the best for visits—it's not so crowded then. You know the Zero One? On West Broadway, just this side of—"

"I know it," I said. I never heard of anyone calling the First Precinct the Zero One before—something about this woman, always about a half-note off.

"Can you make it around ten in the morning?" she asked. "From there, it's only a little jump into the Tunnel and we can—"

"I'll be there," I said, cutting the connection.

I waited almost two hours—she didn't come out.

"I can drive," Hauser told me. "It would be better, anyway—I got a lot of stuff I use in there, and—"

"I'll meet you on West Fourth. You know, where the basketball court—"

"What time?" he asked.

"Say about nine-forty-five? Tuesday morning. Okay?"

"Yeah. You found out anything yet?"

"Not yet," I lied. "See you then."

Doc scanned the psych report quickly, not even wasting a minute to comment on the blackout surgery I'd performed to convert every mention of Morales' name to a blank space. He snapped a gooseneck lamp into life and held the report in his lap. Doc never looked up. He grunted once in a while, checked off a couple of spots on the paper with a red marker. I blew smoke rings at the ceiling, not interrupting.

"Okay, hoss," he finally said, looking up. "What do you want to know?"

"Could this guy be a sex killer?" I asked.

Doc rubbed the back of his head, his mouth twisted into a grimace. "That's too big a question," he said. "Bottom line? If psychiatry could predict human behavior, the Parole Board wouldn't make so many mistakes."

"Come on," I said. "Don't you guys do that all the time? What's the standard for locking somebody up in Bellevue? Dangerous to self or others, right? How could that be anything but a guess?"

"Sure," he said. "That's the standard. But it's way too broad for what you're asking. You just want to know if this guy's *dangerous*, that's an easy one. Yes. *Hell* yes! He's as tight as a stretched strand of piano wire. He sees the world real clear—black and white, no grays. Violence is part of his personality. It's almost his only means of self-expression, the way an artist paints or a musician plays. He seems to process information differently too."

"What's that mean?"

"The brain's a computer," Doc said. "Data comes in, it gets analyzed—much faster than this," snapping his fingers, "messages go to the body, the body reacts. That's all processing is. This guy," he said, indicating the papers in his lap, "he gets the same data as everybody else, but he comes to different conclusions."

"Meaning he's crazy?"

"Not at all," Doc said, deciding to answer more than I asked, as usual. "Trauma of any kind can cause a processing change, especially if it's early enough. Or severe enough. There's this guy, Bruce Perry, he's down at Baylor, in Texas. He's just starting to publish now, so I can't evaluate his stuff completely yet. But it looks like he can actually document *past* trauma in *current* brain patterns . . . and in a sleep-state, no less. That would revolutionize every treatment modality in the world—there's nothing cultural about brain waves. He pulls that one off—and from what I've seen so far, I'm betting he does—he wins the Nobel Prize, no contest."

"So, what this guy Perry does, it's like a lie detector?" I asked.

"I don't quite follow that, hoss."

"Say somebody is all grown. An adult, okay? Then they all of a sudden remember being abused as a kid. Like a flashback. It happens all the time. And there's the usual crap—How do you prove something like that? What kind of evidence would there be of incest that happened twenty years ago? This guy, Perry? It sounds like he *could* prove it."

Doc rubbed the back of his head again, thinking. I waited. "You know what, Burke? You might just be right. I mean, it wouldn't be *that* easy. . . . You could maybe prove past trauma occurred, but not exactly what it was. But it's a start, sure enough."

"Okay, so this guy Perry's a fucking genius—what's that got to do with *my* man?"

"We already knew some stuff," Doc said, still ignoring my straight questions. "Even after they're grown, abused kids are different. A lot of them *stay* different too. Hyper-vigilant. Distrustful. The prisons are full of people like that, right?"

"Right," I answered, meeting his eyes, knowing who he was talking about.

"It doesn't mean they can't be good citizens, lead normal lives. Even accomplish great things. It's just that they'll always be . . . different."

"So, if this Perry guy could hook my man up to one of his machines, he could tell if there was some significant trauma in his background?" I asked, getting Doc off the track he wanted and back onto mine.

"Sure. But that wouldn't necessarily tell you much. This . . . person, he probably experienced trauma many times in his life. He's a hard man, working in a hard trade. It's not like TV. Most cops, they really can't turn it off and turn it on. They become suspicious. Aggressive, even hostile. It's the best way for them to function on the job. Some of them, they just can't go home, take off the badge and the gun, and turn into Ward Cleaver. The job has so many built-in stressors. What job gives you more broken marriages, more alcoholics? And there's temptations too—it's hard to work for wages when the people you arrest are making millions. There's always easy money lying around if you're a cop. And on top of everything else, you've got Internal Affairs snooping into your life. Dangerous? Hoss, *most* of them are."

"Doc, I appreciate all that. But . . . okay, just tell me this: could my man do it?"

"Sex murders? Yeah. Yeah, he could. His definitions of right and wrong, they could be skewed that bad. He doesn't smoke, doesn't drink. . . . I wonder if he uses foul language—"

"Every other word," I told him.

Doc took a short breath, went on like he hadn't heard me. "His kind of rigid, Calvinistic personality structure could easily lead him into a hatred of what he sees as impure women. And if you combine that with impotence—"

"What makes you think he—?"

"I don't. Necessarily. But you'll notice he doesn't seem to have any regular relationship with a woman. He's thirty-eight years old. Never married."

"Plenty of guys never get married," I said.

He gave me a look. I ignored it. "Here's what *doesn't* fit," Doc said. "There's no iron-clad rule, but when you find a serial killer with this sort of rage against women, they usually target victims who fit their fantasy of 'bad' women, understand? The most likely targets are strippers, topless dancers, prostitutes . . . like that. And, from what you tell me, none of the victims were in the business."

I smoked another cigarette in silence, tracking it through. "Doc," I said. "What if he's gay? Wouldn't that account for it? I mean, if he's gay and doesn't want to deal with it—*can't* deal with it? That'd make him all those things it said in the report, right?"

"Ummm," Doc mused. "It could . . . especially if he believes homosexuality is morally wrong. If he repressed it strongly enough, you'd see the kind of overmacho behavior this guy exhibits. But those types, if they turn to violence, it's almost always against gay men. Still . . ."

"Thanks, Doc," I said, getting up to leave, holding out my hand.

He gave me the psych report. "If there's any way I could talk to him—even for a few minutes—maybe I could . . ."

"We'll see," I lied.

The basketball court on West Fourth is one of the city's major arenas, almost on a par with Rucker Playground uptown. The freelance guys who work the top courts are as professional as any in the NBA—when it comes to the city game, maybe better. The city game is all about styling and profiling. Flash is the hallmark, but they still count the points at the end . . . where heavy money always changes hands.

Some of the playground names are still legend—Helicopter, Connie, The Goat—their feats magnified by time. I know a guy who claims he once saw The Goat soar above the rim, jam one down with his right hand, catch it coming out the bottom of the net with his left, and slam it home again with *that* hand before he touched down.

The city game is way past rough—anytime they call a foul, they call the paramedics too. Once I was watching a football game on cable—Australian Rules, the announcer said. None of the players wore helmets or pads, but they threw themselves at each other like they were armor-plated. An Aussie was in the same bar, and we struck up a conversation. He was in town to do a deal with someone—it was that kind of joint. He tried to explain the action to me, but I wasn't following all of it. I saw one player use a judo move to throw an opponent to the ground, then dive on him head-first. I could almost hear the ribs crack. "What do they have to do to have a foul called?" I asked the Aussie.

He thought about it for a moment, obviously puzzled. Then he said, "Well, if they were to use a weapon . . ."

That hour of the morning, the court was being used by stay-in-shape amateurs. The game was so weak there was no betting going on. I leaned my back against the chain-link fence, looking down Sixth Avenue, waiting for Hauser. I heard a double-honk of a horn, looked at the source and saw a window going down in an electric-blue Ford Explorer four-by. Hauser's face showed in the window. I walked over, got into the passenger seat. He hit the gas and lurched out into traffic.

"Very subtle ride you got here," I said.

"Yeah!" Hauser replied, taking it as a compliment. "And the boys really love it."

"Take the next right," I told him, then gave him directions to where Belinda would be waiting.

"Check this out," Hauser said, his face animated as he pushed the eject button on his radio. A cassette tape popped into view, still in the slot. I thought he was going to put in a new one, make me listen to some lame music, but he just left it there.

"What's it supposed to do?" I asked him.

Hauser grinned, pushed a button on the radio. No music came out. He waited a couple of seconds, then pushed another. "What's it supposed to do?" came out of the speakers. In my voice.

"The whole truck is wired," he said. "I've got other stuff too. Even a minicam in the back. I could sit back there for hours. I can see out, but nobody can see in. It's just perfect for surveillance."

"What if somebody wants to listen to the radio?" I asked him.

"As long as the tape cassette is in the slot, it works," Hauser said. "I can *play* the tapes too—all I have to do is push it in."

"This must have cost a fortune," I said.

"Not so much," he said, a slightly defensive tone in his voice.

"It's awesome," I assured him.

"It's great in bad weather too," he said, still not satisfied.

"I sure wish I had one," I said. That seemed to calm him down. Which was a good thing. I quickly discovered Hauser wasn't one of those guys who could talk and drive at the same time—he almost splattered a pedestrian because he was so busy talking. Apparently, he couldn't talk without making eye contact. I made up my mind to ride in the back seat on the way to Jersey.

Belinda was right in front of the precinct. She was wearing jeans tucked into mid-calf black boots, her upper body covered in a white turtleneck, a jacket over one shoulder. When we pulled up, I got out, opened the passenger door for her. She climbed inside, and I slid into the back seat.

"Belinda Roberts, J. P. Hauser," I said by way of introduction.

"I'm pleased to meet you," Belinda said.

"Same here," Hauser said, turning to face her, holding out his right hand for her to shake. Belinda started to reach for his hand, then gasped as Hauser just missed crunching a taxicab at the intersection.

"Take the Tunnel," I said to Hauser. "Then we want the Turnpike south."

In the Tunnel, Hauser and Belinda got to talking about courthouse personnel: judges, clerks, court officers, ADAs. "Moltino's a major asshole," Hauser said.

"Big-time," Belinda agreed.

I put my feet up on the big back seat, leaned back, closed my eyes.

My eyes flickered open as Hauser was pulling off to the side of the road. I could feel the trooper somewhere behind us. "Fuck!" Hauser said. "That's just what I need—*another* goddamn ticket."

I looked back over my shoulder out of the corner of my eye. The trooper was Central Casting: tall, square-jawed, his Mountie hat canted at just the right angle. He walked around to the driver's window—Hauser already had it down.

"Sir, you were clocked at—"

"It's my fault, officer," Belinda said, leaning across Hauser, arching her back so she could look up into the trooper's eyes. Or to show him how eager her breasts were to bust out of the white turtleneck. "I'm on the job," she said. "Going down to the state prison to interview a witness." She pulled a thick leather wallet out of her jacket, handed it over.

The trooper flipped it open, saw the badge, gave Belinda a sharp look.

"Call it in," she said, flashing a dazzling smile. "It's not my boyfriend's badge, it's mine. I don't even *have* a boyfriend," she said in that pouty little-girl tone I'd heard her use before.

"May I see your license and registration, sir?" the trooper said to Hauser.

He took it all back to his cruiser. A few minutes passed. He walked back over. "Sir, you were clocked at seventy miles per hour. Since you have no prior record, it is our policy to issue a warning at this time. Please drive more carefully in the future."

"Thank *you*," Hauser said fervently.

The trooper leaned into the window a bit, handed Belinda's wallet back to her. Then he straightened up, threw a half-salute and went back to his cruiser.

As Hauser pulled away, Belinda snapped open her wallet. A white business card popped out. She put the card in another jacket pocket, cranked her seat way back so she was almost reclining, looking up at me.

"Nice work," I told her.

"Well, you can usually tin a Jersey cop," she said, smiling. "We'd do the same for them on a traffic thing."

"I don't think it was the badge that did it," I told her.

"What else *could* it be?" She smiled again, taking a deep breath.

We got off the Turnpike at Exit 8A. Belinda directed Hauser from there. I knew a faster way, but I didn't say anything.

You almost never see prisons in the middle of cities. Jails, maybe, but prisons, they always want them out in the sticks. But Trenton State Prison is so old that it was there first—they had to build the city around it. We turned off Federal Street into the visitors' parking lot. Hauser looked at the dark monster looming above us: endless stone walls aged into a single definitionless mass, a filthy gray-black slab. "It's right out of a movie," he said. "A fucking horror movie."

Belinda went up to the window first, leaned in to talk to the guard. When she motioned to us, Hauser and I went over too. We each showed ID—Hauser his press pass, me my phony bar card: Juan Rodriguez, Abogado.

"I told them you were George's lawyer," Belinda whispered. "And that J.P. was covering the case. This way, we get a contact visit."

"What's that?" Hauser asked her.

"If you're not an attorney, or a cop, or whatever—if you're just family or friends—then the visit is over the phone. Not a telephone, just a receiver you pick up on one side of the glass. The guy you're visiting does the same. A contact visit is when you can touch—no barriers."

"Piersall. George Piersall," the speaker squawked.

"That's us," Belinda said, standing up to lead the way.

The place was chambered, like the hatches in a submarine. As we walked through each set of doors, they closed behind us before the next one opened. The guard in the first chamber ran over our bodies with a hand scanner. It beeped for keys, the metal clip on ballpoint pens . . . anything. Hauser took out one of those giant Swiss Army knives, the red ones with enough attachments to build a house from scratch. The guard shook his head, gave Hauser a look. Hauser stared back blankly until the guard dropped his eyes. "You get this back on your way out," he muttered.

The next chamber had a metal detector we had to walk through. Then a guard led us around to the conference room. Most of the room was taken up by a long table with a wooden divider running lengthwise: attorneys on one side, clients on the other. There were also a few smaller tables scattered around, the space between them the only privacy permitted.

"There's a better room, for lawyers," Belinda said. "They let cops use it too. But I didn't want to try and talk them into letting the three of us in."

"This'll do fine," I said, casing the room. Over in the corner, a muscular black man in a blinding-white T-shirt was huddled forward, talking to another black man in a business suit. The muscular black man looked up. His eyes passed over my face like it was a blank wall.

"Hey!" A man's deep voice, greeting someone. It was Piersall, spotting Belinda. He walked over so slowly it was just this side of a swagger, a blond man with a neat haircut. His eyes were dishwater blue, set close together, his nose almost too small for his face. He smiled at all of us—his teeth were either all capped or factory-perfect. I made him at around six feet, maybe an inch over. About a hundred eighty-five pounds, most of it in the upper body. A good-looking, confident man—I could see a woman leaving a bar with him *way* before closing time.

He sat down, pulled a pack of smokes from the breast pocket of his prison-issue short-sleeved green shirt. He put the cigarette pack on the table, then he turned to Hauser, extended his hand.

"I'm George Piersall. You must be the reporter, right?"

"J. P. Hauser," Hauser acknowledged, shaking hands.

"And you?" Piersall asked, shifting his eyes to me. "You're with Fortunato?"

"Juan Rodriguez," I said. "At your service."

"Where do we start?" Piersall asked.

"You're not contesting the Jersey conviction?" Hauser replied, setting the table.

"No. Not actually. I mean, it wasn't at all like they said in the indictment, but the plea offer was so good I just couldn't pass it up. I don't care about this one—I'll be going out on it quick enough. The thing is, they already dropped a detainer on me. Instead of parole, they'll just load me into a van to start another bit."

"The woman in New York?" Hauser asked. "The one on University Place? You said you—"

"Doris," Piersall interrupted. "Her name was Doris."

"Okay, Doris," Hauser agreed. "You said you . . . knew her. Before it . . . happened?"

"I did. I mean, not like we were friends or anything. I met her in a bar. We got to talking. And we went back to her place. After that, I called her a couple of times, or she'd call me. If neither of us was busy, we'd get together. You know, no big deal . . . But I *liked* her, you know what I'm saying? She was a nice kid—no reason for anyone to get rough with her."

"You think that's what happened?" I asked him, leaning in to catch his eye. "Somebody played too rough?"

"It could be," Piersall said quietly, staying right on my face. "She liked to play a little hard. Not over-the-top stuff, you know . . ."

"Spell it out," I said.

"Just little games. A slap in the face, grab her by the shoulders, hold her hands down while we did it. That's all."

"Somebody spotted you leaving . . . the night she was killed?" Hauser asked.

"Yeah. I'm not denying that. But even the autopsy report said she could of been murdered anytime—from just before I left to almost twenty-four hours later."

"Any possibility she was married? Or had a jealous boyfriend?" I asked him.

"Who knows?" He shrugged. "A girl like that, picking up guys in bars—it was probably just a matter of time anyway."

"So you figure she asked for it?" Hauser put in, the faintest undertone to his voice.

Piersall caught the undertone. Recognized it and batted it back over the net in one smooth move. "Not . . . *that*," he said, "God forbid," ducking his head slightly, like a man trying for composure. "I mean, she was asking for trouble, okay?" he said. "Not to be *killed*. What I was trying to say, she was taking some risks, see?"

"So what it comes down to," I said, "is you didn't do it. That's no help. You got anything else?"

"No," Piersall said, his face open and frank. "I wish I did. What we have to do, we have to find the guy who *did* do it—that's my only hope."

"We'll find him, George," Belinda said, her voice calm and certain.

"I know, baby," Piersall told her, reaching for her hand, squeezing it for a second. He leaned back in his chair, finally lit the cigarette he'd had in front of him since we started talking.

"This is too crowded," I said, standing up. "With all of us pumping questions at you, we're not gonna get anywhere."

"I can—" Belinda started to say.

"No, it's okay. You and J.P. run through it. I'll step out for a while. I got some paperwork to look over anyway."

"Good to have met you," Piersall said, standing up to shake hands.

"Likewise," I told him.

"**K**amau Rhodes," the loudspeaker barked. I walked over to the side room marked VISITORS.

"Got more than one client in here, huh, counselor?" a fat guard commented.

"It's a living," I said.

I walked into a long, narrow room, sat down on a round stool bolted to the floor, and looked into the murky Plexiglas, its surface smudged beyond redemption by generations of handprints—the only way to say hello or goodbye in that room, hands touching each other's through the barrier. I picked up the phone on my side of the barrier. Across from me was the muscular black man who'd been in the Contact Visit Room. We stared at each other for a long minute.

"Dragon," I said.

"Burke," he replied.

A long minute passed.

"I got your kite," he finally said. "Was that him?"

"Yeah," I said. "What's the word?"

"He's in PC," the black man said. "Been there for almost a week."

"He selling tickets?"

"No."

"Turn rat?"

"No. It wasn't like that. He's not pussy either—it wasn't a voluntary."

"Tell me."

"Somebody tried to take him out. A hammer job, with a shank for backup. His luck was running good—four cops were just rolling down the corridor—routine surprise shakedown—they saw it happening. All your guy got was a knot on his head."

"They pop anyone for it?"

"No. They were pros—hoods and gloves, long sleeves. Half a dozen other guys got between them and the cops—they got clean away."

"So why'd they lock Piersall up? Was it a race thing?"

"No. And it wasn't about a debt or a diss—it was a stone-cold paid-for hit. Word is, the RB was on the job."

RB. The Real Brotherhood. A white warrior gang with branches in max joints all over the country. Like the black and Latino gangs, all race did was get you in the door—what kept you there was performance. Some of them would stab you for stepping onto the wrong part of the yard, but most of them were businessmen—it would take something important to get them homicidal. Something like the prison drug concession, or a piece of the sports book. They also did debt collection and contract-kill work—inside the walls, there isn't much difference.

The RB is small, so it has to play very hard to get respect. It only takes a few seconds to kill a man, but a reputation is forever. If they took money to drop Piersall, they'd get it done, no matter how long it took.

I knew them. Some of them, anyway. If the prison administration doped it out the same way Kamau was telling me, they'd keep-lock Piersall until he was discharged.

"You got anything else?" I asked him.

"He don't mix much. Kind of standoffish. He don't play an attitude, but he don't back down either. He's short, anyway, from what I hear."

"Short here," I told him. "A full-book detainer's waiting on him, though."

"Oh. He don't act much like that. Walks soft—like he don't want to blow his go-home."

"Okay. You sure he wasn't messing with the RB?"

"Dead sure. That happens, they leave word all over the blocks . . . so when they take him out it's a message. Wasn't nothing like that this time. He was just strolling the block when they jumped him."

"He's got money on the books," I said. "Can't you still buy—?"

"Not from the RB," he said. "There ain't enough money in here to bodyguard a man on their hit parade. There's no win—they'd never forget. Your man's gotta stay in lock-down until his hearing. If the RB's got a contract out on him, he can't walk the yard anyway. I don't like his chances, even in PC. You know how that works."

I did. "Protective Custody" is a joke—a little plastic squeeze-bottle full of cleaning fluid, a match . . . and nobody hears the screams. He still had to eat, too. And they let them out an hour a day for exercise. All of them at once.

"Thanks," I said. "Anything I can do for you?"

"Tell the Prof I send my respects," the black man said.

Back outside, in the waiting room, I left a hundred dollars on the books for Dragon. The guard gave me a look. I gave him one back—anything else would have made him suspicious.

In another few minutes, Hauser ambled out. He spotted me, sat down on the bench.

"I think—"

"How'd you get Press plates on that truck?" I interrupted, not wanting him to do any talking there. "I thought they never gave them out to freelancers."

"I'm a reporter, just like anyone else," Hauser replied, his jaw set. "That stuff is blatant discrimination. Took me a few appeals, but they finally gave it up."

"Right on," I said.

He searched my face for sarcasm, didn't find any. Said "Yeah!" under his breath, still pumped from the memory of that battle.

It was another half-hour or so before Belinda came out, her face tight and determined. I caught her eye. She came over to us. We all walked out together.

Everyone was silent with their own thoughts until we got back on the Turnpike. Belinda took off her seat belt, shifted her body so she was facing sideways. "Did you understand what George was saying?" she asked, directing the question at Hauser, turning just enough so she was including me in the answer.

"About what?" Hauser replied.

"About serial killers. Like George said, the one thing you have plenty of time to do in there is read."

"I've read that stuff too," Hauser said. "It sounds like a motley collection of guesswork."

"But what about the part . . . where he said the killer would have to keep doing it?"

"Even if that *is* right, how's that going to help?" Hauser asked her. "According to you, the police *already* know there's a maniac out there. And they haven't charged Piersall with any of the crimes."

"That's just the point," she said. "They know if they charged him they'd look stupid. What better alibi could a man have than to be in prison when it happened?"

"And it's not a copycat either," Hauser said. "There was nothing in the papers about that 'signature' thing. *Nothing.*"

"But *you* know about it," Belinda said. "And once you print it, the pressure's gonna be on."

"I *don't* know about it," Hauser said. "Don't get me wrong—I'm not saying it wasn't like that. But I can't print a rumor—that's for guys with their own columns. Or the ones who take pipe jobs from friendly cops. I'm going to poke around on my own, see if I can find someone to corroborate your information."

"But you're gonna stay on it . . . ?"

"To the end," Hauser promised.

"What about you?" Belinda asked, looking right at me.

"Till the end of the week," I said. "Like we agreed."

Belinda wanted to be dropped off at the courthouse on Centre Street. We did that, then headed uptown.

"Something's real wrong," Hauser said suddenly.

"Pull over somewhere," I told him, seeing how tense he was, not wanting to wait to hear it.

Hauser found a spot just past Canal. He docked the four-by in one sweet smooth sweep. Parallel parking in a rig like that was no easy feat—I guess he could drive good enough when he wasn't talking.

I hit my window switch, lit a smoke. "Go," I said.

"I think she's involved with him," Hauser said. "I think it's personal."

"Because . . . ?"

"Just little things, at first. The way she looked at him, certain things they said . . . like it was a coded language. And she wanted some time alone, at the end."

"So?"

"So I hung around. They went into the Conference Room—the one she was telling us about, for lawyers."

"And . . . ?"

"And I got to talking with one of the guards. About this profile of corrections officers I'm planning to do for *People* magazine."

"That's a nice assignment," I said.

"Yeah." Hauser smiled. "Wish I had it. Anyway, I got a nice look inside that Conference Room. There was only the two of them in there . . . and they were going at it pretty hot and heavy."

"Hot and heavy—that means different things to different folks. Maybe they were just kissing goodbye."

"They were kissing all right," Hauser said. "And her hand was inside his pants. Somebody paid the guard. . . . At least that's the way it looked. The one who let me take a look—he knew what I was going to see."

"There's a couple of ways that scans," I told him. "Maybe she started out working, then got herself all excited. Serial killers turn some women's cranks. Most of those freaks get more fan mail than rock stars. Ted Bundy, he got married on Death Row. Even that slime, the one who tortured kids to death out in Washington State, he had some women all worked up. You see it all the time—prison bars make some people hot. Cops fall for a suspect, guards risk their jobs for a prisoner. It happens."

"And the other way is . . . ?" Hauser asked.

"That she knew him before, on the quiet."

"Either way—"

"Yeah," I interrupted. "Either way, she could be the one."

"Doing the . . . *killings*?"

"It wouldn't be a first," I told him. "Remember that guy Bianchi? He was half of a team—the Hillside Strangler, right? Wasn't there some crazy woman who tried a copycat murder to spring him?"

"Jesus."

"Yeah. Jesus. Me, I don't know. But it adds up, right? What do you think?"

"I think it's still a great story," Hauser said, his mouth set in a grim flat line.

"There's another player in the game," I told him. "When you get time, look through this." I handed him the copy of Morales' psych report.

He scanned it quickly. "This is . . . ?"

"The cop who's been dogging my steps ever since I got on this one."

"You think . . . ?"

"Read it for yourself," I told him, opening the door to get out.

W hen I called in late that afternoon, Mama told me Fortunato was looking for me. I didn't bother with telephones—it was easier to go over there. I grabbed the subway at Canal. My legendary luck held—a derelict was planted in one corner of the car I boarded, doing a great imitation of a time-release stench bomb. Every time he shifted position, a new wave of sickening odors wafted over everybody else. Everybody changed cars at the next stop, preferring the cattle-car crowding to the alternative. I went them one better—I changed trains.

Waiting for the F train at the West Fourth Street station is a group activity around rush hour. I drifted down toward the end of the platform, figuring I'd get a newspaper. The newsstand had a vast collection of porno magazines on display behind some yellowing Plexiglas. I looked them over, thinking that maybe Vyra was right. The magazines weren't about women at all, they were about body parts—*Juggs, Big Butt, Gash*—reminded me of those charts of cows they have in butcher shops, the ones with dotted lines separating brisket from tenderloin.

Because I didn't give a damn how long I waited, the F train rolled through smoothly, precisely on time, dropping me off at Forty-second and Sixth. I spent the ride admiring a new look—a black man with a perfectly sculpted short natural was wearing a robin's-egg blue tuxedo jacket over a pleated-front white shirt and knife-edged jeans, but that wasn't what was attracting all the attention. Instead of laces, his gleaming black shoes were held together by a row of gold collar bars—he just threaded them through the eyelets and screwed on each individual cap. Half a dozen teenagers were scoping the man's style. By tonight, avant-garde would be five minutes ago.

I climbed out of the subway and walked over to Fortunato's office, still taking my time. The receptionist took my name, picked up the phone, and buzzed me in a few seconds later.

Fortunato was at his big desk, a cigar already in his hand. I walked in, sat down. "You're looking for me?" I said.

"Yes. I wanted to . . . straighten some things out. Between us, I mean."

"What things?"

"Look, you may have gotten the wrong impression from our last conversation. Or I may have spoken out of turn. If I did . . . or if you took it that way, I apologize. I just wanted you to know that Julio always spoke highly of you. And when I said we knew who . . . was responsible for his death, I was speaking generically."

"What's that mean?" I asked, playing my role.

"It means we know where it came from, that's all. The direction it came from, not the actual person. And that's old business. Old, *finished* business. Are you following me?"

"I don't follow people unless I get paid," I told him. "And I don't like them following me."

He took a puff on his cigar. His hand was shaking, just a shade past a tremor, but easy enough to see—if you were looking for it. "I'd like you to stay on the case," he said. "George likes you. I do too. You've only got friends here, understand?"

"Uh-huh."

"What do you say to two more weeks, same rate?" Fortunato asked. "No reports, no checking in . . . just nose around, see what you can find out. Do we have a deal?"

"When I get paid," I told him.

S oon as I saw his shadow, I knew I was in the wrong part of town—I'd never make it back across the border in time for a call to Mama to do me any good. I cut south on Park, working my way east, hoping to pick up the IRT local, give me a few options with each new station. I never got there—Morales caught up with me on Fortieth, wrapping a thick arm around my shoulders, chesting me into a parking lot, against the wall. His face was all blotchy, red and white—his eyes were swirling. I could hardly hear him talking through clenched teeth.

"You're in the big time now, huh, cocksucker?" he snarled, his face right in mine.

"What?"

"Don't you fuck me around!" he said, ready-to-snap tight. "Don't you play with me. Push me, just keep pushing me, I'll take your heart! Understand me? Got that fucking straight now?"

"Say what you got to say," I told him, as calm as he was crazed, the way you gentle your voice when a dog growls at you—a big dog, off-leash.

He nostriled a deep breath, mouth not moving. "Now you work for Raymond Fortunato, huh? You playing with gangsters, punk? Or, maybe, you're working on a special case? Am I getting close?"

"You'll never be close, Morales. For that, you'd have to have a clue."

"Oh, I got a clue all right, pussy. I got more than one. I know who hired you. And I know what for. Here's a free one—on the house. Walk away. Walk away fast, and don't look back, understand? You ain't a real player, Burke—you're just a fucking poker chip. Not even a blue one. Me, I'm gonna sweep the fucking table, see? *Everything* goes. You stay in it, you go too."

"I don't know what you're talking about," I said quietly. "You're spooking at shadows. Maybe you oughta see a shrink."

I thought that last crack had done it. His eyes narrowed down so far I could only see a little piece of liquid in the folds of the sockets. A thick, violent vein pulsed in his neck. I could hear his teeth grind. Saw his right hand twitch, clenching and unclenching. I knew his pistol was close—I could feel how bad he wanted it.

A long three seconds passed. His hand came up so fast I didn't see it, an open-handed slap to the left side of my face. It rocked me—my hands came up on their own. Morales stepped back, an ugly smile on his face. "Come on, *chiquita*," he whispered. "Make it easy."

I dropped my hands.

"*Maricón*," he sneered. "I knew you was nothing but a no-balls cocksucking fucking faggot piece of shit."

I just watched him, back inside myself again. Back inside, where nobody could hurt me. I was good at it by now—I'd had plenty of practice when I was a kid.

I held Morales' glare, breathing shallow through my nose, calming myself in case he came at me again. If he did, I'd take it.

He hawked up a thick glob, spit it at my feet. Then he grabbed at his crotch, said "Pussy!" one more time and walked away.

I went down to Jersey to see Frankie fight that Friday—I got a ride down with Hauser.

"I didn't know you were interested in prizefighting," I said when he first mentioned it.

"I got to go down in that area anyway," he said mysteriously. "If you're sure you can get back on your own, no problem."

On the drive down, Hauser was uncharacteristically silent, not even rising to the bait when I tried to get him to speculate about Belinda.

I left the side window open, smoked in silence. We passed right by the Trenton exit, but it wasn't close enough to feel the heat.

We picked up the tickets the Prof had left at the door, found our seats just past the Golden Circle, where chumps get to sit at little tables and get called "sir" by the hostess the same way they do in the casinos.

Frankie was first on the card. I told Hauser I'd be right back, then I walked around to the locker room. Frankie was lying down on a table, face-up, a towel over his eyes. The Prof was talking a mile a minute. Clarence sat quietly on a bench.

"When he walks away, he's gotta pay, understand?" the Prof said. "Take what he gives you. He plays that way, break his back, Jack!"

"What's that all about?" I asked Clarence.

"This guy we are going to fight, he is very cute, mahn. He has this trick he used all the time in the amateurs. What he does, when it gets tough, he just turns his back and walks away. . . . Then he *spins* and throws a right hand over his left shoulder. He has hurt many fighters with that move. My father, he wants our gladiator to *chase* him, stay very close, see?"

"Yeah. Frankie's in good shape? His mind is right?"

"His spirit is strong, mahn."

I walked out, leaving all three of them in the same positions as when I came in: Frankie lying back, the Prof whispering his incantations, Clarence watching. And watchful.

It was another forty minutes before they got it on. Frankie came into the ring first, wearing his black-and-white convict's stripes. He stood still, waiting, but I could see he'd already broken a good sweat. The Cuban's corner made Frankie wait, but they couldn't drag it out too long—Montez may have been undefeated, but he wasn't ranked—didn't even hold one of those cheesy belts they give out for showing up enough times in some states.

When he climbed through the ropes I could see he was much bigger than Frankie, looking even bigger in a white satin robe with glitter dust on the wide lapels. The announcer called out his weight at two twenty-nine, but he looked fifteen over that to me.

At the bell, Frankie came out faster than he had before, almost at a trot. He bounced into a crouch, came up firing with the right hand. Montez spun, catching it on the bicep. He stepped to the side, smoked a fast left jab a couple of times, then backed off. Frankie pursued, like he always did, but he was moving sharper now, more focused. He pinned the Cuban against the ropes, but the bigger man clinched and the ref took his time breaking them.

They got back together in the center of the ring, and Frankie went right back to work, throwing murderous hooks, his hips torquing every blow. Montez suddenly stopped, turned and just walked away. . . . Frankie charged after him, throwing a long right that caught the Cuban in the back of his head. Montez put both hands on his head and tried walking away again—Frankie rammed a vicious shot to his liver, and Montez went down. Some of the spectators booed and hissed, but the ref started the count.

Montez never got up.

The ref raised Frankie's hand. Two of the Cuban's handlers jumped into the ring and started for Frankie. . . . Frankie whirled to face them, a ghastly smile on his face. They stopped in their tracks.

"That's why it says Protect Yourself at All Times," the ref said to the Cuban's corner, loud enough for everyone to hear. "He turns his back, it's on him. There's no disqualification."

The crowd boiled a little bit, then simmered down.

"It's all right to do that? Hit someone in the back?" Hauser asked me.

"If they *turn* their back, sure. Otherwise, you could buy a breather anytime you wanted one . . . like calling a time-out."

"Okay," Hauser said, whatever sense of morality he had about the whole thing appeased. "I'm going to take off now—I'll get in touch with you in a couple of days. You know where to reach me if anything jumps."

"Same here," I said, signing off.

When I went back to the lockers, Frankie was already in the showers. I didn't see the guy he KO'ed anywhere around. That was good—sometimes boxers don't want to leave the fight in the ring.

"We smoked the dope," the Prof crowed. "We downed the clown. We got one, maybe two more to do, then we *ride*, Clyde."

"He looked good," I acknowledged. "Seems like he's faster too. Or sharper, maybe."

"It's all *focus*," the Prof confided. "Frankie's on the case, Ace. He's gonna play that tune straight to the moon, I can feel it."

"Me too," I said.

"What's wrong, schoolboy?"

"Who said—?"

"You don't need to *say* nothing, Burke—I can read your cards like they face-up."

I took a deep breath. Let it out. Spun it a couple of times in my mind. Then I said, "Here's what I know . . . so far," and told him the truth.

The ride back to the city was relaxed. Almost sweet with certainty, with triumphs assured. A future for Frankie . . . maybe one for us too. The Rover hummed through the night, Clarence at the wheel, the Prof riding shotgun. I was in the back with Frankie.

"I wish it would never be over," Frankie said.

"Tonight?" I asked him.

"Not *that* fight. I mean, not any particular fight. Just . . . fighting. I feel . . . right doing it. Like it's what I'm supposed to do."

"You can't fight forever," I told him. "You stay too long at the fair, you know what happens."

"Schoolboy's right," the Prof said, leaning over the back of the bucket seat. "This is about money, honey. We get the green, then we split the scene."

"I . . . guess so," the kid said. "I suppose I don't need to worry about it until the time comes, right?"

"Right," I assured him.

Saturday morning, I got up early. It was still dark out when I loaded Pansy into the Plymouth, figuring I'd give her a chance to run around a bit. I had plenty of time stretching out ahead of me—I was happy enough to take Fortunato's money, Piersall's actually, I supposed—but I wasn't going to *do* anything for it.

"Walk away," Morales had told me, so crazy-wild with rage that I couldn't even ask him what he meant.

But when the Prof weighed in on the same side, I knew it was the right one. "Some mysteries don't need solving, schoolboy," he said. "If the price is too high, just roll on by—with that stone-crazy motherfucker Morales in it, *somebody's* gonna die."

That's the thing about dynamite—once you got it lit, you better throw it away . . . fast.

I drove in a gentle, leisurely loop, checking the mirrors for tags, not surprised to find them empty. I went east on Houston, then south on Forsyth. I spotted a glowing dot of red. Refocusing, I could make out a pair of young men on one of the stoops. Very alert young men, sending off a signal as clear as a neon street sign flashing in the night—Keep Moving.

I drove the length of Allen Street. A hooker in black hot pants and yellow spike heels stepped off the curve, stuck her thumb in her mouth, and shot a hip at me in a halfhearted attempt to make one more score before it got daylight. At least a half-dozen working girls had been taken off that same block. Got into cars, got dropped off in the river. Streetside hooking, it's like playing roulette, with only the double zero paying off—the reason you don't see too many old hookers isn't because they lose their looks.

An old Chinese woman crossed in front of us at a light, a long pole across her shoulders with a bag suspended from each end. Like the yoke her ancestors had probably used in the fields—only this one helped her carry two giant clear plastic bags full of abandoned bottles. She was heading for the recycling center, where she could turn her harvest into cash.

I looked to my left. The cement railing next to me was topped with a line of wine bottles, carefully arranged like a menorah with the sacred Night Train as the center candle. The old woman passed them by without a glance—those bottles weren't any more recyclable than the losers who left them there.

Central Park had more room, but there had just been another bunch of rapes there. At that hour, it would be lousy with cops. Or should be, anyway. Besides, Pansy was a perimeter dog—she never ran far, even off the leash.

I took a left on Delancey, then cut left again on Chrystie, heading for this vacant lot next to the Manhattan Bridge. It used to be a hobo jungle, home to the homeless. A pair of activists had even pitched a big tepee there and lived in it—walking the walk, you had to give them that. But then some low-level drug dealer thought he'd been burned by one of the homeless guys. He came back at night with a few gallons of gas, did some burning of his own. One of the residents died. The city tore everything down, then bulldozed it. The evacuation was peaceful—the only way the cops would shoot to kill would be if the homeless occupied the stadium where they held the U.S. Open—sacred ground to our last pitiful excuse for a mayor. We got a new mayor now. The city's the same.

I parked on Chrystie and climbed out. Ahead was a stop sign. The only way you could turn was right—to the left was a one-way discharge road for traffic exiting the Manhattan Bridge. A good spot—perfect sight-lines in all directions. I snapped the lead on Pansy's collar and crossed Canal Street to the vacant lot. Pansy's huge head whipped back and forth, a low rumble came from somewhere inside of her.

"What's wrong with you?" I asked her.

She just growled some more. Looking down, I could see the fur standing up at the back of her neck. I swept the street with my eyes. It wasn't empty—it never is—but there wasn't anything spooky around.

Once we got across the street, I unsnapped Pansy's lead. She loped away from me, moving in wide figure-eight loops, checking out the territory. Legend has it that Neapolitan mastiffs came over the Alps with Hannibal—if they were all as clumsy as Pansy, I'm surprised they didn't flatten the mountains. She crashed through piles of litter with abandon, occasionally scaring up a rat. She wasn't fast enough to catch one, and none of them were stupid enough to hang around, so every bout ended in a draw.

I leaned against what was left of a metal railing, lit a smoke, watching the morning light break over the top of the tenements to the east. Pansy appeared and disappeared over and over again in the shadows, her dark-gray coat blending perfectly. I heard the motor-cycle before I saw it, the unmistakable sound of a Harley backing off through its pipes. The rider didn't even slow at the stop sign, just downshifted and turned left, going against one-way traffic, heading right for me. The driver's head was covered with a dark helmet and full face shield, but I knew who it was.

Morales pulled up to the curb. Sat on his bike watching me through the face shield for a long minute before he turned off the engine. He climbed off the bike slowly, pulled the helmet off his head with both hands. He kept those hands empty as he closed the ground between us, moving with the confidence of a man who could handle anything he was likely to run across. Which told me one thing for sure—he hadn't seen Pansy.

But I had. The big dog started to amble over to me. I threw her the hand signal for "Stay"—she stopped dead in her tracks, rooted and alert.

I turned to face him, keeping my hands well away from my body. He came closer, pulling down the front zipper of his leather jacket, taking his time.

"What?" I asked, opening my hands wide in the sign language for that question.

He halted a few feet away from me, grabbed his left wrist with his right hand, spread his legs wide to brace himself. "You're slicker than I thought," he said, his voice strangely calm.

So are you, I thought—tailing me on a motorcycle was smarter than I gave him credit for. "I can't keep doing this," I told him aloud. "Guessing what you're talking about every time."

"That's okay, punk," he said. "I'll do the math for you. I can't be in two places at once, you already figured that out for yourself. And you know I'm working solo too, right? You're a slippery sonofabitch, I'll give you that. You know I'm on you, so you use me for an alibi. I had the roles reversed—I guess you knew that too. I thought you were doing the work. Now I know better."

"You don't know *anything* better, Morales. Why don't you just lay it out, give me a chance to set you straight?"

"I'm already straight," he said, still relaxed. "It took me a while to put it together, but now I got it. And I'm gonna leave you on the street until I finish it. Leave you out here, dangling in the wind. Either you're running this whole thing or else you're just a tool. Don't matter to me—anytime I want, you're going down."

"You're out of control," I told him. "I don't know what you got your nose open about, but it isn't me. I'm not in it."

"It's gonna be real easy," he said. "Anytime I want. Just find you alone—like now. You wouldn't be the first ex-con who resisted arrest."

I made a waving motion with my right hand. Pansy broke out of the shadows and started walking toward me, rolling her shoulders, moving with more confidence than Morales could ever put out, a "You talking to *me*?" expression on her face. Morales' head spun on his thick neck. "What the—!"

Pansy kept coming, padding forward noiselessly. Not playing anymore—working. I pointed to my left, keeping my hand stiff. Pansy hit the spot, turned to face Morales.

"You better keep him back," Morales said, his right hand flickering against the zipper to his leather jacket.

"She," I told him. "Pansy's a girl."

"Pansy? Looks like you and the dog got your names switched. You sure her real name ain't Burke?" Morales sneered. Not giving ground, playing by jailhouse rules—you turn your back, you get stabbed. Or fucked.

"She's *my* girl," I said. "You see how it is. Don't do anything stupid."

"You better back her off," he warned. "She'd never make it. . . ."

I stepped to my right, putting more distance between me and Pansy, widening the triangle, letting him see the truth. "I'm gonna say something to her," I told Morales. "Don't listen to the word—it don't mean what you think. She's gonna lie down, understand? Just relax. . . ."

Morales took a step back with his right foot, ready to draw, but he didn't say anything.

"Pansy, jump!" I snapped.

The huge Neo dropped to the ground, but her eyes stayed on

target, pinning Morales. She looked pretty harmless lying down, but I knew the truth—Pansy could launch out of that position as fast as a badger charging out of a burrow.

"You see how it is?" I asked Morales. "No way you get both of us. Not quietly, anyway. And it's gonna cost you something if you try."

Morales slipped his hand inside his jacket. Slow, watching Pansy, ignoring me. The pistol slid out. He held it against his waist, barrel pointing to the side. A semi-auto, not a revolver—I'd forgotten that they let NYPD boys carry nines now. "Take your best shot," he said. He was calm saying it—a hundred eighty degrees from the maniac I met in the parking lot a few days ago. Crazy then, calm now. Dangerous always.

"There *is* no shot," I said. "Like you said . . . another time, right?"

"I can get you alone. Anytime. Get you where there aren't any witnesses."

"That's what the Rodney King cops thought too," I said.

A thin smile played over his lips, but his ball-bearing eyes pinned me as tight as Pansy's pinned him. "I don't know how dirty you are," he said. "I don't know exactly what you done. So I'm gonna do you a solid—for old times' sake. *Drop* this shit, Burke. Drop it now. Stand aside. Don't get in my way."

"You want me to stay away from this Piersall thing, you got it," I told him. "I wasn't really gonna—"

"You know what I mean," he said. "Don't pull my chain. You chumped me off, but you can't middle me. There *is* no mother-fucking middle on this one, understand?"

"Just tell me what you want me to do."

"Do the right thing," he said in his piano-wire voice. "Do the right thing. Or else, the next time you see me, you're gone, understand?"

"No," I told him, as honest as I'd ever been with a cop in my whole life.

"Then you're a dead man," Morales said, backing away.

I snapped my fingers. Pansy came to her feet, walked over to stand beside me. Morales straddled the bike, switched on the engine. He pulled on his helmet, watched us through the face shield for a while. Pansy watched back, immobile as stone. Morales suddenly twisted the throttle and the bike shot off, still going the wrong way on a one-way street.

Maybe I was too.

I picked up a *Daily News* on the way back to my office, read it through while Pansy was up on her roof, looking for coverage of last night's fight. Not a line—I'd have to wait for a later edition.

Morales said he'd been my alibi. All I could make of that was that he must have been at the fights. Didn't make sense. He could tail me around lower Manhattan early in the day easy enough, especially if he didn't care about red lights or one-way streets. He had my car pegged. But so what? Even if he ran the plates, he'd only come up with Juan Rodriguez, the guy who lends me his car whenever I want. Juan Rodriguez is a hell of a citizen. Pays his taxes, stays out of trouble.

I'm Juan Rodriguez. It's not illegal to change your name if there's no intent to defraud. I did it a long time ago. Got a lawyer, did it right. You fill out this petition, explain why you want the name change. Then you publish a public notice that you're doing it, so if any creditors are out there they can move on you.

Actors do it all the time. Some people just don't like their names. Jews used to do it so they could get jobs. Irish guys did it so their mothers wouldn't know they were prizefighters instead of dockworkers. It's no big deal. Costs a few hundred bucks and then you're done.

When I filled out my petition, I said I wanted to honor the foster family who took me in when I was a kid. The judge liked that—it showed respect.

The foster parents I had when I was a kid, their name wasn't Rodriguez. And if I ever found them, I'd pay my respects all right . . . show them how well I learned what they taught me.

So I changed my name. From Anderson to Rodriguez. The only place I ever saw "Burke" written down was on my birth certificate. Baby Boy Burke, it said.

A train of lies, running on a crooked track. When I ran from that foster home, they locked me up. They kept doing it until I learned how to survive out here. Learned from the Prof, mostly.

"Stay low, bro—low and slow. Walk light, keep out of sight," he'd told me. I did just that, switching names, switching games. I'd used up the Anderson name years ago—too many people wanted to know how to find him. Rodriguez was the next step.

There'd be others. I know how to do it now.

Morales could find all that out if he did the work, but it wouldn't bring him any closer.

No way he had me on 24-7. He'd told the truth about working solo. He didn't have a partner anymore—the psych report would have chilled that for sure. And even if he was on the rubber-gun squad, he'd have plenty of free time. And his own collection of unregistered pieces too.

I'd met Hauser near his office. Took the subway there. And I didn't come back with him. Unless Morales had a partner—hell, lots of partners—he couldn't have done it. When you take a subway and have a car waiting at the last stop, the trail goes cold.

So he knew about Frankie. That was the only way. He could have stumbled across it, just following me, but I didn't think so. It had to be something else. We didn't have a written contract with Frankie—it was a handshake deal. I couldn't work it through, how Morales would have figured it out. But he had to know—so that's the way I'd play it.

It was a little past noon when I walked over to Mama's. I didn't much care if Morales picked up my trail from there. In fact, part of me wished he would . . . something about that "alibi" crack he'd made earlier. For once in my criminal life, I'd be happy for some surveillance.

On that Saturday afternoon in late September, I was as legit as I'd ever been. All paid up—clean, sober, and square. Dead even. Unless you looked back into my life—then I was dead wrong.

Before all this started, I thought I knew Morales. Not the way you know a man, the way you know an animal, know their limits. Dogs could be vicious or they could be sweet . . . but they could never fly. That's the way I knew Morales. He was an over-the-top, head-breaking, bend-the-rules, shake-and-flake, never-take, blue-badged dinosaur street-beast. He might shoot drug dealers in the back, but he wouldn't take money from them. "He's so honest he squeaks," McGowan told me once. "Those IAD quislings don't even give you a look, you're partnered with a guy like that—they know he'd arrest you his own strange self."

Could I see Morales as a killer? Sure. In spades. He was high-tension taut, so tight he was brittle. It wouldn't take that much to snap him out, send him off.

It wasn't just the psych report. When he'd braced me in the past, it was always a game. Macho-posturing, make-my-day crap. He was hostile, but always on the safe side of rage. In that parking lot in Midtown, he was stressed way past full boil. Before, he'd been calm. Not centered, the way Max is, but still within himself.

Nobody could switch like that. Unless . . . I threw it out as fast as it came up. Morales was no multiple personality—near as I could tell, he didn't even have *one*.

The white-dragon tapestry was flying in Mama's window. I went in the front door, just in case Morales was watching. Mama wasn't at her register—her post was covered by Immaculata, dressed in one of those Mondrian silk dresses she wears every once in a while.

"What's up, Mac?" I asked her.

"Mama is in the back," she said. "With Flower. Teaching her. I can do my work anywhere," she said, flicking a long-nailed hand at a stack of paper, probably case-summary reports on some of her clients. "So I told her I wouldn't mind taking the front."

"How's business?" I asked her.

"Booming," she replied. "Unfortunately. Hard times only increase stress—a lot of marginal families lose it when the money gets too hard to find."

Immaculata works with abused children and, sometimes, their families. "Mama's business, I meant," I told her, not wanting to get into Immaculata's stuff.

"Who knows Mama's business?" She smiled.

I walked into the back, looking for Mama. Nothing. I asked a couple of her so-called cooks—they gave me blank looks in exchange. I started for the basement. One of the cooks held up a "Stop!" hand. The guy by the back door said something in Cantonese. The cook halting me stepped aside.

At the bottom of the steps, I spotted them. They were seated at a black lacquer table that was much higher on Mama's side than the child's. The table didn't slope—it had been built with a stagger in the middle, like a stair step. I walked over quietly, not wanting to disturb the clear silence. Mama's part of the table held only a black vase with a single white lily standing. She rested one elbow on the table, cupping her chin in her hand, watching Flower. The little girl's tabletop had a stone inkpot, a pad of blotters, and some sheets of heavy, textured paper. Her hand held an ivory stylus. They both looked up as I approached and I could see they were dressed alike, in matching kimonos of plum-colored silk with a black design on the left chest wrapping around to the sleeve.

"I apologize for disturbing you," I said, bowing slightly.

"It is okay," Mama said, nodding her head in acknowledgment. "Almost time to rest. Have tea, yes?"

"Thank you," I said.

"Thank *you*," Flower said, giggling. "My hand hurts."

"What are you working on?" I asked the child, squatting down so my face was level with hers. I could see both Immaculata and Max in her face—and I gave silent thanks that she was clearly going to favor her mother.

"Calligraphy," Flower said gravely, pronouncing the word with all the assurance of her seven years.

"Very important," Mama said. "First others', then your own—that is the way."

"I don't get it," I told her.

"We are learning haiku," Mama told me. "Very good discipline. Very important for balance. We practice the old ways, to master them."

"When I learn to write properly, I can write my own words," Flower said, repeating a past lesson with pride.

"Yes," Mama said. "Haiku is search for perfection. Each person has his own. All life, you work on it. Perfection is not what you ever get . . ."

". . . it is what you reach for," Flower finished for her, a grin on her little face.

"Yes!" Mama said, returning the child's smile.

"I thought haiku was Japanese," I said to Mama.

"Copy," Mama hissed. "Copy like they copy everything else. All root knowledge is from Chinese—they only copy."

"I understand," I said quietly, switching off the subject before Mama got wound up. Stupid of me to forget Mama's prejudices. It took me years to understand that tribalism was stronger than racism could ever be. I learned it in Africa, but sometimes I forget. "What haiku are you doing?" I asked the child, looking over her shoulder at the meticulous characters she had drawn, surprised to see them in English.

"I am just practicing now," Flower said gravely. "So that the pen becomes my thoughts."

"This very old haiku," Mama said, pointing to the original from which Flower was copying. "Haiku is precise. Always five, seven, five. Syllables. In English, must be the same."

I looked over her shoulder. The words were written on rice paper that looked older than me. Written in a sharp-edged calligraphic hand. Mama's?

the ferret, hunting
eyes on the ground, never hears
footsteps of the hawk

"You understand?" Mama asked, watching my face.

I stood there a long time, watching the haiku until it turned liquid in my vision. "Yes," I told her, bowing.

Getting what I came for.

Upstairs, we all sat at my table in the back. Mama brought tea for everyone. She knows I hate the stuff, but I sipped it anyway, not wanting Flower to learn anything bad from me. Immaculata smiled slightly, raising her eyebrows as I sipped.

"Very good lesson today," Mama said to Immaculata.

"Thank you, Mama," Immaculata said. "Max and I are very grateful for what you teach our daughter."

"My daughter too," Mama said. "Granddaughter, yes?" It wasn't a question—she didn't expect an answer.

"Max teaches you too?" I asked Flower.

"Yes. My father is a wonderful teacher," she said, quickly glancing sideways at Mama to see if she'd accidentally offended the dragon lady—it was easy enough to do.

"He teaches you to fight?" I asked her.

"Everybody fights," Immaculata put in. "Max is teaching her one way to do it. Understand?"

"Yes," I said, nodding my head. I'd never been a champ at talking to women, but three generations in one sitting was making me blunder even more than usual.

"Flower teaches too," Immaculata said. "She taught Max some signs."

"How could—?" I started to say.

"When she was just a little baby," Immaculata went on as if I hadn't spoken, "when she would cry to be picked up, she would always wave her little hands. I thought it was just random movement, but, one day, she moved her hands when she wasn't crying. And Max went right over and picked her up. She knew. He did too. She has all kinds of signs now. Signs of her own. Only she and her father use them. I am very proud," Immaculata said formally, her eyes wet.

Flower reached across and held her mother's hand—it wasn't just Max's signs she could read.

I spent the rest of that Saturday in my office, hunting in my head. No matter how I spun it out, I came up empty.

When I looked up, it was dark. I split whatever was left in the refrigerator with Pansy, smoked a cigarette to settle my stomach and lay back on the couch, eyes closed.

There's a few light-years' distance between fantasy and replay— the distance between imagination and imagery. Doc once told me about a guy he had in the max-max loony bin Upstate. A big black guy named Norman. This Norman, he stabbed a lot of people—that was his thing. They put a half-dozen diagnoses on him, with medication to match—nothing worked. So Doc detoxed him—brought him off the chemicals slow so he wouldn't crash.

And without the drugs, Norman was a real sweetheart—just kicked back in his cell all day long, a gentle smile on his face. It had all the shrinks puzzled. So Doc asks him, What's going on in there?

Norman tells Doc he goes to this planet every day. Time-travels inside his head. This planet, Ludar, he called it, it's a beautiful, peaceful place. The sky is rose-colored, and the grass is white, pure white, like snow. Everybody does something on Ludar. Norman, he was a farmer—he raised gold—it grows out of the ground on Ludar. Norman has a wife there. Some kids too. It's a perfect, holy place. Nobody starves, nobody's homeless. Nobody even gets mad.

So Norman's not really in his cell, see. He's on Ludar. He only eats twice a day. For fuel, so he can go back to where he wants to be.

Doc told me Norman really went there. He had so much detail that it had to be real. In his head, real. Doc told me he asked Norman, it sounded so perfect, could he go there too? Norman got real sad behind that. He really liked Doc, and he wished he could have given him better news . . . but most people couldn't go to Ludar— that's just the way it was.

So Doc started to trace it back, find out where Norman got his flight plan to Ludar. They had Norman when he was a kid, the same way they had so many of us. In one of the places they put him, Norman picked up a knife and started stabbing. That was to protect himself—even the guards knew that. Some of those kiddie camps, it comes down to the same two choices as prison.

So they started him on medication then—to gentle him down, keep him quiet. But it never worked. Sooner or later, Norman would start stabbing again.

Doc didn't bother too much with those paper-and-pencil tests—he just asked Norman flat-out: How come you stab so many people? Norman said they were keeping him from going to Ludar. They had no right to do that—he wasn't hurting anybody going there. That's when Doc put it all together. It wasn't *people* keeping Norman off Ludar, it was the medication. When the dose got too strong, Norman couldn't teleport himself off this lousy planet. So he started slicing and dicing. Then they'd switch his medication, and, for a while, he could go home. Doc wrote NO MEDS! on Norman's chart. And Norman, he never stabbed anyone again. He never got out of prison either, but it didn't matter. Norman was off medication. And on Ludar.

Fantasy is something you wish would happen. Flashbacks are something you wish never had. I didn't need an imagination to be somewhere else—I'd been there. All I had to do was remember, play the images out on my own screen.

I went there, stayed a long time. When I opened my eyes, it was early Sunday morning. I had nothing to show for my trip inside my head. And my back felt as cold as the killer's trail.

I went out to resupply. Came back with a pint of ice cream, a bag full of warm bagels, a thick wedge of cream cheese, and a quarter-pound of Nova lox. Pansy loves the stuff. Maybe she's West Indian in her heart and Jewish in her soul . . . although Mama insists she's a giant Shar-Pei.

I stepped out on the fire escape, standing well back in the building's shadow, invisible from the ground at that hour. When I finished the last bagel, I punched Mama's number into the cellular phone.

"It's me," I said.

"Two calls," she answered. "One man say his name J.P. The other was that woman."

"Either one say it was important?"

"Both say."

"Thanks, Mama. I'll call later."

"Watch the sky," she said, hanging up.

On the street, I looked around for a pay phone before I tried Belinda.

"What's up?" I asked her when she answered on the first ring.

"You don't know?"

"No. I *don't* fucking know. You wanna tell me?"

"Oh Jesus. Not on the phone. Can you meet me—?"

"I don't have a car anymore," I told her.

"That's all right," she said. "I have one. You know . . . Wait! Are you on a safe phone?"

"In the street," I said.

"Yeah . . . okay. You know Benson Street? The alley behind the—?"

"I know it," I told her. "What time?"

"Midnight, okay?"

"Okay."

I rode the underground to Midtown, got off a few blocks from Hauser's office. I tried a pay phone on him too.

"It's me."

"Where the hell have you been?" he barked, an urgent undertone in his voice. "Can you meet me—?"

"Say where and when."

"My office," he replied. "ASAP."

The door to his office was slightly ajar. I pushed it open the rest of the way and crossed the threshold, rapping gently on the door at the same time. Hauser's eyes were on some papers on his desk—he jerked his head up sharply. "What'd you do, fly?" he asked.

"I was in the neighborhood," I told him. "What have you got?"

"Sit down," Hauser said, standing up himself. "This could take a while."

I took the seat he offered, lit a smoke, settled in. Hauser was pacing back and forth behind his desk. "Go," I told him.

"Those psych reports—the ones on this cop, Morales. You read them carefully?"

"Carefully as I could," I said, wary now.

"He's a Catholic. Did you see that?"

"Yeah. So what? There's all kinds of Catholics."

"Hispanic Catholics, they generally don't stray as far from the church as others."

"Nobody *generally* slaughters women either," I said. "Is that your idea of a connection?"

"You see where he doesn't have any kids?" Hauser went on like I hadn't spoken.

"Yeah. And if you're gonna tell me maybe he's gay and can't deal with it, I'm already on that trail."

"He's not gay," Hauser said, a dead certainty in his voice. "Did you look at the cross-references on the report?"

"There weren't any," I told him flatly. "I gave you everything she gave me."

"Yeah, there were," he said. "Look at the bottom of the last page."

I ran my eyes over the paper. All I could see was a small box out-lined in black, like an obit:

```
VS = 1
LOD79-I = 2
HOSP80-Dx81-Rx = 3
```

"What's all that supposed to mean?" I asked him.

"The first reference is to vital statistics. Date of birth, parents' names, like that. Next is line-of-duty injuries. The last one is all hospitalizations, communicable diseases—any inpatient stays, including the E-Ward."

"Yeah, okay. But what good's that do us? Belinda never gave us—"

"She probably never had it," Hauser interrupted. "But there's more than one way to get documents out of One Police Plaza. Here, take a look for yourself." He handed over a long printout on thermal paper, like a continuous feed from a fax machine.

I ran my eyes over it, still coming up empty-handed. "Okay, so he was born in 1956 in Camden, New Jersey. And he had an operation to fix a hernia once."

"In the same place," Hauser said.

"In Camden? So what? Maybe he just likes the home-town doctors."

"I don't think so," Hauser said quietly. "I went down there myself. The next morning, after the fight. It wasn't a hernia operation he had in that hospital—it was a vasectomy."

"Okay. So?"

"So it was in 1982. After he was out of the Army—did you know he was an MP there?—and while he was on the cops. If it was an old hernia, the VA would have paid for it. And the cops *damn* sure would have—NYPD's got the best health-insurance plan in the world. So why would he go all the way down there?"

"Just to keep it a secret?" I asked him, puzzled. "What's the big deal about a vasectomy? I had one myself. It only takes a few—"

"He's a Catholic, Burke," Hauser said again, impatience showing around the edges of his voice. "A practicing Catholic. A vasectomy, that's birth control big-time. Permanent. Probably a Mortal fucking Sin, for all I know."

"So he's playing hide-and-seek with the church," I said. "How does that connect to what we—?"

"How could he be gay?" Hauser asked, a tight urgency to his voice. "If he's not having sex with women, why would he worry about pregnancy? A vasectomy would stop him from making babies—it wouldn't have anything to do with protecting yourself against AIDS. There's no other reason to have one, right?"

Okay, so much for that brilliant theory, I thought to myself. "That's real interesting," I said out loud. "But I don't . . ."

"There was no DNA in the bodies of the murdered women, right?" Hauser said, excited now, his volume knob cranked up toward the high end. "And we figured, Piersall probably wore a condom . . . for the one on University Place. But the others, while he was in jail, there was no sperm in any of them either. A vasectomy would do that."

"You mean . . . ?"

"DNA only works on nucleated material," Hauser said. "I checked it out. Blood, sperm, skin tissue—that'd all do it. But there's no DNA in seminal fluid, understand? Even with a vasectomy, you still discharge, don't you?"

"Sure," I said. "You just shoot blanks."

"And they can't get DNA from that. So . . . it could be she's right. It could be that Morales is our guy."

"Our guy for the other murders?"

"Our guy for this one," Hauser said, tossing a copy of the *Sunday News* at me. I looked down at the headline he'd circled in red:

The headline said something about a "Society Murder" but I didn't linger on it, just flashed down to the facts. Loretta Barclay, wife of shipping magnate Robert Barclay, was found in the pool house of her Scarsdale mansion by the maintenance man early Saturday morning. She'd been killed sometime late the night before, while her husband was in Bermuda, finalizing some international deal. She'd been stabbed repeatedly, well past what it would have taken to kill her. There were "signs consistent with a sexual assault," according to the cop they quoted. Nothing of value had been taken from the house or grounds. The police had no suspects.

"What makes you think Morales—"

"I got a friend up there in Westchester. A *friend,* not a source, understand? A state trooper. They think it was someone from the woman's past . . . something about another identity. But that's a blind alley, I think. There's something they found—something that didn't make the papers."

He stepped closer to me, dropping his voice almost to a whisper. "They found a red ribbon," he said. "Inside the body."

I ran back to my cave, double-backing twice, making certain-sure I wasn't followed. Pansy could tell something was wrong. I spent a few minutes gentling her down—I wanted to work in quiet.

I should have figured it—Hauser is notorious for persistence. I know he ran a marathon once—no training, just did it. Took him almost five hours to finish, and a hell of a lot more time before the chiropractor was finished with *him* . . . but he did it. I had the right horse for the course, but my hand wasn't holding the reins—Hauser was going to run wherever he wanted. And as fast.

That's what I needed to do too—run. No matter how strong your backup, true surviving is always a do-it-yourself project.

I did the same thing I used to do when I was a locked-up kid— ran away in my mind. Not to Ludar—I was never *that* crazy—but to a place where they couldn't hurt me. I would look at a spot on the wall until it was all I could see. It would get bigger and bigger, then it would go deep, like it was three-dimensional. The first bunch of times I did that, it was like diving into a clear, deep pool, but one I could breathe in. As long as I stayed down, they couldn't hurt me. After a while, I realized I could *do* things down there. Think-things, mostly. I could hold a question in my hands before I dived into the pool. Sometimes, when I came up, I had the answer.

Morales couldn't have done the murder up in Westchester County. He was watching the fights in Atlantic City. Watching me. He said he was my alibi—that he had watched the wrong man. So he must be thinking I was in on it, somehow. Maybe my job was to draw him away . . . get him off the scent?

No, that was stupid—I didn't know he was following me. And I damn sure couldn't *rely* on it.

So maybe Morales was telling me I was off the hook. He knew I couldn't have done the killing—he was right there with me—the timing couldn't work.

Was he doing me a favor, warning me off?

Why would he?

It didn't make sense—didn't add up.

Unless . . . ?

I sat in front of a mirror, looking into the red circle I'd painted on it years ago. The spot widened, got deeper. I took that *Unless* in my hands and dived in.

The answer came—so fast and hard that it knocked me right back to the surface.

Unless Morales had never been in Atlantic City at all.

Unless he was sharper than I ever thought—planting the lie deep.

Unless I was *his* alibi.

I took the subway to within a few blocks of a taxi garage in the Village. Luck was with me—the dispatcher I usually deal with was on duty. I showed him my Juan Rodriguez hack license. He nodded, not saying a word. I handed him four fifties—he handed me an off-the-books cab. The deal was always the same: I'd keep the cab for twenty-four hours or less. When I returned it, I'd also hand over whatever was on the meter. The dispatcher would keep that, plus the two bills. An expensive rental, but a perfectly anonymous, untraceable one—in this city, a yellow cab is invisible.

I pulled out of the garage and was waved down almost immediately. A guy and his girl wanted to go to an address in the East Nineties. I dropped them off, said "Thank you, sir," for the nice tip, and grabbed the FDR for the Willis Avenue Bridge.

Soon as I hit the Bronx, I flicked the "Off Duty" overhead lights on. That wouldn't surprise anyone—a Yellow Cab might . . . sometimes . . . take a fare to the South Bronx, but it would never pick one up there. If you were a Yellow Cab driver, getting back into Manhattan was all you thought about—the Bronx was for gypsy cabs.

I parked in front of the gym, locked it up and went inside.

"Greetings, my friend," Clarence said, peacocking in a tangerine linen jacket over an emerald green silk shirt.

"The Prof inside?" I asked him.

"Only temporarily, mahn. The workout is over. We will all be leaving soon."

"I'll wait out here," I said.

"You are troubled?" the young man asked. "Can I—?"

"No, it's okay, Clarence. I just need to ask the Prof something."

"If it is a question, my father will have the answer," he said confidently.

I heard the Prof before I saw him, rattling on about the next fight. When he spotted me, he dropped the rhyme-time patter, closing the space between us quickly.

"What is it, Burke?"

"I gotta talk to you," I told him. "This thing . . . it's getting out of control."

"Come on," he said, gesturing to Frankie and Clarence to follow. The Prof led the way outside to the loading dock. He and Frankie sat down, Clarence stood, not wanting to risk a blot on his outfit. I gave the Prof a look, sliding my eyes just slightly to the right, where Frankie was sitting.

"He's with us," the Prof said, saying it all.

"I need some cover," I told him. "Tonight. In the Benson Street alley, behind the Family Court downtown. I'm supposed to meet her at midnight. And the wheels are coming off."

"Coming off what, schoolboy?"

"Morales has been on me—*dead* on me—for a long time now. There was another killing, up in Westchester. Same night as the fight, but real late, after midnight. I didn't know about it—it didn't make the papers, not the early ones anyway. Morales moved on me Saturday morning. He said he was at Frankie's fight. Watching me, all right? He said I was gaming him—that he was my alibi for the killing."

"He thinks you . . . ?"

"Prof, I don't know *what* the fuck he thinks. First I thought he was accusing me of being in on it . . . like this Belinda was my partner or something. He warned me off . . . said *everyone* around would be going down."

"Cop's doing you a favor?" Prof sneered. "That's a natural-born lie."

"Yeah, that's what I thought too. Except that . . . up in Westchester, the killer left the signature . . . the red ribbon inside the body. No way Piersall did it, so it had to be Belinda, right?"

"Or this guy Piersall, he's really innocent . . ." the Prof mused.

"Sure," I said. "He pulls some hooker out of a truck stop in Jersey, cuts her up for the sex-fun of it—few weeks later, he's rehabilitated? No way—it *has* to be Belinda. She's got something going with Piersall—Hauser saw it."

"If you're sure, then—"

"But what if it was Morales?" I said, confusing myself even more than the Prof. "What if he's skating? What if he wasn't down in Atlantic City at all? He could be setting me up to be *his* fucking alibi, right?"

"If that's true, he has to know about Frankie," the Prof said. "Unless he's got partners, he couldn't—"

"He's got no partners," I said. "I'm sure of it—he's out there by himself."

The Prof regarded me steadily, his dark-brown eyes gentle on mine. "This ain't us," he said. "I got no beef with an honest thief. You want to rob, it's just a job. You can steal, still be for real. But when you hurt folks for fun, it's time to run or gun, son."

"I'm with you," I said. "And I'm all for running. But I'm not gonna do it blind. Whoever it is, they got their eyes on me. There's no sense in getting out of town. I'm safer here—more places to slip into. There's a big piece missing. I find it, I can get lost, understand?"

"Okay, we do it today," the Prof said. "Let's get rolling. You want Clarence to stay with—?"

"No, I'm okay," I said. "That cab over there's mine—for a while, anyway. If you can do the other thing, cover me tonight—"

"You're covered, homeboy," the Prof said, leaping lightly off the loading dock to the ground.

"I'm in too," Frankie said.

"You don't know what this is about," I told him.

"I know about taking a partner's back," the kid said. "I mean, I *heard* about it. I never saw it myself, not till you guys came along." His eyes cut off the ring, holding me in place. "I'm in," he finished in a flat no-argument voice.

The Prof nodded. Frankie jumped to the ground. We stood together in the shadow of the building, not talking. It felt like the prison yard: standing around, huddling against the chill that was always there, even in the summertime. Gun towers somewhere above us, the real danger right there on the ground, surrounding us even tighter than the filthy stone walls.

I cupped my hands to light a cigarette, using the few seconds to scan, an old prison-yard habit. The match flickered bright red in my hands. A different flash in the corner of my eyes, silver. What the . . . "Down!" I yelled, driving my shoulder into Frankie's chest, taking him down with me. His body spun just as I hit him, a split-second before I heard the shot. I stayed on him, trying to flatten against the ground. Chips flew from the brick wall over our head. A quick burst of shots rang out, so close they blocked my eardrums. Clarence, lying prone, his pistol held between two hands braced on his elbows. Sounds of a car peeling out.

Then it was quiet.

"High on the shoulder," the Prof said, kneeling over Frankie. "In and out," he said, pointing to Frankie's leather jacket.

"I'm . . . okay," Frankie said, biting into his lower lip.

"You see them?" I asked Clarence.

"No, mahn. Just the car. A dark car. Sedan. I may have hit it—I don't know."

"Let's get him to the hospital," I said. "Quick, before the cops come."

"In this neighborhood?" the Prof sneered. "Don't worry about it. We'll get him over to Lincoln, tell the Man it was a drive-by. Kids in a Jeep, random fire—you know how it goes. Get in the wind: we'll be there tonight."

Nobody had said anything, but we all knew—Frankie wasn't the target. Somebody out there had me in their sights—somebody way past threats. Whoever it was, they knew about Frankie. Knew about the gym. Maybe knew about Atlantic City.

Homicide fixes things. I used to believe in it, like a religion. But when you deliver a murder, it always comes wrapped in razor-wire—you handle it wrong and it cuts deep. And any mistake you make is the only one you get.

Guns are too easy. They *make* it too easy. Squeeze a trigger, take a life.

Even if I could make myself do it, I'd be guessing. It could be Belinda. It could be Morales.

And if I guessed wrong, I'd be dead twice.

There's a special curse reserved for Children of the Secret. We decide to survive, to pay whatever that costs. Some of us turn dangerous, but that's not the real curse. The real curse is friendly fire—when your hate turns your aim wild and you cut down anyone who tries to be on your side.

I never thought I'd do that. I would rather die than hurt anyone in my family—my true family. A family of truth, not of biology.

I never had a parent until the State took me. And what they did to me, I will never forgive. If the State was a person, I would have killed it a long time ago. Killed it or died trying, I have that much hate in me.

Sometimes it spills over. I don't feel anything about those killings in the Bronx years ago. I don't feel anything about going into that house. I don't pretend anymore—I don't pretend I went in there to save a kid. I went in there for me, focusing my hate down so narrow it lasered right through the darkness. When I was done, a dead kid was in the pile of bodies I'd made.

Ever since, I've been trying to blame the State for that too. But I knew better. And maybe Morales did too.

About eleven that night, I was still thinking about it. I have guns. Cold guns, impossible to back-track to the source. Fine guns, in perfect working condition. And I know where to get more. That used to be a feat in this city, but any punk can get one now—it's a fashion accessory, part of the Look.

Don't get me wrong. New York has gun-control laws. Real tight ones too. You want to carry a pistol, you have to have a damn good reason—like being a rent collector for a slumlord or needing something to show off at penthouse parties. If you work in a dangerous neighborhood, you can probably carry a piece legit. But if you *live* in one of those neighborhoods, that's too fucking bad, Jack.

Getting my hands on a gun was no problem. But I couldn't do it. Not out of guilt, out of fear. Afraid of what I might do . . . start fixing things with bullets. I had tried that. Tried real hard. But the only thing I could kill with guns was people.

And not the people who had hurt me so deep when I was a kid, only secondhand substitutes.

I took a long piece of razor-edged dull-gray plastic out of my desk drawer. One end was wrapped in friction tape, double-sided so it would be sticky wherever I grabbed it. The way you use it, you stab deep, then you twist it, hard. The plastic will cut into anything, but it snaps real easy—you leave a big chunk inside.

I took my old army field jacket down from a hook. It's a burglar's special, custom-made by a tailor I know over on Broome Street—the old man's been making them for years. It's got a Kevlar lining, several thin layers—for bullets. The sleeves are heavily padded, with a layer of chain mesh inside. That's for dogs—no matter how well they're trained, most of them will take a sleeve if it's offered. The inside pockets are perfect for stashing stuff like jewelry or cash. But it wouldn't hold a stereo or a TV set—an outfit like this isn't for amateurs.

I slipped the plastic knife into the left sleeve, anchored it in place with a piece of Velcro loop. The jacket is designed to get past any street cop's pat-down—no bulges. The knife didn't show. Neither did the speed key for handcuffs resting flat just under the back panel.

There's a place for a set of lock picks, another for a couple of pairs of surgeon's gloves with the talcum powder already dusted on their insides. I left the lock picks, kept the gloves.

I climbed into a pair of chinos, pulled them down over a pair of work boots. Not for construction work, for my work—thick crepe for the soles, steel caps for the toes.

You see kids dressing this way all the time now: big baggy pants, torn sweatshirts, clunky lace-up boots. Industrial-look gear, it's the in thing now. Makes sense when you think about it. Kids copy the life *style*, not the life. A while back the boys were all sporting thick gold-chain ropes, four-finger rings, ultra sunglasses. Even fake beepers. All to look like drug dealers, the ultimate ghetto role model. Those kids didn't deal drugs—and the ones modeling industrial gear this year don't work jobs either.

In America, the more useless it is, the more we love it. Those monfucious 88 Double-D cups you see on some of those poor little bitches who went way over the top with the implants so they could be headliners in the strip bars—you think they're there so those girls can nurse entire litters?

Amateur criminals are like thrill-killers. All they really get out of crime is a sick little buzz—that's their pathetic loot. You show me some geek night-stalking in a Ninja outfit, I'll show you a full-race disturbo. The first rule of stalking is to blend. When I walked out the door that night, I looked like just another ex-soldier in the army of disconnected men who pound the pavement until they merge with it.

Me, I was going to work.

It takes a different head to use a knife. Guns, they're a video game you play in your head. A knife is personal.

If it was Belinda, if tonight was when it happened, the knife would have to do. Harder to make a mistake when you're working close.

I walked up Broadway in the opposite direction from the traffic flow, stopping in doorways to scan behind me. It looked clear. Felt that way too.

I made the right into Leonard Street, staying on the south side of the block so I could see into the alley. No cars. Just the usual soggy piles of litter around the pair of big blue Dumpsters awaiting the early-morning pickup.

Leonard Street runs past the Criminal Court on Centre, then crosses Lafayette past the Family Court. It's a one-way street. Most folks could say the same thing about the courts.

I watched the alley mouth. Usually you could see right through to Franklin Street on the other side, but the view was blocked by a pair of semis, backed in side-by-side, like they were waiting for the off-loaders. I wasn't going in there until I saw her. With the semis parked at one end, it was even more of a box than usual—it'd be too easy to block the opening and just hose it down.

I could make out the outline of a homeless man. He was lying on a bed of flattened cartons, shrouded by a tattered old parka, about ten feet away from the alley's entrance. Couldn't tell if it was the Prof, but I figured that for his best spot. I watched the man steady for a few minutes—he didn't move.

It was quiet in the street. All the action was a few blocks away in either direction. To the east, night arraignments at the Criminal Court—a dull-gray mass that squeezed everyone tight, sometimes extruding a lucky chump, mostly just grinding, grinding. To the west, the whole bullshit "downtown" scene, with its grunge-dressed club kids all looking exactly the same different.

A few minutes before midnight, a white compact—Toyota? Honda? no way to tell—nosed its way around the corner from Lafayette. The car slowed, came to a stop just past the alley, then reversed and backed in. Backed in deep—if you passed by the alley, it would be hard to spot. The headlights blinked off. The driver's door opened. The interior light came on. One person inside—or maybe just one person visible above the windshield line.

Someone got out, wearing a bulky jacket and a slouch hat. Belinda? Hard to tell in that light—I gave it a little more time. Whoever it was took off their jacket, then bent forward and leaned on the car's front fender. Then they extended one leg backward, flexed it. Did the same to the other. Like warm-up exercises for a race. When my night vision kicked in, I could see it was her. When she turned sideways and stretched, reaching her hands way over her head, I was sure.

I slipped out of the doorway, walked back up the block, crossed the street and started back down. When I got to the alley, I turned and walked in.

"Hi!" she said when she spotted me, pulling the hat off her head and waving it like I might have to pick her out of a crowd. It would work just as well as a signal to someone across the street, but I was already committed . . . had to trust my own backup.

I kept walking, closing the distance between us.

"Thanks for coming," she said, her voice a little higher-pitched than usual.

"Like I promised," I said in reply.

"You want to sit inside?" she asked. "It's getting a little nippy out here."

I didn't answer, just walked over to her car and opened the door. The light went on inside—the car was empty. "You leave the keys in the ignition?" I asked.

"Sure. How come . . . ?"

I reached in, pulled out the keys. Then I went around to the back of the car and opened the trunk. No light went on, but I had my pocket-flash ready, one of those mini-Mag lights that don't take up space but cover a lot of territory. The trunk was empty. Too empty for a car anyone used. I dropped the flash, bent to pick it up. Came away with a read on the license. A Z-plate—the little white car was a rental.

"Satisfied?" she asked, hands on hips.

"Yeah," I told her, stepping past where she stood. I opened the car door again, took the keys in my hand and stuck them into the ignition. But as I backed out, I slid the keys out of the ignition and dropped them softly to the floor.

I stood next to her. Close enough to smell her perfume, a biting citrus cover-up. Her eyes were dark in that alley, unreadable. "You wanted to meet," I said.

"He did it again!" she whispered. "In Westchester. It was in the—"

"I know."

"He's gonna get crazy now. He must *be* crazy—they'd never let him investigate an out-of-town case—he *has* to know that."

"Morales, you mean?"

"Who else? Who else *could* it be? George isn't gonna make it, Burke. He's not gonna live to take advantage of this."

"What do you mean? If the cops—"

"It's too late for that," she said, urgency overamping her voice. "There's a contract out. On George. In the prison. They're gonna kill him!"

"Who?"

"Who? I don't *know* who—what does it matter? Whoever Morales got to, whoever he paid. It's gotta be *now*, before it's too late."

"What do you think I could—?"

"He's gotta get *out*, do you understand? Out! Out and away. After this is all cleared up, he can come back in. Surrender himself. After they find the real killer and clear him."

"How could I—?"

"You could do it, Burke. I know you could do it. People have escaped from there before—there has to be a way. All it takes is money, right? I've *got* the money. If you would only . . ."

"There's a big risk—"

"It doesn't matter," she interrupted urgently. "Whatever the chance, we *have* to take it . . . before it's too late for anything."

"I'm not talking about a risk for *him*," I told her. "It's a risk for anyone who helps, inside or outside. He's gonna need a getaway driver, a change of clothes, some hair dye and a razor. And a place to hole up. A *local* place—if he tries for the Turnpike, they'll have it roadblocked."

"I know, but—"

"And he can't go back to his house. Can't go *near* it. Or near anyone the cops know about. Your best bet is out of the country. Central America—Costa Rica, maybe Honduras. And that takes *long* green, understand? Enough so he can keep paying the tab month after month."

"I can get all that. From Fortunato—he says there's a way to 'invade' the trust or something. I don't really understand it all, but he said we could get a couple of hundred thousand, easy."

I lit a cigarette, cupping my hands to give me an excuse to scan. Nothing was moving. It was so quiet in the alley I could hear pieces of paper rattling every time a faint breeze came by. Escaping from Trenton State Prison . . . it could be done—I know guys who have pulled it off. The joint is an old catacombs, with secrets only the convicts will ever know. There's lots of ways out of prison: Your case gets reversed on appeal, you score a parole, you get a pardon from the Governor. You can wait for Work Release and then just not come back. You can get yourself into an outside hospital and make your break from there. All those ways, it takes juice. The old way—over the Wall—that takes something else. I got the cigarette going, turned to look at Belinda. "Why me?" I asked her. "You know what it takes, and you say you've got the ticket. Why don't you just go do it?"

"I *will* do it," she said. "You want me to wait outside, drive the getaway car . . . anything . . . I'm down to do it, all right?"

"So you need me for . . . what?"

"To set it up. Somebody has to pull strings in there. George isn't going to escape if he's locked in solitary—that's where he is now. He doesn't know enough about how the place runs. But you do. You could get it done."

"And I get . . . ?"

"Money. A lot of money," she said. "And anything else you want . . . from me."

I spent most of my younger years doing time—now all I wanted was to buy some. "It'll take a while," I told her. "Couple-three weeks, *minimum.* You can't wait that long, there's nothing I could even *think* about doing."

"That's okay. That's *good,* honey. . . ."

That last word was a test flight. I nodded—not shooting it down, but not turning on the landing lights either. "I need the money—"

"Up front," she said. "I know."

"Soon as I have it, I'll—"

"Can't you get started now? You know I'm good for it."

"I know that," I lied. "But there's no way I tell people inside the walls about you—I have to keep you completely out of this, for your own protection."

"Okay . . . I understand. I'll talk to Fortunato tomorrow. It'll take a few days, but—"

"That's okay," I said. "Just let me know when you've got it."

"You're a doll," she said, standing on tiptoes to kiss the corner of my mouth. I felt her tongue flickering soft against my lips, opened my mouth just a fraction, put a little pressure into my kiss-back. "Can I give you a ride anywhere?" she asked, another test flight.

"No thanks. I'm going over to the courts," I said, pointing to my right. "There's a few things I can do. Preliminary things. Whatever little cash that costs, I can front myself."

"Okay," she said, opening the door to her car. "I'll call you as soon as—"

"Take care," I told her, turning my back and walking away, toward the courts.

I was halfway down the block when I heard a car pull out of the alley. I turned, looked over one shoulder. The white car was speeding up the block. I trotted back to watch just as it made a hard left through a red light.

I crossed Leonard and took up my old post, just in case Belinda made another pass. After ten minutes, I figured she wouldn't. Still watching the homeless man asleep on his hard pallet, I crossed over to the alley. Standing over him, I said "All clear," in a calm, quiet voice.

The figure in the parka-shroud stirred. "I do not see how they do this every night, mahn. I myself would rather be in jail." Clarence rolled onto his side and got up stiffly, rotating his neck to work out the kinks. His pistol was in his hand. He caught me looking at it, said, "I could not draw it from such an uncomfortable position, mahn. It was better to be ready."

"So where's the Prof?" I asked him.

"This way, mahn," Clarence said, walking into the alley. I followed him, one pace behind and slightly to his side. He walked up to one of the Dumpsters, smacked the side of his hand against it three times. The Prof's head popped up. Clarence and I each took one of his hands, pulled him free. A sawed-off shotgun dangled against the Prof's chest, held up by a loop of rawhide around his neck. When he landed on the ground, he make a quick motion with his right hand—the scattergun disappeared into the folds of his coat. "When it gets down to the clutch, I never lose my touch," the little man said, a wicked grin on his face.

Clarence pulled out a cellular phone, punched a single button. After a couple of seconds, he said "Come on," into the speaker.

Just as we were about to exit the alley, I heard the squeal of tires. Car coming, fast. "Chill," the Prof said. "It's Frankie Eye, and that's no lie."

Sure enough, a charcoal-gray Lincoln Town Car pulled to a jerky stop at the curb. The door opened and Frankie got out gingerly, favoring his left arm, which was wrapped and cradled in a white sling. He walked around the back of the car, opened the rear door and slid in. The Prof followed. Clarence took the wheel, I got the shotgun seat.

The Lincoln pulled away, a lot more smoothly with Clarence at the wheel.

"The fuck's all this?" I asked the Prof, nodding my head in Frankie's direction.

"I'm okay," Frankie answered for him. "The bullet went right through—just took a piece from inside my upper arm, under the shoulder. No bones broken, nothing. The docs cleaned it and packed it, gave me a shot. Just a butterfly thing, no stitches. I got to wear this sling for about three-four weeks, that's all."

"Yeah, terrific," I said. "But what's this about you driving? And where'd you get this car?"

"I can drive fine," the kid said. "My right arm's perfect. And I scored the ride from a guy I know in the neighborhood. A good guy—we go back—I was inside with him."

"And he wouldn't get upset if you wrecked his car? Or if we got stopped and the cops impounded it?"

"Nah," Frankie said, "he's cool. Besides, it's not really his car—they clouted it over in Brooklyn. Soon as we get it back, it's going straight to the chop shop."

"Just fucking beautiful," I muttered, realizing any cop in the city had Probable Cause to stop us. "You at least switch plates?" I asked Frankie.

"Sure," he said, sounding offended. "I ain't stupid."

"You got a registration to back up the plates?" I asked him. "You got an FS-20 . . . an insurance card?"

"Noooo, I guess not," he said, looking sheepish.

"You realize they could nail you for that?" I asked him. "Put points on your license . . ."

"I . . . don't have no license," he said, head down. "I mean, Upstate, I never learned . . ."

"Hey, schoolboy," the Prof interrupted. "Frankie here, he's a bit slow to be turning pro, but—"

"Right on," I agreed, stopping the word flow from the Prof before he got on a roll. I extended my palm to the back seat for Frankie to slap. "Thanks, kid."

"That's okay," he mumbled.

"He dealt himself in, Jim," the Prof said. "He wanted to play, wouldn't stay away."

"Where can we drop you, mahn?" Clarence asked, his face in the mirror a study in calm repose.

I looked up, saw we were on Sixth Avenue in the Thirties. "Thirty-fourth's okay," I told him. "I'll get you tomorrow, fill you in. It's coming down now. Real soon."

"Soon's we know, we'll show," the Prof said.

The car pulled to the curb. I opened the door, stepped out, leaned back inside. "Thanks again, Frankie," I said to the kid.

"I'm with you," he said in reply. Saying it the right way—*after* he'd come through, not before.

I returned the cab, then made it back to my place on foot. Stopped to make a phone call, lined up reservations for tomorrow.

I caught an early flight to Syracuse out of La Guardia the next morning. I paid for the flight with the American Express Gold. Juan

Rodriguez doesn't have credit cards, but Arnold Haines does. Pays every bill right on time, too. Arnold's a better citizen than I could ever hope to be, and he's got one big advantage over Juan—he can visit an RB soldier in prison without raising any eyebrows.

I rented a plain tan Ford Crown Vic at the airport and started the drive to Auburn, a max joint in the middle of the state.

They let me inside without a glance—Arnold's been on the Approved Visitors List for quite a while.

The Visiting Room was on the open plan. It was half-full. About as much as you would expect—Auburn's a hell of a distance from the city, where most of the convicts came from.

They brought him down quick enough. Silver looked good, healthier and sharper than when I'd last seen him. He was used to jailing, and he never jailed alone—most of the RB's membership is doing time in one joint or the other.

"How's Helene?" I asked, shaking his hand.

"She's good. And she's close by. Thanks to you, brother," he said, still gripping my hand.

"You need anything?"

"A few magazine subscriptions maybe. I could pass them around to the guys when I was done with them. A library, like."

"You got it."

"I appreciate you coming," Silver said. "But there's gotta be more for you to make the trip, right?"

"Right," I said, leaning close to him, dropping naturally into the side-of-the-mouth style of convict-speak. "I heard there was a contract out on a guy down in Jersey. Trenton State Prison. Guy's name is Piersall. George Piersall."

"If it's Brotherhood business, I can't—"

"I'm not trying to call it off," I said quietly. "I'm in it, but not on his side, okay? The whole thing smells. Smells bad. If there's something out on this guy, I think it's a setup."

"You want—?"

"I don't want anything," I told him. "He's in PC now, this guy."

"That won't—"

"I know. But if there's word out—*if*, I said—then you should know there's more players in the game. More than you know about.

This guy, he's also got an escape planned. That's gonna take juice. Inside juice. Which means somebody's gonna get left holding the bag, understand?"

"Yeah. If it's a contract, outside money, maybe we could wait. But if it's a Brotherhood thing . . . ?"

"It's not," I assured him.

"Piersall. What kinda name's that?" Silver asked, his eyes on mine.

"He's white," I said. "And, far as I know, he's not a player. He's got no crew. He's not into juggling. He wouldn't make a play on the sports book or the drug action. He's short, real short, but there's a New York detainer on-and-after. He's not going anyplace, but he wouldn't start something up down there just before they transfer him. What's the point?"

"So you want . . . what?"

"I want to know if somebody paid for a hit. And I want you guys to watch your backs if that's the case. Okay?"

Silver lit a cigarette from the pack I'd left on the table. "Okay," he said finally.

We spent a couple of hours catching up on old times. The time I did, the time he was doing.

I was back in the city by nightfall.

I stayed up late, watching some pro wrestling on the tube with Pansy. She wasn't into it like she usually was. Maybe the product was getting weak—if it couldn't entertain Pansy, I didn't have much hope for its future.

I watched with my eyes closed, one hand on Pansy's neck, my old girl and I, reassuring each other.

I knew something I hadn't told Belinda. Hadn't mentioned it to Silver either. If there was a pipeline out of Trenton, the RB was collecting the tolls. The last three to get out, they'd all been members. The *federales* took one of them down soon after—nailed him backing out of a bank in Nebraska with a pistol in his hand. They pumped so many steel-jacketed rounds into him they could have used a magnet to drag him to the coroner. The other two, they were still at large. It wasn't like the old days, when Rhodesia was the safe harbor. And the Stateside white-supremacist groups were lousy with FBI agents and semipro informers. I don't know where the other two had gone to, but they did get gone. It didn't look like they were dead—the thing about being an ex-con is that they only need to find a tiny piece of your body to make an ID.

If I set up an escape, I'd have to work with the Brotherhood. And if they had an open contract, I'd be handing Piersall over to the lions.

This whole thing was a black diamond solitaire: plenty of facets, but no light. Belinda, Piersall, and me. Three liars, lying.

And Morales . . . ?

When I got up the next morning, it was past eleven. But that was okay—I finally had something I could do.

Sitting in Mama's restaurant, I went over it again with Max. He was down for the job, but he wanted to drive. I nixed that—I needed him for better things.

We took my Plymouth to the Bronx. I didn't care who knew where I was going for this part. But I checked the mirror anyway. . . .

Nothing.

"You seen Clarence around?" I asked the black man with the fancy Jheri-curl at the gym's front desk.

"The West Indian dude? Dresses real nice?"

"That's him," I said.

"He's in the back," the black man said. "With the little guy—the rhyming man."

"Much obliged," I said.

He stood up, not blocking my path, but coming close enough. "You the heat?" he asked, his tone friendly.

"Sure. And this is my partner, Charlie Chan," I said, nodding my head over at Max. The Mongol regarded the black man calmly, hands open at his sides.

"Yeah . . . okay," the man said, standing aside.

I found them all in a side room off the main area, clustered around a new-looking big-screen TV with a VCR wired in. They were watching a fight tape—I couldn't tell which one. We stood there, watching. Then I recognized it—it was Frankie's first fight, the one with that guy Jenkins.

We took seats, watched in silence as the Prof ran the tape in slow-mo, rapping to Frankie. "Okay, honeyboy, you see that? You see that overhand right? That move is chump from the jump, son. Telegraphing's bad enough, you sending him fucking Parcel Post!"

"I see it," Frankie said.

"*Everybody* saw it, fool!" the Prof snapped. "You been gettin' by on toughness, kid. You keep climbing the line, tough ain't gonna be enough. Soon as you get out that cast, we gonna—"

"I could work with one hand," the kid offered. "On the heavy bag—"

"No way, José." The Prof slammed the door on that one. "We got nothin' but time, boy. Just lay in the cut, stay out the rut, okay?"

"Yeah, okay," Frankie said. "But if I'm gonna get paid, I should—"

"Do what the boss says," the Prof finished for him.

We watched the end of the fight. Half of what the Prof was rapping didn't make sense to me, but Max seemed to follow it easily. Maybe having no audio was a help.

When the tape was finished, I pulled Frankie aside. "I could use some help on something," I said, keeping my voice neutral.

"Sure! I mean, if it's okay with the Prof."

"Let's ask him," I said, putting a hand on Frankie's shoulder, walking him into a quiet corner.

"**H**ow's this?" Frankie asked me, a wide grin spreading across his face. He was at the wheel of a white Cadillac Eldorado coupe, parked in the open area on West Street, south of Fourteenth, just off the Hudson.

"An El D. is all right with me," the Prof endorsed, offering the kid a high-five.

I didn't ask him where he got the car—right about then, I didn't want to know.

"You sure the ho' will show?" the Prof asked me.

"She's a Hoosier, brother," I told him. "Never passed Hooking 101—she won't even look in the back seat. Take my car," I told him. "If Morales makes a move, you're clean, okay?"

"Let's play," the little man said.

Max and I folded down the back seat so it was flat—a nice feature to have in your car if you wanted to carry a set of skis. We climbed in, then lay down with our feet toward the back of the trunk, Max behind the passenger seat, me behind Frankie.

"This is gonna be just fine," I said to the kid, pulling a light army blanket over me and Max. If you looked into the back seat, all you'd see would be a big empty space. "Keep the windows up," I said. "We got to do at least one drive-by, so I can be sure you pick out the right one."

"Got it," the kid said, pulling away surprisingly smoothly for an unlicensed amateur.

On Tenth Avenue, I leaned close to Frankie's ear. "Look, kid," I told him, "the way these girls work, it's always from the passenger side of the street. They'll come over, lean into the window, see what's happening, all right?"

"Yeah."

"It's almost impossible to see into these windows with all that tint they got on them. I'm gonna just slide up . . . here! Okay, now, slow and steady. You're a man looking for a piece of ass, checking out the merchandise, okay?"

"I got it," the kid said, a little tightness in his voice.

We made her on the second pass. Roxanne, still working the same block. Couple-three weeks, she was probably the veteran girl on that stroll by now.

"You got her?" I asked Frankie. "The white chick in the red shorts, white top?"

"Yeah."

"Okay, one more spin, you make the swoop. I'm going under the blanket now. We hear the car door close, we know you got her. Head for West Street, downtown—we'll make our move soon as we hear you say 'hotel,' right?"

"Right."

I slid back, lay next to Max. Felt the Caddy make a couple of turns, then slow to a crawl. Then stop. Faint hissing sound as the passenger window zipped down.

"Hi, honey. You lookin' to party?" Roxanne's voice? No way to tell—after a while, they even *sound* alike.

"That's *exactly* what I'm looking for," Frankie said.

"Where'd you like to go?"

"Around the world," Frankie told her, his voice deeply laced with the self-important ego of a mid-level Guido. "And I got the cash for the ticket."

"Ummmm," the whore purred. "That costs a little bit, honey. Would a C-note bother you?"

"*Nothin'* bothers me," Frankie bragged. "Except wasting time. You comin' along or what?"

I heard the door open, heard it slam shut. Felt the Caddy move off. Heard the snap of the central locking system. Okay.

"I know a good place, honey," Roxanne said. "It's just over on—"

"Yeah, well, fuck a whole bunch of that outdoor shit," Frankie said. "I got a nice place. All fixed up. You're gonna love it."

The Caddy made a left turn, heading downtown.

"I dunno, honey," the whore said. "I mean, I'm supposed to call my man if I go off the block. Maybe we could just pull over and—"

"Your 'man,' " Frankie said, his voice dripping sarcasm. "You mean your pimp, right? You got a nigger pimp, bitch?"

"Hey! Be nice," Roxanne purred. "I got rules, just like you. And I really gotta—"

"When you see my hotel room, you won't be—" Frankie started. I tapped Max's left shoulder and the warrior slid out of his hiding place so smooth and quick I almost didn't see it. By the time I pulled myself out of the back, Max had his right hand completely over the whore's nose and mouth, his left resting on her collarbone. Frankie was driving straight ahead with his good hand on the steering wheel, calm as a rhino watching a jackal.

I pulled myself up so my lips were close to her ear. "Roxanne," I whispered, "it's okay. Nobody's gonna hurt you, all right? All we need are some answers. You give us the answers, we let you out, with a hundred bucks for your trouble. My man is gonna take his hand away from your mouth. Slowly, now . . . okay? Just be nice and calm. The doors're already locked. Nobody can see into the windows. You act stupid, you scream—anything like that—your neck's gonna get broken. Okay?"

She nodded her head vigorously.

I tapped Max's shoulder again. When he turned, I held up one finger. His big hand came off the whore's mouth. Slowly, like I had promised.

"Don't turn around, Roxanne," I said quietly. "This'll only take a minute. You okay?"

"Yes," she said. Her voice was steady, her breathing shaky. Close enough.

"You know my voice, don't you?" I asked.

"No!" she said quickly. "I swear I don't—"

"It's all right," I told her gently. "Nobody's mad at you. A while back, you asked me to do a job of work for you, remember? You got word to me through Mojo Mary?"

"Yes. But I—"

"Shhhh," I soothed her. "Like I said, nobody's mad at you. You used to be an actress, didn't you? That story of yours, about wanting someone to dust your man, that was pretty slick. Very believable. You have a lot of talent, girl."

"Thanks," she said, turning around despite the warning, looking me full in the face. No longer afraid, now that I'd recognized her talent. The left side of her face was bruised, the whole eye socket discolored. "I did act, you know. In school. When I first came here, I—"

"I know," I told her. "But right now, we're working on something. You were hired to do a job, that's all. The same as me. The woman who hired you—"

"She told me—"

"The one with the blond wig?"

"Yes! Rhonda. She said all I had to do was *tell* you, that's all. There wasn't anything else."

"I know. This man of yours, the one that was supposed to be in jail? What was his name? What was the name the blonde bitch told you to tell me?"

"Hector," the whore said. "She told me to say Hector. On Riker's Island. I wasn't really gonna—"

"That's all right, girl," I said, handing over a hundred-dollar bill. "Here, take this. Your man treats you like that," I said, touching my face where hers was bruised, "maybe you should get on a bus instead."

"My man didn't do this," she said indignantly, touching her own face. "It was that nasty cop—the one asking all those questions about Rhonda."

"What kind of questions?" I asked, gentling my voice so I wouldn't spook her.

"Like . . . where did I meet her, did she live around here. Stupid questions—like *I* would know where she cribbed. I told him the truth—I never saw her before she showed up one day. He was scary. I was just standing around, you know, blasé-blasé, just taking a rest, okay? He like *charges* up, snatches me by the arm. I thought he was a crazy man, like I was being kidnapped or something, but one of the other girls, she knows him, she told him take it easy, okay? God, I thought he was gonna *kill* her, the way he looked. Anyway, he drags me by the arm into his car, right there on the street, and he starts asking me questions. I answered him straight. Every one. So he asks me again. The *same* questions. I was getting real scared, so I told him, you know, time is money. Then he just started to *break* on me. For nothing. He slapped me so hard I thought he knocked a tooth out. He's one of those guys who *hates* us, I can tell. You know, the kind who drive by just to curse at us. They never buy— they just like *look* at us. It's disgusting."

"I'm sorry that happened," I told her, signaling for Frankie to pull over. We were just north of Canal, with a big wide spot to pull over. Perfect. "Here's where you get off," I told her.

She stepped out of the Caddy. Once she got her feet on the ground, she remembered her trade. "How am I gonna get back?" she demanded.

"Take a cab," I told her just as Frankie tromped the gas pedal.

Roxanne wasn't the first person who tried to hire me for homicide. Most of the hit man stories are myths anyway. You want someone to knock off your wife so you can marry that nineteen-year-old secretary who spends more time working under your desk than on hers, your chances of finding a pro who'll take your money, take her life, and keep his mouth shut—that's about zero. You ask around in too many bars, the next guy you'll meet will most likely be an undercover cop.

During the boom times of the mid-to-late '80s, some of those yuppies actually bought the bullshit along with the stocks and bonds, convincing themselves that power ties and five-thousand-dollar wristwatches were amulets, protecting them against having to pay up when their notes were called. They used money like steroids, bulking up their egos to where they were easy marks. For people like me.

I remember one especially. Young guy, on the sweet side of thirty, tanned and toned, as smooth and cold and hollow as a ceramic vase.

"It happens," he told me dismissively. "I was margined to the max, and I couldn't make the call. So I got involved in this bust-out scheme. You know what I'm talking about?"

"Sure," I told him. It was the truth. You buy a restaurant—just on paper, you're never going to actually run it. Then you use the joint's line of credit to buy everything: industrial refrigerators, china, cash registers. Even soft goods, like Kobe steaks from Japan and mega-lobsters from Maine. It's all on the come—cash in thirty days. Then you turn around and sell it. Sell it *all*—at a deep, deep discount, say 70 percent off. You take the cash and you walk. Run, sometimes.

"Yeah," he said, not convinced but wanting something more important from me than just demonstrating his superiority. "Anyway, one of the guys turned weak. . . . He's been making noises about . . . going to the authorities. You understand my position?"

Better than you do, sucker, I thought, nodding my head in agreement.

"Yeah, well . . . I need some work done. And I was told you could . . ."

I nodded again, very somber, very reassuring. They never come right out and say it. They want you to ice a man or burn a man—means the same thing. Top him, drop him. Dust him, cap him, ace him or waste him. Blow him up, blow him away. Clock him or Glock him. Smoke him. Grease him. Chill him, plant him. Cancel his ticket, or punch it. Take him down, take him out, take him off the count. So many words—it's like they had an ad agency on the job full-time.

At ground zero, they say it straight—tell you to go out and *do* the motherfucker. . . .

I told him I could handle it. Told him what I'd need up front. "That's the way it's done," I said. And the with-it twit went and got the money.

Got himself taken too—I didn't think he'd call a cop. I read about it a few weeks later. When the guy the yuppie was worried about went to the *federales*, he started a bear market in informing. The sucker I'd been dealing with was too late—by the time he was ready to turn, his information was selling at a deep discount, and all he really bought was some time inside.

Maybe he'll learn something inside besides how to improve his tennis game. I tried to think of a way I could have cared less, but I couldn't come up with one.

But those other people, they had really wanted the work done. This thing with Roxanne was bogus—it had mousetrap written all over it. There was no work to *be* done: they just wanted me on tape agreeing to do a murder—a handle to twist me with.

For what? To blackmail me into helping Piersall escape? That was crap—no matter what they had on tape, it wouldn't be enough to make a case. Most cops would just laugh at it.

But I couldn't see Morales laughing.

I thought about Mama's haiku. Footsteps of the hawk. There was truth in it, I knew. When the cops search a room, the one place they never look is *up*. They look under the beds, behind the doors, all that. But they never look up. They could find a roach on the ground, but they'd never find a spider on the ceiling.

Morales was a cop. All cop. Every chromosome a cop. He'd never look up.

But if he was the hawk, he wouldn't need to.

L ate afternoon by the time I got over to Mama's place. White dragon in place, quiet. I came in through the back, thinking of how well Frankie stood up—how he dealt himself in on a bad hand—thinking, What kind of man does that?

I knew the answer when I walked into the restaurant, saw Mama and Max at a table. With Clarence and the Prof. And Frankie.

Frankie inside Mama's. With us—that was the Prof's vote. And I had too much respect for him to veto it, even if I wanted to.

I sat down at the one large round table in the place. The sauce-splattered old sign Mama always keeps on it—Reserved for Party of Eight—was gone. The table was never used unless we all needed to face each other at the same time. Didn't happen often.

If I needed any proof that Frankie had been dealt in, watching him work on a bowl of Mama's hot-and-sour soup closed the issue. Her soup was only for family—no exceptions.

"Is my boy an actor or what?" the Prof crowed.

"He was perfect," I acknowledged. "Good as De Niro."

"Joe Pesci," the Prof rasped.

"What?" I asked.

"Joe fucking Pesci," the Prof said in his the-subject-is-closed voice. "The *best* actor on this planet, bar none. He gets the call, he does it all. Man's so slick he could play a goddamned telephone booth and motherfuckers be putting quarters in his mouth."

"I didn't know you were such a movie freak," I said.

"I am a movie *critic*," the Prof announced grandly.

"Yeah, okay, I stand corrected," I told him. "But you're right on this one—you weren't there, I was. And Frankie was *smooth*. He played his role like a champ."

"I . . . like doing that," Frankie said, looking up.

"Scamming?" I asked.

"No. Acting. I mean, I know that wasn't *real* acting . . . but I really liked it. Playing a part. Being something else . . . I don't know."

"It's a mug's game," I told him. "It's all who you know, who you blow."

"Joe Pesci never kissed ass," the Prof announced, defending his man with vehemence.

"How the hell would *you* know?" I challenged.

"It's in his face, ace," the Prof said. "Kissing ass, it marks you, bro—easy to read as a true ho's greed."

"Yeah, sure . . ."

"Hey, schoolboy . . . you ever see *Casino*? How about *Goodfellas*? You ever see *My Cousin Vinnie*? You ever see *Raging Bull*?"

"I seen that one," Frankie put in. "De Niro, he was awesome. He . . . I dunno . . . he *feels* it, I guess."

"De Niro?" the Prof snorted. "He ain't no turkey, I'll give you that. The dude is strange, but he ain't got no range."

"De Niro could play anyone," I said. "He's a genius."

"Who could he play?" the Prof challenged. "A priest, a gangster, a crazy man? Sure. But he's always De Niro, see? No matter what, he's always himself. Joe Pesci, that's the real deal. Listen up, bro, my man Pesci, he gets to be whatever you see. He could be playing Malcolm fucking *X* if he wanted to."

"Yeah. Okay, you win," I surrendered. I looked around the table. "What's going on?"

"Investment," Mama said.

Max balled his fists, rolled his shoulders like a fighter coming in, shook his head No, tapped his left shoulder.

I nodded agreement, said, "Okay, Frankie can't fight for a while, right? What's to talk about?"

"We got an offer," the Prof said. "For Frankie's contract."

"From who?" I asked him.

"Rocco Ristone," the little man said. Saying it all with those two words. Ristone was a major player, just a cut below the big boys in the promotion racket and pushing them hard from behind.

"He came to you?" I asked.

"No, he came to Frankie. Tell him, kid."

"After the last fight, couple of days later, he came to the gym," Frankie said. "Asked me if I was under contract. I told him I was. Told him to who, when he asked. He asked me, what was I getting? I told him I got a hundred-grand signing bonus, all expenses, and the Prof cuts my purses one-third across."

"Damn," I said admiringly. "That's a whole *string* of lies."

"Ain't it, though?" The Prof smiled, extending his hand, palm up. I slapped it, but I wasn't satisfied.

"How'd you know how to play it?" I asked Frankie.

"From reading the papers. And the fight magazines. I figured, if he knew I was under a contract, he'd have to buy it out."

"You *want* to be bought out?" I asked quietly.

"No. I just thought I would put some protection on the Prof. On all you guys. Make them think there was real coin around."

"So what's to discuss?"

"Frankie," the Prof said. "We got Frankie to discuss. He stays with us, keeps knocking motherfuckers out, we maybe—*maybe*—get him a shot at one of them plastic belts in a couple of years. Maybe not. With us, you know he ain't never gonna get a *real* title bout unless he *loses* a few times, right? No way one of those punks is gonna have a *fight* when they can get millions just for showing up."

"With all respect, my father," Clarence said. "There are no guarantees, yes? Even if Frankie were to go with this Ristone man, he might not . . ."

"Well, we could still train him and all. . . ." The Prof's voice trailed away as he caught the look on Frankie's face. It added up—no way Ristone was going to let us stay in the game if he bought us out.

I looked over at Max to see if he was following this. His face is a mask to most people, but I can read it. Max hears the same way a blind man sees. He was with it—staying inside himself, waiting.

"How much we got in this?" I asked the Prof.

"Well, you, me, Clarence, Max . . . and Mama now, we each put in five. We got those two dinky purses on the up side, got some expenses on the downs—call it a wash. I figure the whole dive cost about twenty-five."

"Frankie was sharp," I said. "He knew how to play it as good as if we schooled him ourselves. Most of these promoters, they take fifty percent, then stick the fighter with all the expenses off what's left. But Ristone, he thinks Frankie got himself a better deal, right? He gets his purses cut one-third, and got fronted a hundred grand, the way Frankie told it." I looked around the table at my family, hell-bound to do the right thing. About this, anyway.

"I say we cut the pie, and cut Frankie loose," I told them. "Ristone has to buy the contract back. Okay, there *is* no contract, but he can't know that. He pays us back our hundred grand, lets us keep five points—off the top, not off the bullshit 'net'—and takes it over. We split the loot, okay? Fifty-fifty on the hundred grand. That way, we each double our money, and Frankie scores fifty large right away. Then we get Davidson to represent the kid. We give him one point of our five points instead of cash. He'll go for it."

"Davidson's a righteous shyster," the Prof said. Meaning: he's a land shark, but for his clients, not for himself. For a lawyer, that's what you want.

"It plays perfect," I urged. "We score, Frankie scores . . . and Frankie stays in the hunt. What do you say?" I finished, looking around.

"One hundred percent on money, very fast. Very, very good," Mama responded, voting Yes.

Max nodded his head in assent.

"You will keep your colors, mahn?" Clarence asked. "I designed them myself, to honor our family."

"Forever," Frankie promised.

"When you get the belt, we all get some gelt," the Prof said, looking hard at Frankie. "Don't forget, boy . . . whatever you get to be, you learned all them moves from me."

Frankie had tears running down his face. He wasn't ashamed of them, played it like a man. "I love you guys," he said.

"Shut the fuck up, fool!" the Prof barked at him.

I was the last one to leave the restaurant. I'd called Davidson from the phone in the back, ran it down to him. He was game to play, said he'd represent Frankie on the contract "and at any and all subsequent proceedings," talking the way he talks, more vocabulary than content. But *his* word was good—straight-arrow, dead-serious, stand-up, go-to-the-wall good. Frankie was covered.

I smoked in silence, alone in my booth in the back. Frankie had been my shot to go legit. My chance to make a living on the straight side of the law. I know all about stealing. All about stinging, scamming, swivel-hipping my way through a mine field. I have great ideas, but I can never figure out how to sell them. Like Phone Sex on Hold, that was my best. You know how they put you on hold when you call most companies . . . you have to sit there and listen to some disgusting Muzak crap, getting madder by the second? I bet, if you could listen to some heavy-breathing bimbo tell you how hot you were making her, you'd sit there patiently for days. The only problem I had was how to know what kind of sex the caller wanted. Maybe I could use that voice-mail thing: press 1 for heterosexual, press 2 for homosexual, press 3 for bondage, press 4 for foot fetishes. . . . Ah, fuck it—it was like all my citizen-ideas—good for a laugh and not much else.

This wasn't the time, anyway. Something was coming down. Something too heavy for me to lift. I was finally hearing the footsteps of the hawk, and I didn't have the firepower to shoot it down. The only thing I could do was not be around when it landed.

"I'm calling from a pay phone," the woman's voice said. "I don't have long. Do you know who this is?"

I knew, all right. Helene. Silver's wife. She'd left a message late last night, saying what time she'd be calling today. "Yes," I told her.

"He said it was a contract," Helene said, her voice as calm as if she were quoting stock prices. "But with the . . . new information, the contract is canceled until further notice."

"I got it," I told her.

"Canceled until further notice," Helene said. "That's what I had to tell you."

"Okay, thanks. Can I do—?"

"Goodbye," she said. I heard the receiver come down at her end.

Hunting humans has its own blood-rhythm, linking predator and prey so deep each can feel the other's pulse. I know—I've been both. That's the jackpot question you ask a little kid who says he's been sexually abused, the one question that brings out the truth—not what did they *do*, but how did it *feel?*

I know how it feels.

When you're being stalked, it's not your feet that get you trapped, it's your mind.

I know that too.

It's a dance, a dance with rules. The rules don't kick in until you hear the footsteps. When that happens, when you're *in* it, you can feel the animal part of you trying to take over and call the shots. That's the right part of you, the part that can save you. Manhunting isn't a chess match—that only happens in books.

But you can't let survival instinct be the boss. When you're up on the high-wire, speed means nothing—balance is everything.

Fear is good. It sharpens your vision, keeps your blood up, forces all your sensors on full alert.

Terror is bad. It shuts you down, closes your eyes tight, freezes you in place.

If you break cover too soon, you're an easy target. But if you rely on your camouflage, you could end up frozen in the headlights.

The worst place to be is in the middle. When elephants fight, the grass gets trampled. I wanted to go to ground, play my trump card—patience. But that wouldn't work now. Belinda and Morales were dancing to the death and I had only two choices: pick a partner and cut in . . . or stand away and be cut down.

A little past five in the morning, the city still dark. Transition time: too late for the muggers, too early for the citizens.

"She's rolling, not strolling," the Prof's voice, on the cellular phone I held to my ear.

I cut the connection, slipped the phone into my army jacket, looked over at Max. The warrior was sitting in the passenger seat of the Chevy Caprice Arnold Haines had rented, breathing so shallow you had to look real close to see it, like a computer in wait-state. I settled back, waiting for the next piece.

It wasn't fifteen minutes later when the phone purred again. "Bitch just touched down, safe in the pound," the Prof reported.

"Mary, she lives there?"

"Yeah. Looks like she's home, but she's not alone."

"Little weasely guy, mustache?"

"That's him, Jim."

"Okay," I said. "We're moving."

"If she don't sing, give me a ring," the Prof said, promising backup. Then he gave me the address.

T he building was off Third Avenue, mid-scale enough to sport a lobby, but no doorman. Maybe one of those co-ops that went all to hell, jacking up the maintenance costs to cover the empty units— first thing that goes in joints like that is the doorman.

We wanted 8-F. I looked at the name next to the bell: Johnson. Maybe that was Rudy the Weasel's sense of humor.

There's lots of ways to bypass a buzz-in system like they have in most apartment lobbies, but the easiest one is to just follow right behind someone who got the green light himself. Too early in the morning to wait for that to happen. Too early to run a UPS or FedEx hustle either. I was about to call it off, go back to the car and wait for a citizen, when Max pointed to the inner doors. I followed his gaze. A pair of heavy glass doors designed to open in the middle, pull-handles on each side. The glass was smudged, like it hadn't been cleaned in a long time. I made a "So what?" gesture. Max took a couple of steps to the doors, put one hand around each handle, and pulled. There was a lot of play in the doors, they bowed outward as Max pulled. I nodded my head, whipped out a flexible plastic strip and worked it into the opening. The 'loid slid in like it was greased, covering the slip-lock, forcing it back inside. The doors popped open.

We walked across the lobby to a pair of elevators. The whole place looked neglected, downtrodden. Maybe they fired the maintenance crew too. I looked up at the floor indicators, rectangular plastic with numbers painted on the inside. Only one of the elevators was working and its number 8 was lit—probably the last time it was used.

I pointed to an EXIT sign to my left. We walked over. I pushed gently, and the door gave way. A staircase, just like I figured.

We started up, me in the lead, Max behind. I walked slowly, testing each step. I went first because I could hear someone on the stairs before Max could feel them. And because I needed to set the pace: if you climb stairs too fast, you could be winded at the top—it wouldn't happen to Max, but I was a good candidate.

The stairwells were dirty, littered with cigarette butts too old to be yesterday's. Half the lights were burned out. I spotted a broken wine bottle on 4, a dead condom on 5.

I pushed open the door on 8, stuck my head out and looked around. The hall was empty. It was quiet—a stale quiet, just this side of rot.

The doors were all painted a uniform cream color. A bad choice—the parts that weren't chipped were mottled with handprints. 8-F looked sticky to the touch. I dropped to one knee, slipped a self-sealing white #10 envelope under the door.

We waited a couple of minutes. No reaction from inside. I pushed a little black button on the door jamb, heard it buzz softly inside the apartment. I stood back so whoever came to the peephole could see me easily. Max flattened himself to my right, his back against the wall.

I could feel somebody at the peephole, but I wasn't standing close enough to be sure. It wasn't my face I was counting on to get me inside, it was the envelope. An envelope with ten C-notes inside, wrapped in a piece of paper that said:

This is business. There's a lot more of this in it for you. I need something done, and it has to be today.

I heard the rattle of a door chain, then it opened. Rudy stood there, bare-chested, his right hand behind his hip. "You sure you—?" he said just as Max flowed through the opening like white-water over river rocks, pivoting on his right foot, the heel of his left hand cracking just below Rudy's breastbone. Rudy doubled over, airless. Max did something to the back of his neck and Rudy slumped to the floor, out. On the carpet next to him, a switchblade, still in the closed position.

I pointed to the hallway. Max glided over to the side of the opening. I knelt next to Rudy, quickly wrapped a length of duct tape twice around his head, covering his mouth. I razored the tape free, then I turned him on his stomach, pulled his hands behind his back and used another piece on his wrists. I looked up just as Mojo Mary came around the corner, naked except for the pistol she held in one hand. She opened her mouth wide, raised the pistol, but Max had her from behind. The pistol dropped to the floor and Mojo Mary stopped struggling.

Max hauled her over to the couch and pulled her down next to him. He held her in place with one hand, his thumb behind her neck, fingers splayed around her throat.

I pocketed the white envelope, then slid the clip out of the little automatic Mary had dropped, worked the slide to see. . . . Sure enough, a cartridge popped out—there'd been one in the chamber. I walked over to the couch and pulled up a chair so I was facing Mary. Max still held her, but his eyes were on Rudy.

"Just stay easy," I said to her, my voice matching the words. "Nobody's going to hurt you," I promised, leaving the *unless* hanging in the air between us.

Mojo Mary took a deep breath through her nose, displaying her high round breasts and showing me she wasn't going to scream all in the same move. Like the Prof said, a pro ho'.

"This won't take long," I told her. "Just tell me what Morales wanted."

"How did you—" she gasped, her face showing fear for the first time.

"I've got people on it," I said, keeping it vague in case Morales worked her over the phone.

She took another breath. "He just wanted—"

"Don't lie, Mary," I warned her. "Don't even try."

"I'm . . . scared," she said. "If he knew . . ."

"He won't know," I told her. "No way he knows. Not from me, not from you."

"He made me . . . suck it," she said, her voice dropping so low I could barely hear it.

"That's part of the job, right?"

"Not his . . . cock," she said, dropping her voice still another notch. "His gun. His pistol. He made me take it in my mouth. It *hurt*. He made me open my eyes. His face was right there. All sweaty and crazy. Then he cocked the gun—I heard it click. He said, if I didn't tell him, he'd do it. He said, I liked blow jobs so much, he'd show me one. A real one. Blow out the back of my head, that's what he said."

"This was in your work crib? The one on—?"

"No. It was in his car. A fancy red car. He stopped me on the street, made me get in. He drove way north, like for the Triborough? But he didn't go over it, he made this turn. . . . I don't know. We ended up in this scary place, like out in the country or something. It was . . . like empty. Just us. He told me, I didn't do what he wanted and he'd leave me there. Another dead whore, who'd care? . . . That's what he said."

I knew where he'd taken her. Ward's Island. Nothing much out there but a hospital for the criminally insane. Maybe Morales was checking out his new home, before he moved in. "So you told him . . . what?" I asked her.

"I told him the truth," Mojo Mary said, hands fluttering in her lap. "Everything."

"Now tell *me*," I said.

She glanced over at where Rudy was lying all trussed up on the floor. "Did you kill him?" she asked.

"If he was dead, what would we need the gag for?" I answered reasonably. "Nobody's getting killed here. Nobody's getting hurt, either. Just tell me, Mary. Then I'll be out of your life."

"I told him that girl, that Roxanne, what she paid me for."

"To get in touch with me?"

"Yeah."

"And about how you met her in Logan's, all that?"

"Yeah."

"You tell him what this Roxanne wanted? From me?"

"Yes. But I—"

"It's okay," I reassured her. "What else?"

"That's all. Really."

"Don't lie anymore," I warned her. "I'm not playing. You know me a long time, Mary—I don't play."

"I'm *not* playing."

"Is *that* when Morales put the gun in your mouth?" I asked. "When you told him that was all of it?"

"Burke, I . . ."

"He wanted to know about the blonde," I told her, not making it a question. Her eyes were little slot-machine windows—I could see the wheels spinning behind them, trying to wait on three-of-a-kind. "You got any doubts I'll do it?" I asked, stopping the wheel. "You don't know who to be scared of, I'll tell you, Mary—be scared of the one who can do it *now*."

"He's a cop," she said softly. "He can do it anytime he wants. I asked around . . . later. Some of the other girls, they know him. He's . . . been with them, you understand? He's not like other cops. I mean, he pays. Pays full price. But he hurts you, that's what they said."

"S&M hurt? Or—?"

"No. He isn't into whips and chains, not like that. He's just . . . rough. Like he *hates* you while he's doing it. One girl . . . You know Irene? The redhead who works in the—?"

"No," I said, not wanting her to stray off the trail.

"Well, anyway, she took a back-door from him. You know, Greek-style. I mean, he didn't *make* her do it. That's what she does and all.

But there's a way to do it . . . a right way, I mean. It really don't have to hurt if you—"

"I know," I told her, guiding her back to the path.

"He didn't do it the right way. Just didn't care. She told him, but he just grabbed the back of her head and like *shook* it," Mojo Mary said, shaking her right fist like it had a handful of hair in it. "Real hard. Like he was—"

"What about the blonde, Mary?"

"He asked me *everything*. About her, I mean. And I told him. It wasn't much, right?"

"You tell me," I answered her.

"It wasn't. I mean, I didn't *know* anything. I mean, I don't street-stroll, you know that. She was buddies with this Roxanne, not with me."

"You told Morales that they wanted to hire me, get some work done?"

"Yes. But I know you didn't—"

"Right. I didn't. What else?"

"He said, if they ever called again—*ever*—I had to call him. Right away, before I went to the meet. He said, if I didn't call him, if he found out I was in touch with them without telling him, he'd find me."

"And did they—?"

"Never!" she said, almost jumping off the couch with the force of it. "No way I'd—"

"Okay," I told her.

"Okay? That's it? You're not—"

"Everybody has to make a living," I told her. "I'm not mad at you. When Morales comes around, tell him the truth. Tell him I was here, asked you the questions."

"If he knows I told you, he'll—"

"That's right," I interrupted. "When the time comes, you decide."

I stood up. Max did too, bringing Mojo Mary along with him. I didn't bother warning her about calling the cops—it wasn't something she'd do.

"I'll leave you to get the tape off," I told her.

She knelt next to Rudy, put her face close to his. "He's breathing," she said, almost indifferent.

"I wouldn't stick you with a body," I told her. "Just cut the tape off real careful—he'll be fine." I nodded at Max. The warrior cracked open the door, checked both ways. Then he stepped out, heading for the staircase. I closed the door behind him, turned to Mojo Mary. "We need a few minutes, make sure there isn't any problem leaving, okay?"

"Sure," she said. "Okay if I go into the kitchen, get a knife? So I can start on—"

"Better not," I said quietly. "I heard you were pretty good with those things yourself."

"Rudy taught me," she said. "Taught me good." She turned her back to me, bent over. A crescent-shaped scar blossomed on one tawny thigh, just below her butt. "That's his mark," she said.

I looked at the scar, not saying anything. Mojo Mary looked over one shoulder back at me, still bent at the waist. I wondered if Rudy was going to wake up with a mark of his own. The cellular phone in my jacket buzzed. Once, twice. Then it went dead. All clear.

"You want to jet, now's the time," I told her, looking down at Rudy.

I dropped Max at his temple, returned the Chevy to Hertz, took the subway back to my place. I picked up Pansy, went down to the garage and pulled out in my Plymouth. Then I drove over to West Street, parked the Plymouth on an open strip of asphalt, slipped on Pansy's lead and walked over to the river.

The Hudson was calm—the water looked like the pebbled glass in those old-fashioned office doors. A giant red cement-barge sat on the water, the name *Adelaide* carefully stenciled on the stern. The captain's wife, my best guess. A brown tug with all-black topsides was pushing the barge upriver, probably to one of the yards in the Bronx, pushing so slow that a passing sailboat looked turbocharged. Another tug with the same brown-and-black paint scheme caught up and ran alongside for a few minutes, then it pulled away in a wide sweep, heading back to base.

I lit a smoke, wondering why I felt so safe out there, open and exposed, a sniper's dream. It hit me all at once. I couldn't run, but I was safe until I *did* something.

They were stalking each other—and I couldn't stay out of the middle. I was a blind leech in muddy swampwater, searching for a pulse. The bigger animals wouldn't chase me, couldn't catch me if they did. But if I didn't find that pulse, I could starve to death.

The cellular phone in my jacket purred, making me jump. I pulled it out, my back to the river, scanning the wide street.

"What?" I said into the mouthpiece.

"I got it!" Hauser's voice, low volume, high energy. Whatever it was, he was pumped.

"Are you—?"

"In my office," he said. Then the connection went dead.

No way to go back to my place, drop Pansy off. I'd been out long enough for Morales to have picked up my trail. Some other cop might have spread some cash around the streets—"Call me when you see this car," like that—but Morales wouldn't do that. When he was partnered with McGowan, he let the Irishman do that kind of work. Alone, he was a blackjack kind of cop, the kind you couldn't do business with. He'd pay a whore for sex, but not for information—Morales expected *that* on the house.

Scaring people isn't the best way if you need them working for you. It's okay when all you need is a piece of information—fear makes some people talk. But it's easy to overdose that kind of thing—easy to scare people so much that they freeze. McGowan knew the difference. Morales didn't. Or didn't care.

Morales wouldn't go on the pad, wouldn't take a bribe to look the other way. But he'd shoot you in the back and lie about it with a straight face. Morales had been out too long. He was rotten with honor, as dangerous as a nerve-gas canister in a subway car— with Morales, the best you could hope for is that the body wouldn't be yours.

I loaded Pansy into the car, headed south on West Street. I made a U-turn at Chambers, heading uptown. I cut east on Little West Twelfth, did some twists and double-backs through the Meat Market, then pulled over and waited.

Five minutes, ten minutes. Nothing. I knew Morales could track—he'd shown me that much—but I also knew he had no patience. I put the Plymouth in gear and headed back uptown.

I found a place to park on Eighth, in the mid-Twenties. I wouldn't leave Pansy in the car, not in this city. A guy I know in Brooklyn, he had a beautiful Rottweiler, kept it in his yard, behind a high wrought-iron fence. The dog would challenge anyone who walked by, but it couldn't get out. Some two-bit gangstah-dressed punk walked up and stood right by the fence. When the Rottie came over, the punk sprayed metallic paint right in the dog's eyes. The Rottie screamed, tearing at its eyes with its claws. The punk was still watching when the cops rolled up, the paint can in his hand, giggling.

The cops called the Animal Control people. They tranq'ed the Rottie, but it was too late—one eye was gone, the other burned right in its socket.

The Rottie lived, but it was blind.

The punk went to Family Court. He told the judge he was walking by the yard one night. He couldn't see the Rottie in the blackness. The dog growled, and he jumped, scared. His homeboys laughed. "Nobody disses me like that," he said. So he came back with the can of spray paint for payback.

The judge put him on Probation.

When he got shot in the chest a few weeks later, the cops put it down to gangbanging. At least that's what it said on the report. They never got to interview the punk—he died in the ambulance.

"No dogs allowed," the slug at the desk said, not even bothering to take the cigarette out of his mouth.

"Where's it say that?" I asked, looking around for a sign. The only one I could see said NO SMOKING.

"Building rules," the slug said.

"I got a pass," I told him, leaning over the desk, a twenty-dollar bill in my hand.

The slug took the money, dropped his eyes like he was reading. I took the stairs—I didn't want anybody running into Pansy on the elevator.

Outside Hauser's office, I turned the handle to the door. It opened easily. I walked inside, Pansy slightly behind me to my left.

"What the fuck is *that?*" Hauser greeted me.

"She's a Neapolitan mastiff," I told him. "Don't worry, she's mellow."

Hauser gave me a dubious look. I threw Pansy the hand signal— she dropped to the floor. "Stay," I told her. It was just to comfort Hauser—staying in one spot was one of Pansy's specialties.

I sat down across from Hauser, his desk between us. I noticed four empty white Styrofoam coffee cups—Hauser had another in his hand.

"You gonna finish that?" I asked him, tilting my chin toward about half a roll with thick butter oozing out the sides.

"You want it?" he replied.

"Yeah," I said.

When he nodded, I reached over and took it, flipped it back over my shoulder without looking. I heard the click of teeth. "Jesus!" Hauser said. "She just—"

"Pansy would catch bullets, you covered them with enough butter," I told him.

Hauser shook his head in amazement—like all real reporters, there wasn't a whole lot that *didn't* interest him. All the urgency he'd shown on the phone was gone—whatever he had, he was going to showcase it, slip a little bit out at a time. I didn't push him, knew there was no point.

"Loretta Barclay," he finally said. "That name ring a bell?"

"The woman in Scarsdale, right? The one who got killed . . . with the red ribbon left in—"

"Right," Hauser said, leaning forward. "The cops have been working on it. And it doesn't look random anymore."

"Because . . . ?"

"Because she didn't exactly come from money, this woman. In

fact, she's got a nice little track record of her own. How does a twenty-year sentence in Indiana strike you? She did three of it, then she went over the wall. Off the grounds, actually—she just walked away. One of the guards went with her. They found him . . . dead. In a motel room in Youngstown, Ohio. He had enough pills in him to drop a horse. Left a suicide note too, but the cops never bought it—it was too soon after the escape. And the woman, she just vanished."

"When was this?" I asked him.

"She was arrested in 1979, tried in 1980, sentenced the same year. She walked away in '83."

"They been after her all that time?"

"Right. The feds too. Turns out she met the guy she married in Boston. When she was dancing in one of those topless joints."

"That's kind of open for a woman on the run," I said. "How could she—"

"She had the works," Hauser cut in. "New face, new chest too. The cops think it had to be the same plastic surgeon. Beautiful work . . . no way to tell unless you had her under a magnifying glass. A lot of those strippers get implants anyway—that wouldn't make anyone suspicious. She dyed her hair, blond to brunette, let it grow real long. I saw a picture of her—a copy of the original they took when she was booked in Indiana. Believe me, her own mother wouldn't have recognized her. If it wasn't for the fingerprints, they never would have tumbled to it."

"So they think it's somebody from her past?"

"They think it *could* be. They talked to the cops here, but there's really no connect to *our* pattern. I mean, they were all killed, all stabbed to death . . . but that's all."

"So the big break, it's just that she was—"

"There's more," Hauser said, his voice tightening. "One of the reasons she got such a short sentence was she rolled over. She named—"

"Short sentence?" I said. "Twenty years? What was the beef, triple homicide?"

"Indecent liberties with a child," Hauser told me. "Forty-seven counts. Forty-*seven*. She was part of a ring, recruiting little girls for . . . movies. The oldest one was thirteen. It was a professional operation—they had a house rented near the state line. She was a dance teacher, modern dance—the kids were her students. When they popped her, she was looking at Natural Life. No question about the kids testifying like there usually is—the cops had the movies, and even an ACLU judge high on marijuana wouldn't have suppressed *that* evidence.

"There were four other people, three men and a woman. She turned them all in. And they all got forever sentences, Life Plus. She got to go to minimum security and then—"

"They got all of them?" I interrupted.

Hauser nodded, like he was glad I was finally with the program. "All but one," he said. "One of the men took off just before they came for him."

"And the cops think he might have . . . ?"

"I don't know. Me, I don't see how it could be. Why would he wait a dozen years? And why would he risk his own freedom just for revenge—the FBI's looking for him too. Besides, it's not like those kind of people have any loyalty. . . ."

"You're right. And when they dusted . . . ?"

"Nothing. Only the prints that should have been there. Whoever did it, he was wearing gloves, I guess."

"So this Barclay woman, she—"

"Not Barclay," Hauser interrupted. "Her real name was Thomchuk. Barbara Ann Thomchuk."

"Yeah, okay. Thomchuk. There's no way her husband could have done it? Even if he was out of town, alibi'ed to the hilt, he could have paid . . ."

"He wasn't playing around on her," Hauser said. "The cops checked. And even if he was, they had a pre-nup, a solid-gold one, drawn up by a top matrimonial firm in White Plains. He could just pay her some money, walk away clean. He wasn't having business problems, didn't owe money to the sharks. He didn't have a drug habit, wasn't a boozer. And *her* life wasn't insured at all, only his."

"So you think the answer's in her past?"

"*Got* to be," Hauser said. "Tomorrow morning, I'll be on it. I already got plane reservations for Chicago—that's the closest airport."

"Let me know," I said, getting up to go. "I think you're on the right track."

When I was doing time—after I hooked up with the Prof and stopped being stupid about my life—I studied this one guy real close. The Prof told me to do that. "Keep a tight rein on your game, schoolboy. You want a clue, watch those who do." The thing about this guy, he was a skinner. A tree-jumper. Slash-and-burn rapist. And he only did kids. I studied him because he could say *anything*, anything at all, and it would come out like he was telling the truth.

What really impressed me was him passing a lie-detector test. The cops came up to the prison—they wanted to question him about some missing kids. This guy, he told them he could lead them right to the kids . . . he said they were all snatched by the same ring of freaks . . . but he'd have to be out to do it. Let him out, no surveillance, and he'd call in as soon as he learned where the kids were hidden. It should have been a slam dunk NO from the cops, right? I mean, who'd take that kind of chance? But what made it hard for them was the way this freak breezed through the test—when he said he knew who had the missing kids, it came up No Deception.

Finally, they decided not to go for it . . . even though they half-believed him. I thought he had some trick, something I could use myself when I was out in the World again. But he told me it was no trick at all. If you don't feel things, you can't show them. You stop feeling deep enough—all the way inside you—and you never bounce the needles.

But it wasn't like he was a pure stone-face. He could laugh—even when he didn't see anything funny. He could cry too—Doc told me he used to do it in group all the time. Did it in court too, faking remorse the same way he faked laughter.

He tried to explain it to me. He said you could cry on cue—all you had to do was think of something bad that happened to *you* when you were a kid, something that made you feel real sad inside.

I tried it. Alone in my cell. Just to see if it worked. I went back, in my head. Went back to being a kid. But then I started shaking so bad I couldn't stop. My teeth were chattering, but the crying wouldn't come. All I got was those red dots behind my eyes, the red dots merging into a haze until I was looking through it . . . a red filter over my eyes. It made me afraid, that haze. Because the only way to make it go away was killing.

And I could never kill the right ones. Could never find them.

So I went dead myself. Went dead instead. At least I tried—I don't always pull it off. But when it comes to flat-faced, no-react lying, I'm an ace.

That's why Hauser didn't know what he'd really said—didn't know he'd given me the code-breaker.

And it wasn't in Indiana.

I knew it then—I was on the spot.

Marked.

Judas-goated right into the clearing. If I walked away, it wouldn't be safety, it would be proof. Proof for the survivor.

I couldn't cover all the bets, not by myself.

I drove to the Bronx before morning light. First stop, the Mole's junkyard. He listened, his eyes somewhere else, absently fumbling with some electronic gadget he was working on. But when he nodded Okay, I knew I could take that to the bank.

Next stop, Frankie. I waited outside the two-family house he lived in. Actually, he lived in the basement, off the books. That's the kind of thing the city would bust a Bronx homeowner for . . . while ignoring the after-hours joints with no fire exits. When Frankie rolled out to do his road work, I pulled alongside in the Plymouth. He climbed into the front seat.

"I want to ask you a favor," I said.

"Okay," he replied.

"What I need—"

"I meant, Okay I'll do it, not Okay, you can ask me," the kid said, his voice low and steady.

"It's not crew business," I told him. "It's just me. And there's nothing in it for you—this isn't about a score."

"I never had no family before," Frankie said. "But I always knew what I would do if I did. I used to dream about it Upstate, the way other guys dreamed about pussy. I can *get* pussy, you understand what I mean? But family . . . ? I know what I'd be if it wasn't for the Prof. A fucking drunk, with no respect, not from anyone. Specially not from myself. I'd rather die like I am right now than live like I was, okay?"

"Okay, kid," I told him, holding out my hand.

After he shook it, I told him what I wanted.

"Let's get off first," the Prof said to me. It was later that night. I was in the passenger seat of Clarence's Rover. The Prof was in the back, his upper body between the two front buckets.

"Can't do that," I told him. "I know it's one of them, but it could be both."

"If murder's the crime, one or two, it's all the same time, school-boy. I don't feature this decoy shit."

"It's the only way," I said. "Here's what I know. They may both be in it, but they're not together."

"Who gives a flying fuck about that?" the Prof challenged, one hand on my upper arm. "Remember where you come from, son . . . same place as me, see? You know the rules. Hell, I *taught* you some of them. Listen to me. You been . . . messed up for a while. Ever since the . . ."

"I know," I told him. I did know. That house in the Bronx. The kid. The dead kid. "Don't you ever feel . . . bad about it?" I asked.

"You don't mean bad, you mean guilty," the Prof replied, eyes holding me as hard as his hand was. "I feel bad. I feel bad about a whole motherfucking *bunch* of things. But guilty? I'm *not* guilty, and I say that to the Lord, not to some cocksucking, ass-kissing, black-robed weasel-faced piece of dogshit scumbag judge. I didn't mean for it to happen—neither did you. And you know that. You know what guilt is, son? It's the evil people *put* on you. Like a hex.

A voodoo curse. Guilt's nothing but loan shark's money, you understand. They don't *want* you to pay it off—motherfuckers live forever on the interest, like the miserable vampires they are, see?"

"Yeah, but . . ."

"There ain't no 'but,' goddamn it," he whispered urgently. "You feel bad, do something to make it right. But this human-sacrifice bit ain't shit. Remember this—they both the same color."

I knew the color he meant. Blue. "Listen, brother," I said. "I know what you mean, and I'm not arguing. I wouldn't disrespect you like that. But here's the thing: if one of them is bent, and I do the other, then I'm boxed. Down for the count. 'Cause one thing's sure, Prof—whoever's doing it, they're watching me. Watching you too—this wasn't hatched up in one night."

"I stand with my father," Clarence said. "Last time, they did what we should do—shoot first. This time, I will be ready, mahn."

"I'm gonna play it out," I told them. "We got two trains coming on the same track from different directions. I'm standing in the middle. All I gotta do is jump out the way just before they hit. I pull it off, and it's done. I don't and I am. It feels . . . right. It's gotta play the way I say."

"Your rhyme ain't worth a dime," the little man said. "But I love you, schoolboy. And I promise you this—you don't jump in time, I'll take what's mine."

Even when I was a little kid, I knew the truth. If I wanted to stand my ground, I'd have to steal some first.

My family is my ground now. All I've got. Everything.

If I screwed it up, if it didn't play the way I figured it . . . then I knew what had to be done. Knew I wouldn't be around to do it.

The Prof can do many things, but he's no assassin. I couldn't let him die trying.

So I did the right thing.

I went over to Mama's. Sat down in my booth and told her everything. She never made a note, but I knew it was engraved in her mind.

If I didn't jump off the tracks in time, Max the Silent would visit the people who had shoved me down there.

It was another three days before it happened. Almost midnight when the cellular phone in my jacket chirped like a damn cricket, jolting me awake. I opened the channel.

"What?"

"She call. Say you call back, quick."

"See you later, Mama," I said.

"You still—?"

I cut the connection.

"Hello . . ." Her voice was trembly, trailing off to a whisper-breath.

"It's me," I said.

"I've got it," she said. "The proof. Certain-sure. And I'm scared. He could be—"

"Say where and when."

"*Now!* Right now. Can you—?"

I said Yes. She gave me the address.

It was on Charlton Street, close by the river. Her name was on the bell: Belinda Roberts. I rang it, got buzzed in. It was a walk-up, four flights.

The door was standing open. Belinda stuck her head out, waved me on. She was wearing only a black jersey bra and a pair of white shorts. I closed the gap between us. As I walked into the apartment, she stepped to one side. I could see from the way it was laid out that it was the only apartment on the floor.

"Have a seat," she said, pointing down the hall. The place was L-shaped, turning a corner as you walked in. The floor was wood, bleached so white it looked unreal. The left-hand wall was all bookcases. The right was all windows, a thick cage of steel bars blocked most of the view. Straight ahead was darkness, the only light a baby spot, its rose-colored light illuminating a big wooden chair. The chair . . . I walked closer, took a look. It was an execution chair, or a damn good replica. Complete with heavy leather straps on the arms and a metal electrode cap. Above it, a glossy black-and-white poster: a photograph of an electric chair—the same chair? maybe . . . At the top of the poster, in blood-red letters:

CAPITAL PUNISHMENT
SOMETIMES IT'S A <u>FATAL</u> MISTAKE!

"What's this supposed to be?" I asked, turning around to face her. That's when I saw the big automatic in her hands. She held it trained on my chest, feet spread in a combat shooting stance, close enough for me to see the sweat on her face . . . and the long tube silencer screwed into the barrel of the gun.

"It's your turn now," she said, holding the gun dead steady. "Remember? Remember when I came to your place? Remember what you made me do? Well, now it's *you* I don't trust. I'm too scared to play around."

"What do you want?" I asked, watching her eyes—so I wouldn't have to look at the pistol.

"I want what you wanted," she said. "To know I can trust. If you're wired . . . if you're with *him,* I'll . . ."

"I'm not with anybody," I told her.

"Then show me," she said. "Do what I did. Take off your clothes. All of them. Slow."

"Watch my hands," I said quietly. "I can't take this stuff off without reaching, you understand? There's no wire. I'm doing what you want. Just don't get nervous, all right?"

"Why would I be nervous?" she snorted. "Because I'm a bitch, is that it?"

"Anybody would be nervous," I said. "I'm nervous. Probably more than you, okay? But I'm not pointing a gun at anyone."

"Just do it," she said. "Do it now."

I removed my army jacket. Very slowly. I dropped it to the floor, knowing the padding wouldn't let any of the metal clank. I pulled my black sweatshirt and white T-shirt over my head, dropped them on top of the jacket. I held my hands over my head, turned around completely.

"Do the rest," she said.

I unbuckled the black chinos, unzipped the fly. I went to one knee, careful to keep my hands where she could see them. Then I pulled off the boots, one at a time. Socks too. When I stood up, the pants fell down. I stepped out of them, waited to see if . . .

"Come on," she said, her voice as unwavering as the pistol she was holding.

I pulled my shorts down, stepped out of them too.

"Step away," she said, her voice deliberately harsh, the way cops learn on the street—keep control of the guy you're arresting—keep the reins *tight*—don't talk, *demand*. "Not to the side, back! More. Get *away* from those clothes—now!"

I backed off. She came forward, closing the gap, walking splay-footed, keeping the pistol centered, perfectly balanced.

"Further," she ordered. The back of my legs touched the electric chair. "Stop," she said.

I raised my hands again, trying to reassure her.

"Sit down," she said. "In the chair."

I did it.

Belinda circled to my left, as careful as a wasp stalking a scorpion. My eyes followed her, but I held my body straight. "Put your arms where they're supposed to go," she said, almost out of my peripheral vision. "I've got to look through your stuff, and I can't do it while I'm holding a gun on you."

I laid my forearms on the broad flat wood arms of the electric chair as she stepped in behind me. I felt the barrel of the pistol in the back of my neck. "I'm going to fasten the straps," she said. "I can do it with one hand. If you move, you're dead."

I sat still, breathing through my nose to keep the panic at bay. I heard the metal-on-metal as the restraints snapped into place. She pulled another strap around my waist. I heard that one snap closed too, somewhere behind me.

Belinda circled back in front of me, walked over to where I'd dropped my clothes. She put the pistol on the floor, started pawing over my jacket. "You got toys, huh?" she said, pulling out the Velcro panel, holding up the handcuff speed key.

"I never leave home without one," I said, hoping for a smile. I didn't get one—she went back to work, rooting through my clothes.

"No lock picks?" she asked.

"Never use them," I replied, still trying for flip.

"Don't worry," she said. "I've got some."

Before I could ask her what the hell that meant, she turned back to her task, her face tightened in fierce concentration. I kept it quiet—maybe after she saw I was clean . . .

Finally, she stood up. "No wires," she said. "No guns either."

"I'm playing it straight," I told her, sick of games, scared real deep, trying to sound calm, keep her from spooking.

"Yeah. Maybe you are." She walked back toward me, pistol in her hand again. "You've got a nice body for a man your age," she said. "Pretty thin, though. You work out?"

"No."

"Too bad. It can make you feel real, real good, you do it right."

"I'll have to try it," I promised. "Now, how about if you take—"

"Just sit there," Belinda said. "It's time you learned what's going on. You have any cigarettes?"

"In my jacket."

She walked over, found my pack. "You want one?" she asked.

"Yeah."

"Okay," she said, coming close, holding it to my lips, striking one of my wooden matches. I took a long drag, smelling her sweat—a sour, ugly smell. What had Immaculata said? Coarse?

She pulled the cigarette away, went back to where she was standing. Then she carefully placed the burning cigarette in an ashtray.

"That's one," she said absently, like she was speaking to herself.

"One what?" I asked, trying to keep her talking.

"Sssshh," she said, bending forward at the waist, arching her back so I was looking directly into her cleavage. "It's a secret. You be a good boy, maybe I'll tell you about it, okay?"

"Sure," I replied, trying to sound reassuring without spooking her.

"You want the truth?" she asked, straightening up, hands on hips, looking down at me. "This is just like the movies, isn't it? Where the detective gets everyone in the room and solves the crime? Well, there's only two of us here. And only one of us knows what's going on. So I guess it's my turn. . . ." She walked a few paces closer, then stopped. "You want me to solve the crime, Burke?"

"Do it," I told her.

"I love him," she said calmly. "George, I love him. Don't give me any funny looks—I saw how you were looking at that painting in Jon's apartment . . . the one on Van Dam. I'm not like that—I'm no groupie—serial killers don't get me hot. It's not what George did, it's what he *is*. My lover. Since we were kids. That wasn't how it was planned, though. You want to know how it was planned?"

"Yeah, I do," I said, staying in my center, willing her to stay in hers too, stable, calm . . . pushing that out at her, a cloud I wanted to wrap around her, a mist on her vision, slowing her pulse with mine. . . .

"The way it was planned, we were the entertainment. Did that ever happen to you? Where you go to a party and you think you're going to have fun . . . and then it turns out you *are* the fun? That happened to me.

"I loved this guy in high school. I mean, I *worshipped* him. I'm the kind of woman, I love you, I'll do anything for you. Anything. I was only fifteen. I didn't know . . . but I should have. When you look back, everything's clear, isn't it?"

I just nodded, wanting her to go on, keep talking until her motor ran down.

She put her hands behind her back, looked down like a bashful kid. "He invited me to this party. I was so excited. But when I got there, it was just him. And some of his friends. They didn't actually . . . force me. He said it would prove I loved him. So I did it.

"But that was after . . . First, they brought us to this big house in the country. All us kids, I mean. This old man was in charge. He was a rich man. A philanthropist, they said. In the foster home, that's what they said. It would be like we were getting adopted. We all went to live there. I was about ten . . . eleven, I don't remember. George was there too. And a bunch of others.

"We were the entertainment. The old man would do things to us. After a while, he made us do things to each other. Sometimes, he brought his friends in. To watch. At first, just to watch. But sometimes, they would do it to us too.

"I'm going backwards," she said. "I do that sometimes. But I'm not crazy—I wouldn't want you to think that. Where was I . . . ?"

"You were the entertainment," I said. "First for this freakish old man. Later for some high-school jock."

"You *are* listening," she replied. "That's good. You're a good listener. Did anyone ever tell you that? I knew you were a good listener, the first time I met you. In Central Park, do you remember that?"

"Yeah. You said you liked my dog."

"I *did* like her," Belinda said, a hurt tone in her voice. "I knew what you were, even back then. A few months later, Morales told me. He told me what you do. He hates you. So he told me what you did. And I thought, one day for sure, I could use that. A man like you."

"What did Morales tell you?"

"He told me you were a hit man," she said, closing to within a couple of feet. "A paid killer. He said you killed a few people. He said you were a liar and a thief and a killer. I knew I would like you."

"None of that's true," I told her.

"Yes it is. I checked. And you know what? Morales, he *helped* me check. And then . . ." She walked in tiny circles, nibbling at her lower lip, looking down, the pistol waving aimlessly in her hand. I stayed quiet. Her head came up: "Where was I?"

"You said you loved George," my voice gentle and soothing, still trying.

"Yes. I love him. That wasn't supposed to happen. They made us . . . do things with each other. Me and George, we did it a lot. Even before we . . . could, like. I mean, before he could even get it up. When he was a boy. That's really when I loved him . . . when we were in it together. Like brother and sister, so close. If I love you, I'll do anything for you."

"What did he want you to do?" I asked.

"Kill," she said, the word as dead as her eyes—a pretty-painted house with no furniture inside. "The case against George, the one in New York, the woman on University Place, it wasn't really that strong. Fortunato said he could get it overturned if he had some-thing—newly discovered evidence, that's what he called it. I was going to mess up the trial. I had this plan. I'd jerk George off on a visit, into a condom. Then I'd plant it inside one of the others. But that was stupid. George told me it was stupid—the only way you get the same DNA is from identical twins—it would lead them right to me. George wouldn't want that. Besides, he always wore a rubber when he . . . AIDS, you know. George always said he wasn't gonna let one of those cunts kill him from her grave. So I used the red rib-bon. It wasn't that hard. To do it, I mean." She had her hands clasped in front of her, still looking down. All of a sudden she dropped to her knees. Dropped hard—I could hear the dull thud when her knees hit the wood. She reached her right hand behind her. When she brought it back around, a long red ribbon trailed from her fingers.

"I did it for love," she said, bowing her head again.

I sat there, strapped in place, working on calm, watching. I had one shot—one thing that might spin her. But the one shot was like a bullet in a derringer—the target had to be close. Her head came up slowly, a tiny bit at a time, her eyes going slowly over me, climb-ing until she was looking into my face. Now . . .

"You have no love, Eunice," I said softly.

She rocked back on her heels like she'd been slapped, face a mottled red-and-white. "You . . ." she whisper-snarled.

"Eunice Melody Moran," I said, moving into the rhythm, trying to wash over her with words, get her spinning, keep her against the ropes, then . . . "You changed your name. Easy enough to do. Just like Barbara Thomchuk did. I don't know about the woman on Uni-versity Place. . . . I guess George did that one on his own, huh?"

"How could you . . . ?"

"I'm not a cop," I said, pushing her, working fast, closing in now. "I'm a criminal. A professional. Just like you thought. Just like Morales told you. There were seven people on the list. In that pyra-mid trust, yes? George was first, so he gets the money until he's gone. You're way down . . . last. By the time you got your hands on that money, you'd be an old woman. I don't blame you. It was brilliant, the way you did it. And I know why you really want George out of prison. You tried to have him hit inside. That was a pretty good plan, but you didn't know who you were dealing with. I do. I know those guys. I can make it happen. Right in his PC cell. One word to the right guys and he's charcoal. I'm no problem for you, girl. We can do this. Together, you and me. All I want is some money. Just a fair price for a piece of work. You were seventh on the list, right? Five people ahead of you, not counting George. And George, he's as good as dead right now. He stays, he escapes, he wins his appeal—it all comes out the same. That's down to five. You did three of them . . . at least three of them, right?"

"Four," she said. "There's only one left now. A man. I just made that up . . . about the red ribbon. I got the idea from George. I mean, he didn't know *why* I was doing it. But he said, if I made them look like sex murders, they'd never suspect a woman did it. *You* didn't suspect it, did you? You're just a man. A weak, stupid man. Chasing shadows, and scared of them too. There never *were* any red ribbons. But the last one, a man . . . I can't make it look like a rape, so . . ."

". . . so that's perfect," I finished for her. "That's the kind of work I do—you said so yourself. A hundred grand flat and I'll do them both, George and the other guy."

"You *do* think I'm crazy, don't you?" she said, a bright smile on her face. "I let you go and you'd run right to your pal Morales, wouldn't you? You're no killer. I asked around—that was all bullshit street gossip. You're a con man, that's what you are."

"I can get it done," I told her. "Why don't you just—?"

"What, just *listen* to you? You're lying. You'd say anything to stay alive. *Do* anything too. I know about that. That's what I did. Did . . . did *anything*. That old man . . ."

"Capshaw?" I asked, trying to get her talking again, trying to catch her in a loop, anything . . .

"Capshaw? Oh yes. Capshaw. He's still making us play. Even dead, he can do that. He has the power. Money, that's the power. He told us. He *showed* us. And I was the last."

"What's this foundation thing?"

"The Adelnaws Foundation? That's his. And his friends' too. He told us about it. In his will, but it only happens if he dies of natural causes. He knew what we were. He knew what we'd do. So he made us wait. Spell it backwards."

I tried to do it in my head. . . . SWANLEDA—didn't make sense. "I don't get it," I told her.

"Swan Leda," she said, offhand, the way you give someone your phone number. "It's from Greek mythology. Zeus turned himself into a swan. So he could rape Leda. Capshaw turned himself into . . . I don't know, whatever he was. Rich, I guess. He turned himself rich, so he could rape us. I was the last one. He called me, and I went up there to visit him. Just before he died. And he told me, about the will and all. I was last on the list."

"But if he told you—"

"Yes! You understand. You really do. That was my gift. Not the list—we all knew about the list—but the names, the *real* names . . . I was the only one who had *that* list."

"He knew what would happen . . . ?"

"Of course he knew. He was my family, like he was my father. In my family, we know what to do. We all knew it, but I was the only one who knew it *all*."

My spine shuddered. I took a shallow breath, tried again, "Look, all you have to do is—"

"*Here's* what I'm going to do, Mr. Burke." She stepped on my words, focused now, her voice clipped and precise. "Listen good. And see if you still think I'm crazy. I'm leaving here soon. I'm going to meet Morales. One-on-one, I told him. And he's too macho-stupid to ever tell anybody else. He's coming to the loft, the one on Van Dam. That's where you're going to kill him."

"Okay, sure. I'm with you. . . ."

"Sure you are, honey. Believe me, you *are* going to kill him. Morales has his notes. Somewhere, I don't know where, he's got his notes. He's an old harness bull, he'll have notes. He's been tracking you for a good while now. Lots of guys on the job know about it."

"Bullshit," I said. "Morales has no friends."

"That's right. That's why you thought he was the one shooting at you. At that gym in the Bronx. That's was me—I'm a very good

shot—qualified Expert every year at the range. I missed on purpose . . . and it worked. See, Morales doesn't *need* friends for this
one," she said, a wide smile on her face. "Because you're going to
kill him. Bang-bang, he's dead. And then you're going to come after
me. Come right here. You were waiting for me. No sign of forced
entry—you must have picked the locks. I bet they'll even find a set
of picks in your jacket. And here's your gun," she said, waving the
automatic. "Silencer and all. A real pro outfit. But I was too fast for
you. I got the gun away from you and shot you. Right between the
eyes. At close range, as we fought over the gun."

"It'll never fly," I said. "Who's gonna believe I was waiting—"

"Oh, everybody will believe it all right," she said. "Why, look!
Here's a cigarette butt. And I don't smoke. Maybe they should
check the saliva, see if they can make a DNA match. They'll have
plenty to work with—head wounds don't hardly bleed at all."

"Anyone can take a—"

"I know. I just did. See, the problem isn't really you, Burke. It's
Morales. That stupid grunt, he's been chasing me for a long, long
time. Only he didn't know it, I don't think. He knew something was
wrong with a couple of those murders, but nobody would listen.
Any other cop, he'd have gone on with his life. But Morales, he
doesn't *have* a life. Sooner or later, he was going to . . . Ah, it doesn't
matter, does it? You and Morales, you're both going to solve my
problems. All my problems."

"It won't work. Why don't you—?"

"Shut up!" she snapped. "You're done talking. The only reason
I'm not killing you right this second is maybe Morales won't show
up on time. He could get in an accident, have a flat tire—I don't
know. But I have to do him before I do you, just to make sure."

"It won't help," I said. "What I know, what I just told you—it's
all written down. If anything happens to me—"

"*Liar!*" she hissed out at me. "Dirty liar. You don't have anybody.
Just other . . . people like you. Thieves. Even if you did leave something, they'd only want money. I'll *have* money."

"What if Morales doesn't show up at all?" I tried. "Or what if he
has backup? You could talk your way out of a lot of things, but not a
dead body in your apartment."

"He'll show," Belinda said. "I got everything I need from you. Well, *maybe* everything. We'll see. . . ."

She pulled the jersey bra up over her breasts, then over her head. She slipped off the shorts, stood there naked. "You think a man can be raped?" she whispered.

"I know they can," I said.

"I don't mean by another man, like in prison. Do you think a woman can rape a man?"

"I don't know."

"You and me, we're gonna find out, honey. Don't go away now."

She walked down the hall, an exaggerated wiggle to her hips, looking over one shoulder, blowing me a kiss. When she came back, she had a blue washcloth in her hand. She got on her hands and knees and started crawling toward me. When she got right on top of me, she raised her head, licked her lips. "I'm going to make you come," she purred. "In my mouth. And I'm going to spit it up on this," she told me, holding out the washcloth. Her eyes flickered under long lashes, looking up at my face. "Looks like you're not just a hit man, Burke," she whispered. "You're a rapist too."

"You're out of your—"

"No," she said. "No, I'm not. I look good, don't I? Isn't this perfect? I'm going to rape you. You're going to get nice and hard, and you're going to come in my mouth. Even though you know what I'm going to do with it. Even though you know you're going to die. You can't help yourself. Just watch. . . ."

She pulled my cock toward her, stuffed its limpness into her mouth, sucked hard. I felt a tremor. *No!* Another, like a little shock wave. I couldn't . . . stop it. I felt myself go crazy, right in my own mind. I couldn't—she couldn't make me. But people *did* make me . . . when I was a kid. I felt that come back at me . . . and then the red dots flashed behind my eyes until they merged into a scream inside me and I snapped my head forward, trying to drive my forehead into the top of her skull. . . . It didn't work—the leather straps pulled me up short. She craned her neck, looking up at me from under her bangs, my cock still in her mouth. She winked at me like we were sharing a joke—then she went back to work. I looked down, looked at her mass of chestnut curls covering my lap. And I went dead.

She tried for another few minutes, licking, sucking, making little noises. But I stayed dead.

Her head came up, lunatic eyes shining with joy. "It doesn't matter," she said. "You just sit here, be a good boy. Maybe, if you're *real* good, when I get back, I'll give you another chance."

She got to her feet, brought her face down to where we were almost touching, closed her eyes, and spit full in my face.

When I opened my eyes again, she was at the end of the hall, dressed in a yellow turtleneck and black pants, a pocketbook over one shoulder.

"See you soon," she said, and blew me a kiss.

Strapped in that chair, waiting, I was cold. Not from the temperature, from inside me. I went into that safe place, the place where ice cauterizes, makes you numb. You can think things there, but you can't feel them. I didn't want to feel. . . . The only option on that menu was Terror.

I had a plan going in—I thought it over first. It was a good plan—no way Belinda was going to kill me in her own apartment—too many risks. How could she explain it to the cops?

But after she explained it to me, I could see it happening.

Getting people out of the way, that was the real plan. Hauser was too much of a news hound to let him stay around. No telling what kind of stunt he'd pull if he thought there was a story in it. The Prof and Clarence, they were professionals all right, but they were my family first. The last time I got them in something . . . that time in the Bronx . . . I wasn't going to do that again.

I wanted to save Max for vengeance. If it came to that, he could take his time, work around the edges, strike when it was safe. Max isn't bulletproof—but if you don't know he's coming, he can't be stopped.

I had my backup ready: brains and muscle both. The Mole and Frankie. Only the Mole is a lunatic and Frankie's down to one arm.

I rocked in the chair, trying to tip it over. Maybe I could get free that way—maybe the crash would say something to the people downstairs. She hadn't put a gag in my mouth, so I figured yelling would be a waste of time. I shoved hard to my right—the chair didn't budge. I couldn't see where the legs met the floor, but I guess it was anchored somehow.

Calm, stay calm. I tried to remember everything I'd learned about escapes. There was a young guy I did time with once. He could get out of handcuffs like he was greased. The trick was to fold your hands over so they were no wider than your wrist—he was always practicing it. He would let you hold his wrist, tight as you wanted. And then just pull it free. I tried, but it was no good. Something like that takes practice. . . .

There was a little play in the waist strap—I had pushed all the air in my lungs into my stomach when I saw what Belinda was going to do—I'd remembered at least that much. But it wasn't enough. . . . I just had more room to squirm, a worm on a hook.

I could feel the baby spot beaming down on me, a hot, focused light. It was so quiet I could hear my heart beat . . . faster than I wanted, but still below the panic line. Maybe Morales would get the drop on her. . . . Then all I'd have to worry about was starving to death.

If there's a way in, there's a way out. I said it to myself, over and over again, a mantra that gave me no peace. If only I had . . .

I heard the deadbolt on the front door snap open. The sound froze my heart. I stopped breathing. A thin beam of light came around the corner.

"Jesus Christ!" It was Frankie, a flashlight in his hand, the lens taped so only a sliver of light came through. He came forward slowly, wary as a stray dog offered food.

"I'm okay," I told him, willing calm into my voice. "But hurry it up, all right?"

He moved quickly to where I was strapped in. I saw the Mole materialize over his left shoulder, his leather satchel in his hand. The Mole pushed Frankie out of the way, held up his hand so Frankie couldn't get any closer.

"You wired up?" he asked me, making a sniffing noise like a bomb dog.

"No."

The Mole nodded, satisfied. He put his satchel on the floor, knelt to open it. Then he carefully examined the straps through his Coke-bottle glasses. He shook his head in disgust, reached in his satchel and came out with what looked like a giant pair of scissors. The scissors had a pistol grip on one side with a wide handle on the other, a spring between them. The Mole worked it under the strap on my left arm, resting the base of the scissors on the chair itself. He leaned forward, grunting with effort, and the thick leather parted. I flexed my arm, working some of the stiffness out while the Mole did the other strap, around my right arm. I could have slipped out then, but the Mole did the waist strap too, and I was free.

"She went out the front door, headed downtown," Frankie said. "We couldn't follow her. I mean, not and get in here too."

"You did the right thing," I told him, climbing into my clothes. "It doesn't matter anyway—I know where she's going."

"Can we—?" Frankie asked.

"You got a car?" I interrupted.

"We got the Mole's . . . truck, I guess it is," Frankie said. "He picked me up in it."

I knew what he meant—the beat-up old panel truck with the name of a kosher butcher on the side that the Mole used to get around in.

"Let's go," I told them.

The Mole drove like he always did, with bat-blind incompetence, like he had a sonar system in his head but it wasn't working too good. The panel truck yawed around corners. Every pothole sent my head toward the roof.

"You have any trouble with the locks?" I asked the Mole.

He gave me a "Don't be stupid" look, sawing at the big steering wheel to negotiate another corner.

We drove up Van Dam slowly, seeing if . . . Nothing—the street was quiet. Morales' screaming-red sports car was parked right in front of the loft. I used Frankie's flashlight on its windshield—it was empty. We turned on Greenwich and doubled back, parking on Charlton—the loft on Van Dam was just through the alley.

"You got a piece?" I asked Frankie.

"No. I mean, you didn't—"

"That's okay," I said. "Mole?"

"I have some grenades," the lunatic replied. In his world, the subject of individual targets doesn't come up much.

"Stay here," I told him. "Frankie'll be back in a minute. Then take off, okay?"

The Mole nodded, as miserly with words as always. I took off down the alley, Frankie right behind. He may not have been a world-class burglar when he was doing houses, but he knew how to move: quick and careful. I located the building, eye-checked it, taking stock. A rusty fire escape ran up the back of the building. The loft was on the second floor. I looked to the rooftops. The buildings were so close together you could travel the length of the block and never touch the street.

No way I was going to ring that bell, ask Belinda to throw down the key. I knew what she'd throw down if she saw me coming.

Frankie saw the look on my face. "What can I do?" he asked, hard truth in his voice.

"One more thing, brother," I told him. "I gotta get on that fire escape. Get on *quiet,* understand? And it's too high for me to jump."

"I'm with you," Frankie said, planting his feet, bending at the knees, cupping his right hand. I stepped into the cup with one foot, jumped off with the other one just as Frankie heaved up with all his strength. For a second, I was floating. . . . Then I grabbed the base of the fire escape with both hands and hauled myself up. I turned from my perch, looked down at Frankie. I made my right hand into a fist, held it right next to my face. Frankie made the same gesture from below, answering. I moved both hands in a "Get the hell out of here!" gesture. Then I turned my back on Frankie and went to work.

took a black shadow-marker out of my pocket, smeared it over my face in a random pattern. I pulled a black wool watch cap over my hair, slipped the black gloves on my hands. The window into the loft was closed, pitch black from years of city soot—I couldn't tell if it was dark inside or if I just couldn't see through the glass. No bars on the window—strange in this neighborhood. I got my hands under the frame, shoved up slowly. Nothing. I braced myself, shoved with all my strength. It didn't budge. I pulled a black silk handkerchief from my jacket, spit on it and rubbed a clear circle on the glass. Still couldn't see anything.

I ran my fingers over the window. Old plate glass, not even Thermo-paned. No wires in it either. In this neighborhood? Maybe a motion detector . . .

I took a deep breath. Let it out slow. Then I took off my jacket, pulled it open like a shield over my face, and kicked in the glass. It shattered easy enough. I came all the way through behind it, the jacket protecting my face and arms. I rolled into the room, staying low, the plastic knife in my hand.

For a second, I didn't move. Didn't breathe. Then I heard footsteps, running. Heard a door slam. I moved along the wall, heading for a patch of light I saw off to my right. I peeked around the corner, looked into that big room with all the Retro crap scattered around. I heard a grunting sound. Who . . . ?

Morales. On his back, head propped against the base of the couch. His shirt was white, but his chest was red, a spreading stain. I ran over, dropped down next to him.

He opened his eyes, looked at me. If he was surprised, he didn't show it. "Bitch shot me," he said through clenched teeth. "Got the drop on me, took my piece. Told me the whole story—like she was getting her rocks off, telling me. Then she just stepped back and fucking shot me."

"Don't talk," I said. "I'll—"

"Bitch shoulda known I always carry a spare," he said, straining with every word. That's when I saw the pistol in his fist, a cheap-shit .25-caliber Raven automatic—the favorite of low-level gangbangers, a perfect throw-down piece. "She had the gun up, ready to finish me—bitch didn't see this one. I was just about to take my shot when I heard the glass go. She took off."

"They'll get her," I said. "It's all over now. Just—"

"I'm done," Morales said. "She caught a fucking lung—I can feel it. She gets away, you're done too. She won't go out the front door—she's gonna use the roof, make a run for it. Take . . ."

His head slumped on his chest, lolling to one side. I put my ear close to his face. I could hear him breathing, but it wasn't much.

"Don't give me up," I said, dropping the cellular phone next to his hand—the same hand I pulled the pistol out of. Then I straightened up and started for Belinda.

I found the inside staircase to the roof at the end of the hall. Flattened my back against the wall and pushed it open with the barrel of the pistol. It moved easy. I counted to five in my mind, then slipped inside. Still nothing. Up the stairs, step-by-step, slowly, slowly . . . all the way to the roof.

She'd be running now. Running hard. She couldn't be sure Morales was dead, couldn't go back to her apartment. Did she have a car stashed somewhere? Money? A passport?

It didn't feel like that. She'd gambled everything on a pair of murders—she'd left me staked out, went off to do Morales . . . but the bridge she built had collapsed under her feet.

I crawled out onto the roof, snaking my way forward using my elbows and feet. Nothing. I stopped, went quiet, listening to the night. The sound of breaking glass wouldn't bring the cops in this part of town—the other apartments were empty anyway. And she'd had enough time to get completely off the block. I couldn't stay around, not with Morales maybe dead right beneath me. I stood up to wide-angle a look at the other roofs, trying to spot a flash from her yellow turtleneck. A piece of brick flew off the chimney a couple of inches from my face. I hit the ground, rolled to my right fast as I could just as another pair of shots smacked into the brick where my chest would have been. No sound . . . She must be using her own piece—the one with the silencer.

I couldn't tell where the shots had come from, but they had to be close.

No more footsteps to hear—now the hawk was on the ground, talons out.

I crawled backward until most of my body was behind the chimney. Would she think she'd hit me, come over to finish me off? No . . . she couldn't be sure. Time was grinding to a stop, everything in slow motion. But I knew it was an illusion—knew time was the enemy too. I counted my options, came down to one.

"It's me, Belinda," I called softly. "I got out of your place. Morales is dead—your plan is shot. We have to do this together now, girl. You and me."

"You're a liar!" Belinda's voice, a viper's hiss slashing through the night. I couldn't follow the sound to the source, but she had to be close. Real close.

"I'm not lying," I said out of the darkness. "I'm too scared to lie. It's over now. You pulled it off. All I want to do is get out of here alive."

"*Liar!*" she hissed again, a robot, locked in by its programming.

"I just want some of the money," I called to her. "Just a piece, okay? We can't stay up here. Sooner or later, the cops are gonna come. I can alibi you. Foolproof. The Chinese restaurant, that's where we were tonight. Together. A dozen people saw us. You were right—Morales wouldn't have any notes. It's you and me now."

"You swear?"

"I swear on my mother's life," I told her.

"Stand up where I can see you," she called back.

"No way. You've got a gun—I don't. I'm not getting myself—"

"I'll throw it away," she promised. "Watch."

Something silver flashed to my left, a high arc. I heard the sound of metal hitting the roof. "I gave it up," she called, her voice closer now. "Now stand up where I can see you."

"You first," I told her. "I can't see where it landed—I'm not letting you run over and pick it up."

"I'm coming," she said, stepping out from behind a maintenance shack, hands in the air.

I stood up too, letting her see me, holding my hands high, easily palming the little .25. We walked toward each other, feet crunching on little stones and litter, maybe ten feet apart, hands still in the air like we were going to slap each other high-fives.

"It'll be okay," she said. "Don't worry. We can still—" Her right hand flashed toward her waistband but mine had less room to travel—I cranked off three rounds into her chest. The cheap little pistol made *pop-pop-pop* sounds. She staggered, fell to her knees, pulled Morales' gun out and fired—missed—just as I put two more into her. She fell on her face. The pistol dropped from her hand.

I ran over, reached under her arm and rolled her over. Her yellow turtleneck was still clean—I couldn't see where the bullets had gone in. "You're liars," she said, voice drained. "Dirty fucking liars, all of you."

I picked up Morales' revolver, knelt down by Belinda. Her raptor's eyes flamed at me. I pointed Morales' pistol at her forehead, squeezed the trigger. The explosion shut off my hearing. Her forehead disappeared.

I ran then, ran hard. Across the roof, down the stairs, Morales' pistol held ahead of me like a talisman against evil. The apartment door was standing open. I found Morales, still in the same position, knelt next to him.

"She's dead," I told him. "I shot her with your throw-down gun. I put another one into her with this," I said, holding up his pistol so he could see it. "I'm taking off—the cops'll be here in a minute."

"I didn't . . . call," he said. "I waited . . . in case you could—"

"Give me five minutes, then," I said. "I'm going back out over the roof."

"You . . . got it," he grunted—in pain, but he was going to make it, I could see.

"I'm out of here," I told him, standing up.

"Your prints . . ." he whispered.

"I was covered," I told him, spreading my hands so he could see the gloves.

"Give me my piece," he said, craning his neck so he could look up at me.

I bent down, handed it over. He took it. Carefully wrapped his hand around the butt, slipped his finger into the trigger guard. "*Now* you're covered," he said, closing his eyes.

I went back to the roof, moved shadowy past Belinda's body. Her eyes were open but the light was out. I walked softly, the tiny flash out in front of me, going from roof to roof. I was almost to the end of the block when I heard the sirens.

I stopped in an alley, reached down, pulled the detachable soles and heels off my boots and walked away on the new ones. A few blocks over, I dropped the pull-aways down a gutter sewer.

A few blocks later, I took off the gloves and tossed them into a Dumpster. Once I slipped a token into the slot for the Spring Street subway, I was gone.

Hauser never got his story. By the time he came back from Chicago, it was all over the news. TV, radio, the papers, everything. Hero cop Jorge Morales had cracked a serial murder case. . . . A rogue female detective was the culprit, and he'd taken her out in a vicious gun battle that saw him catch a slug in the chest. He lost a lung, but he was going to make it. Politicians knocked each other over trying for photo ops standing next to his hospital bed. NYPD loved him. If they had questions about the bootleg cellular phone or the extra gun, they kept them to themselves.

I called Helene from a pay phone. "The contract's back on," is all I said.

When Hauser called the prison to set up another interview with Piersall, they told him Piersall wasn't going to be having any visitors. Seems he was out of PC only one day when somebody shanked him—he was DOA by the time they got him to the prison infirmary.

Frankie's got another fight coming up in ninety days—Ristone got him a match with a tomato can. The big buildup had already started. No more real fights for Frankie until he had a string of setup KOs under his belt.

Hauser told me he wasn't done. "This Adelnaws Foundation stinks," he said. "Did you know this guy Capshaw had a conviction for child molesting? Almost forty years ago, in Toronto. And this foundation, it's on the Internet, the server's over in Finland somewhere. I'm gonna take a look."

"Be yourself," I told him.

It was good advice I gave Hauser. But it was a couple more weeks before I took it myself. Vyra called from the Vista. And I climbed in the Plymouth and drove over to see her new shoes.

A NOTE ON THE TYPE

This book was set in Caledonia, a face designed by William Addison Dwiggins (1880–1956) for the Mergenthaler Linotype Company in 1939. It belongs to the family of types referred to by printers as "modern," a term used to mark the change in type styles that occurred around 1800. Caledonia was inspired by the Scotch types cast by the Glasgow typefounders Alexander Wilson & Sons circa 1833. However, there is a calligraphic quality about Caledonia that is completely lacking in the Wilson types.

Dwiggins referred to an even earlier typeface for this "liveliness of action"—one cut around 1790 by William Martin for the printer William Bulmer. Caledonia has more weight than the Martin letters, and the bottom finishing strokes of the letters are cut straight across, without brackets, to make sharp angles with the upright stems, thus giving a modern-face appearance.

W. A. Dwiggins began his association with the Mergenthaler Linotype Company in 1929, and over the next twenty-seven years he designed a number of book types, the most interesting of which are Metro, Electra, Caledonia, Eldorado, and Falcon.

Composed by North Market Street Graphics,
Lancaster, Pennsylvania
Printed and bound by Quebecor Printing Fairfield,
Fairfield, Pennsylvania
Designed by Virginia Tan